ROGUE ANGEL™

AleX Archer

THE SPIRIT BANNER

A GOLD EAGLE BOOK FROM
WORLDWIDE®

TORONTO • NEW YORK • LONDON
AMSTERDAM • PARIS • SYDNEY • HAMBURG
STOCKHOLM • ATHENS • TOKYO • MILAN
MADRID • WARSAW • BUDAPEST • AUCKLAND

If you purchased this book without a cover you should be aware
that this book is stolen property. It was reported as "unsold and
destroyed" to the publisher, and neither the author nor the
publisher has received any payment for this "stripped book."

Recycling programs
for this product may
not exist in your area.

First edition January 2010

ISBN-13: 978-0-373-62141-5

THE SPIRIT BANNER

Special thanks and acknowledgment to
Joe Nassise for his contribution to this work.

Copyright © 2010 by Worldwide Library.

All rights reserved. Except for use in any review, the
reproduction or utilization of this work in whole or in part
in any form by any electronic, mechanical or other means,
now known or hereafter invented, including xerography,
photocopying and recording, or in any information storage
or retrieval system, is forbidden without the written permission
of the publisher, Worldwide Library, 225 Duncan Mill Road,
Don Mills, Ontario, Canada M3B 3K9.

This is a work of fiction. Names, characters, places and incidents
are either the product of the author's imagination or are used
fictitiously, and any resemblance to actual persons, living or dead,
business establishments, events or locales is entirely coincidental.

® and TM are trademarks of Harlequin Enterprises Limited.
Trademarks indicated with ® are registered in the United States
Patent and Trademark Office, the Canadian Trade Marks Office
and in other countries.

Printed in U.S.A.

Titles in this series:

"I'm considering putting together an expedition to find the Khan's lost tomb."

"Don't bother," Annja said, missing the quick flicker of surprise that flashed across Davenport's face when she didn't even glance up from her drink.

"Why not?" he asked.

"Because he more than likely didn't have one."

Davenport sat back and watched her for a moment. "What if I told you that the Mongols did build a secret tomb for their Great Khan? That they filled it with an amazingly diverse treasure trove, loot from the hundreds of cultures he conquered? And what if I said I had in my possession the journal of a man who had intimate details of the burial process and a map to the location?"

Annja smiled. "I'd say you better hire someone to authenticate the map and the writings pretty darn quick. Hell, I'd be happy to do it for you myself just to prove to you the ridiculousness of the very idea."

Davenport nodded. "Good. You can start first thing in the morning."

Annja stared at him blankly for a moment, and then it dawned on her that she had been neatly led right where Davenport wanted her to go.

The
LEGEND

...THE ENGLISH COMMANDER TOOK
JOAN'S SWORD AND RAISED IT HIGH.

The broadsword, plain and unadorned,
gleamed in the firelight. He put the tip against
the ground and his foot at the center of the blade.
The broadsword shattered, fragments falling
into the mud. The crowd surged forward,
peasant and soldier, and snatched the shards
from the trampled mud. The commander tossed
the hilt deep into the crowd.
Smoke almost obscured Joan, but she continued
praying till the end, until finally the flames climbed
her body and she sagged against the restraints.

Joan of Arc died that fateful day in France,
but her legend and sword are reborn....

1

Mongolia
1245

Father Michael Curran, Special Vatican Envoy from His
Holiness the Pope Innocent IV to the People of the Felt
Walls, stared at the waves of oncoming riders and did
what he could to keep the fear from showing on his face.

Not that there wasn't good reason to be afraid. They
were at least three days' hard ride from Karakorum, where
Guyuk, the grandson of Genghis Khan and the current
ruler of the Mongol Empire, held court over his subjects.
In the years since the death of the Great Khan, the empire
had fractured. More and more tribes were returning to the
old ways, fighting and competing against one another.
The Naimans were one such group and Curran's party
was deep in a contested area that the Naimans claimed as
their own. The distance from the capital meant that no one
was going to come charging in to save them. To make

matters even worse, the honor guard that Guyuk had sent with Curran for this trip into the Hentiyn Nuruu Mountains numbered less than thirty men, while the Naiman warriors currently charging their position appeared to number in the hundreds.

As the enemy swept forward, Curran could see that each man stood high in the stirrups, guiding his mountain pony with his knees, leaving his hands free to use his bow with the unerring accuracy that had made the Mongol army so feared. True, these were not the famed warriors of the Great Khan—just a lesser khan's raiding party— but he knew they were deadly just the same. The thunder of their horses' hooves mixed with the screeching wind that whipped across the open plain, and the priest no longer had to wonder what hell might sound like. Now he knew, beyond the shadow of a doubt. Hell was the uncanny silence as the enemy thundered toward them. Hell was the thrumming of the enemy's arrows as they filled the sky above him, so thick that for a moment he lost sight of the sun itself. Hell was the thump of the shafts as they met leather armor and human flesh. Hell was the cry of the injured and the dying as they fell into the snow around him.

The Naimans harbored years of resentment against the unification brought to the plains by the army of Genghis Khan some fifty years before. They had caught the small group in the open, crossing a wide valley between two separate mountain peaks, leaving them with few places to run and little to use as cover of any sort. Curran had to admit to himself that it was a marvelous piece of strategic planning. Volke, their group's leader, had been too confident in his belief that no one would dare to attack a party under Guyuk's protection. But the harsh winter and the lure of overwhelming odds had apparently filled the enemy with daring. Curran knew the old adage usually held true: desperate men will do desperate things.

Having been forced into a desperate move, it now seemed that this group of raiders was determined to make certain that no survivors were left behind to report their audacity to the ruling khan.

Volke shouted something in Mongolian, but the wind whipped his words away before Curran could make sense of them. It didn't matter, though; they hadn't been directed at him, anyway, but at the other Mongol warriors in their small group. As one, the soldiers around him wheeled about and sent their sturdy ponies charging for the mountain pass they'd emerged from a half hour before. The priest would have been left behind if one of the warriors hadn't snatched the reins of Curran's horse out of his hands as he thundered by, forcing him to follow suit.

As they raced away, Curran fought to remember the man's name.

Tamaton?

Tanguyuk?

Tamarak!

That was it. Tamarak was one of the older, experienced warriors assigned to the expedition by the khan himself and ordered to personally see to the safety of the envoy. Curran had resented it at first, seeing Tamarak's presence as a sign that the Mongols still did not trust him. But now he was thankful to have the man at his side.

Curran knew that if they could reach the pass behind them, they could lose their pursuers in the mazelike passage across the mountains or take shelter in the many caves lining the passage walls. Either one would more than likely grant them the time and safety they needed to regroup and restore their wounded. If they could hold off until dark, they might then be able to sneak across the valley without the Naimans being the wiser.

Curran's group was tired—they'd been traveling for days already—while the enemy appeared to be fresh. It was obvious to Curran that the enemy had the advantage. That didn't seem to matter to these hardy warriors, though. They would either succeed or die trying, apparently; and for the first time since he had come to live among them, the priest felt a sense of admiration for their tenacity and sheer courage in the face of overwhelming odds.

Their horses thundered on through the snow while the enemy closed inexorably from behind.

After a time, it was obvious to everyone, even Curran, that they were not going to make it. Volke shouted again and the small entourage turned to fight.

Curran watched their pursuers come on with fear in his heart but with courage on his face.

As the enemy closed the distance, they split ranks, sending half of their forces sweeping to the left while the remainder went right, enveloping Curran's small group in a wide circle two ranks deep, with each rank moving in opposite directions. From out of those ranks the arrows came again. Curran watched Volke topple from the saddle with more than a dozen black shafts jutting from his now-still form. Kaisar and Jelme, his senior lieutenants, met the same fate seconds later. In moments, the enemy had effectively stripped the small band of its most experienced leaders. Curran had no doubt that the tactic had been intentional. Cutting off the head to kill the body was a strategy as old as war itself.

If someone didn't do something soon, they were all going to die, the priest realized. Apparently the men around him felt the same way, for there was a sudden shout from one of the more experienced warriors and the troops spurred their horses and charged the enemy. Trained to act with the others, Curran's horse followed suit. The Jesuit was about to meet the enemy whether he wanted to or not.

"Lord, protect your humble servant," the priest whispered under his breath as he drew his sword and went to meet his death with his head held high in the manner of the Savior he revered.

The two groups slammed together with thunderous force. Men shouted, horses screamed, and Curran found himself slashing to and fro with his weapon, striking out at anything within reach, fighting for his life just as savagely as the enemy sought to relieve him of it.

For just a moment, he thought they might win. Their sudden concentrated attack had surprised the enemy and they burst through the first rank without stopping, surging forward, but in the next moment a heavily mailed fist holding the pommel of a sword smashed into Curran's face, toppling him from his saddle. He struck the ground hard, and as he lay there unmoving, the wind knocked out of him, he felt a stabbing pain in his left leg. Curran screamed in agony. Darkness loomed and then swept over him like the tide.

HAVING FULLY EXPECTED to die when he'd lost his grip on his horse, Curran was surprised to regain consciousness sometime later. With consciousness, however, came an awareness of the pain his body was experiencing and surprise quickly turned to regret. In that first instant, he was convinced that death would have been a better alternative to what he was currently experiencing. He screamed aloud against the pain and passed out again.

The second time he regained consciousness, the cold

had wrapped him in its chilly embrace, dulling the pain to a minor roar, and he was actually able to open his eyes.

He immediately wished he hadn't.

The dead were everywhere. They covered the ground in front of him and as far as he could see on either side. After stripping the bodies of anything of value, the Naimans had followed the traditional steppes custom and left the dead where they had fallen. Now their eyes stared unseeing and their blood stained the snow in thick patches of crimson-black. The bodies of his companions mingled haphazardly with the corpses of the horses on which they'd ridden, neither man nor beast being spared in the midst of the fray.

He shifted his position and a lance of roaring pain shot up from his left leg and threatened to plunge him into unconsciousness once more. He fought against it, knowing that if he succumbed, he'd most likely freeze to death.

When the dizziness receded and he could think clearly again, he looked down at his leg. He turned away almost immediately. The sight of the dark shaft of an arrow jutting up from his thigh and his own blood staining the snow was almost too much for him to bear.

He couldn't ignore it, though. He was going to have to deal with it, and soon, if only to keep from bleeding to death. Steeling himself, and taking a deep breath to keep from vomiting, he looked down at his leg again.

The arrow had hit him high on the back of the thigh and had gone all the way through his leg at an angle, exiting about an inch above the knee. He could see that the edges of the head were barbed, which meant he wasn't going to be able to pull the arrow back in the direction it had entered. Nor could he remove it the other way; the feathered shaft would prevent it.

He was going to have to break the shaft on one side or the other and then pull the rest of it free.

The very thought of it made him shudder.

Why bother? he wondered. Even if he could get the shaft out and stop the bleeding, he was only trading one method of dying for another. There was no way he could travel in his condition, and if nightfall caught him here on the plain he was sure to freeze to death. It seemed God had saved him from a quick, sure death only to fall victim to a long, lingering one.

But Curran was not the type to go down without a fight.

The wind was picking up and the snowfall that had dogged their march earlier that morning had started anew. Never mind the brutal cold that threatened to steal his every breath. If he didn't do something immediately, he wasn't going to have the strength left to try anything at all.

He tore several strips of cloth off the shirt of a nearby corpse, folding some a few times to create makeshift compresses and laying the others out where he could reach them without difficulty. Working quickly so that he wouldn't have time to think about it, he rolled partially on his side, exposing the feathered end of the arrow. Taking it in his left hand, he gripped his thigh tightly with his right, holding it steady. Curran took a deep breath and then snapped his left hand sharply to one side, breaking the wooden arrow in two just above the fletching.

He screamed against the pain, but managed to remain conscious. The motion had started the wound bleeding again. With shaking hands, he stuffed several of the compresses against the open wound and then tied it off with one of the strips.

He was breathing heavily now, the pain making it difficult to concentrate, but he pushed through it, knowing he had no choice but to finish what he had started.

Gingerly placing his leg flat on the ground, he took hold of the tip of the arrow, wrapping his fingers around the barbed edges to give him more leverage. He gritted his teeth and pulled.

With more than a bit of resistance, the rest of the shaft slid free.

He tossed the broken shaft of the arrow aside, packed the wound with some snow and the rest of the compresses to stop the bleeding, then tied the whole thing off just as he had the entry point.

When he was finished, he slumped on the ground, sweating, exhausted and in considerable pain.

After some time—he didn't know how long—the pain receded to a manageable level. He pushed himself back up into a sitting position and took a look at his handiwork.

Blood had dried around the edges of the makeshift bandages, but it looked like as if the wound had stopped bleeding.

Maybe he was going to make it, after all.

A soft snort to his immediate right made him nearly jump out of his skin. He slowly turned his head, not wanting to jostle his injured leg but at the same time afraid of what he might see. To his vast surprise, he found the horse he'd been riding standing a few feet away, rooting through a partially opened saddlebag for something to eat.

"Thank you, Lord," Curran whispered.

If he could get on the horse, he had a fighting chance at survival.

Like the other Mongol steeds, his was a short-legged, shaggy beast that had seen its fair share of death and was unmoved by the carnage around it. Losing interest in the saddlebag at its feet, it raised its head, catching sight of Curran in the process. It trotted over and nuzzled him, looking to be fed.

"Good boy," the priest whispered, petting its nose with one hand while grabbing onto the straps of the saddlebags it still wore with the other.

Using the straps for support, he hauled himself upright, using the strength of his arms and his one good leg. It took several tries, but at last he was standing on one leg, his arms wrapped around the horse's neck to keep from falling.

He rested in that position for a moment, praying the horse wouldn't make any sudden moves and dump him back down on the snow. When he'd caught his breath again, he reached for the pack still hanging around the horse's hindquarters, right where he'd loaded it earlier that morning.

Working slowly and carefully to limit jarring his injured leg any more than necessary, he untied the drawstrings of the pack and withdrew the ceremonial robe he'd worn when appearing for his audience with the khan in Karakorum. The material was quite thick, something he constantly complained about when wearing it, but now he was silently thankful. He slipped the material over his shivering form and slumped against his horse, already exhausted and he hadn't even tried getting himself up into the saddle.

A sudden sound to his left drew his attention.

He straightened up, trying to see.

Only the dead stared back at him.

The sound came again, a low moan, but this time he saw the fingers of a nearby form twitch in conjunction with it.

Another survivor!

"Hey! Hey, you! Can you hear me?" Curran called out in the Mongolian he'd picked up during his two months in Karakorum.

The strange croaking sound that came out of his parched throat surprised him. Until that moment, he hadn't even been aware of his tremendous thirst. He coughed, then used a handful of snow to wet down his lips and throat before trying again.

"Are you okay? Can you walk?"

There was no response.

He knew he hadn't imagined it. That meant the man was either too injured to respond or simply couldn't understand him.

Curran had no choice; he was going to have to go over to the injured man and take a look. He considered climbing astride the horse, but decided the effort required to get up and then back down again was probably too much for him. Instead, he got the horse moving slowly in the direction he wanted it, using the animal as a makeshift crutch for support as he hopped along on his good leg. When Curran was close enough, he pulled the horse to a stop and dropped down in the snow next to the wounded man.

He rolled the body over and discovered that it was the man who had saved him earlier, Tamarak.

The feathered shafts of two black arrows jutted from deep in the man's stomach and a sword blade had taken a bite out of the left side of his head. Given the barbed tips, Curran had no way of removing them. He'd been able to remove his own only because the arrowhead had come all the way through his flesh. These were embedded deep in the muscle. Pulling them out was likely to cause more damage than leaving them in. The best he could do was to make Tamarak as comfortable as possible and to stay with him until the end.

An end that could come faster than either of them wanted if they didn't find some shelter and protection from the cold.

He dragged the other man closer to the horse, where, to his surprise, the animal got down on its knees, allowing Curran to haul both himself and Tamarak's unconscious form onto the horse's back.

The beast climbed to its feet, and for the first time since the Naiman war party had been sighted, Curran felt optimistic about his chances for survival.

As if in answer, the wind swirled around him and the falling snow began to thicken. The storm was here to stay, apparently.

Curran took a moment to get his bearings and then turned the beast about to face the direction in which they had been fleeing. There were caves back in the pass itself and it was Curran's intention to hole up inside one for shelter from the storm.

He'd worry about how to get back to Karakorum in the morning.

First, they had to survive the night.

SEVERAL HOURS LATER Curran sat in a cave that was deep enough to filter out the winds howling outside. There had been a few sticks lying just inside the entrance. He combined them with some of the extra clothing from his pack, and made a small fire to keep them warm. It was still cold, though not as bad as it would have been had they been trapped outside. It would serve to keep them from freezing to death.

At least until the fuel ran out, he thought, and then just

as quickly pushed the image away. The Lord will provide, he told himself. The Lord will provide.

At least we won't starve to death, Curran thought, with a glance at the corpse of his horse where it lay just within the entrance tunnel. The poor beast had collapsed after carrying so much weight through the freezing cold weather without rest. Curran hadn't yet managed to get up the nerve to start carving up the carcass. He didn't mind eating horseflesh. He'd been forced to do so during other missionary journeys he'd been on and it hadn't been all that bad. It was just that this particular horse had been instrumental in saving his life and it felt disrespectful to treat its remains in such a fashion.

Still, when the time came, Curran had little doubt that his reticence would quickly vanish. Starving to death wasn't on his list of endings to this saga.

The dead horse was proof of what they had endured to reach this point. The trail had been difficult to find without the Mongols to guide him. The ever-increasing fury of the storm had cut their already-slow pace to a crawl, as did the times that Curran lost his grip and toppled off his patient mount. Thankfully, the horse had traveled this way before, and when he finally stopped trying to control it and just gave it its head, it took him where he wanted to go.

With the help of the firelight, Curran had cleaned Tamarak's head wound and had broken off the jutting ends of the arrows to keep the wounded man from accidentally driving them deeper into his body.

After that, there wasn't anything to do but wait.

The snow had continued to fall and the entrance to the cave was half-covered from the heavy accumulation. Curran didn't mind, as it served to keep the heat from the fire trapped in the cave, warming him and his unconscious companion, while still allowing the smoke to escape.

Unable to sleep, Curran took out his worn leather journal and began to write, recording the events of the past several days in as much detail as possible to ensure that there was some record of what had happened to him should he not make it back to Karakorum. He'd been doing the same thing since his mission had started many months before, and what had once been an annoying chore had turned into a soothing balm for his spirit.

At the very least, it gave him something to think about other than the pain in his injured leg, he thought ruefully.

It wasn't long before Tamarak, delirious with fever and pain, began raving aloud. At first Curran ignored it, knowing there was little he could do for the man, but then something Tamarak said caught his attention and he listened more carefully.

What he heard amazed him.

If it was true, he was being given the secret of the ages!

I really need a miracle now, Lord, he prayed, as he turned to a clean page of his journal and began writing frantically, trying to get it all down just in case the good Father decided to deliver on his request.

2

Mexico

Annja Creed was knee-deep in sacrificial victims when the shooting started.

At first, there was only a single gunshot, which was easy enough for her to ignore. After all, the sound of isolated gunfire was relatively common at a dig site this deep in the jungle. Someone fired off a weapon at least once a week. The reasons for doing so varied, but they usually had something to do with the local wildlife. Just last week, Martinez had found a twelve-foot python in his bed and had fired off four shots before he managed to hit the thing. A few days before that, the cook—a guy by the name of Evans—had used his shotgun to drive off the howler monkeys he'd caught raiding the food larder. The monkeys still managed to get away with the chocolate bars he'd been hording.

But when the first couple of shots were followed by an entire volley of gunfire from several different weapons, Annja knew something was seriously wrong.

For the past three weeks, Annja and the rest of the dig team working on behalf of the Bureau of Cultural Studies had been carefully excavating the ruins discovered at Teluamachee, about a hundred and fifty miles outside of Mexico City. A recent earthquake had cut a swath through the jungle, knocking down trees and natural earth formations with equal abandon, exposing a set of long forgotten ruins hidden in a narrow valley deep in the jungle. A scout for a local logging company had discovered the site and, thankfully, had enough respect and admiration of his heritage to report the location to the bureau rather than selling that information on the black market. The bureau wasted no time in assembling a team of experts—including Annja—asking them to come down and take a look at what they had found.

Annja had been in between assignments when the call had come in and she'd wasted no time in agreeing to join the team.

The main dig site consisted of a large three-story temple complex in the standard step pyramid formation, with several smaller buildings lining the east and west sides of the courtyard extending south from the base of the pyramid itself.

A few hundred yards to the west of the main structures was the site's cenote, a deep, water-filled sinkhole that the Mayans considered a link to the rain gods, or Chaacs. Sacrificial victims and precious objects had been tossed into the sacred well as offerings during the site's heyday as a way of protecting the populace and bringing good fortune. To the dig team's delight, the earthquake that had uncovered the primary dig site had also drained the cenote, exposing its secrets to the light of the sun for the first time in centuries.

Annja was down in "the hole," as they had come to call it, erecting a grid made of nylon rope and stakes across the entire area. This would allow them to record the precise depth and location of every object they removed from the muck-covered bed at the bottom of the sinkhole. That information would then be fed into a 3-D simulation program that would provide them with a computer model to work with in analyzing the artifacts.

It was important work, which was one of the reasons Annja had volunteered to do it, despite the ankle-deep puddles and stinking muck that covered the bottom of the cenote. From where she stood she could see the skeletal remains of at least five different individuals and more than a handful of ceremonial objects, such as knives, bowls and statuettes. The items they recovered from the cenote would probably tell them more about daily life at the site than the ruins themselves. It was like a window into the past, one she looked forward to peering through.

But right now she needed to forget about the past and focus on the present.

She looked up toward the rim of the cenote, expecting to see Arturo, her partner for the afternoon, peering over the edge and frantically signaling for her to come up, but there was no sign of him.

Had he run off? Gone for help? She didn't know. Thankfully, the rope she'd used to climb down into the hole was still where they had left it, hanging against the interior wall of the cenote. It was tied off at the top around a nearby tree trunk and so Arturo's help wasn't required for her to get back to the surface. It would have been helpful, but not necessary.

She slogged over to the far wall, being careful not to step on any of the remains scattered about her feet, and took hold of the rope. Planting one foot against the interior wall of the cenote, she began to pull herself up hand over hand, walking her feet upward as she went.

She hadn't gone more than a few steps up the wall when a shadow blotted out the light from the setting sun above. Startled, Annja looked up. She was just in time to see Arturo hurtling down toward her, his arms and legs flailing wildly, his mouth open in a silent scream.

Annja let go of the rope, dropped the few feet to the bottom of the cenote, and flattened herself against the wall, trying to make herself as small as possible.

Arturo's body missed her by mere inches and then hit the bottom with a loud, mud-filled splash. His sightless eyes stared back at her, accusing. So, too, did the bullet hole in the center of his forehead that was leaking a thin stream of blood into the muddy water where he lay.

She could hear voices above, shouting in Spanish. She couldn't make out everything that was said, but the word *cenote* came through loud and clear a few times and she knew they were headed her way, either to see if Arturo had been alone or to be certain he was dead.

If they looked in and caught her here…

Annja didn't need to finish the thought to know she was in deep trouble. She had only seconds to find a place to hide. Any moment now someone was going to stick their head over the edge and see her.

Her chances of surviving for even a few minutes after that were slim to none.

Without hesitation she took a deep breath and threw herself down into the water at her feet, burrowing into the mud and muck beneath and throwing it over her body, trying to cover herself up as much as possible. There wasn't anywhere else she could hide. The dark fatigue pants and top she was wearing would help, she knew, as would the deep shadows accumulating with the close of day near the walls of the cenote itself. If she could just stay out of sight for a few moments, she might be all right.

For the time being, at least.

She kept one ear turned to the side, listening, and just as she suspected, she heard two voices talking together somewhere above her. An argument ensued for a moment, the voices rising and falling rapidly, and then they fell silent.

Annja didn't move from her place of concealment. She was unable to tell if they had left or not and didn't want to take the chance of being caught unexpectedly in the open.

Her caution saved her life.

Bullets suddenly thumped into Arturo's unmoving form and it took all she had for Annja not to flinch as the gunshots echoed around the enclosed confines of the cenote. The rope she'd intended to use to reach the surface was thrown down a few moments later. Laughter drifted down from above and then moved off until she couldn't hear it anymore.

Annja pulled herself out of the muck and took a deep breath, not only to fill her lungs with air but to keep her startled wits about her, as well. It wouldn't do anyone any good if she lost it now. There were too many people in the camp above who'd need her protection.

And that was precisely what she intended to do.

She reached out and placed her finger tips on Arturo's throat, checking for a pulse, wanting to be sure. She would have been highly surprised if he'd survived the fall, never mind the gunshot wound to the head, but stranger things had happened and she didn't want to leave without being certain.

In the end, it turned out to be wasted effort.

Arturo was dead.

Gently, she brushed the side of her palm down over his eyes, closing them, and then stood. A glance upward told her she was alone and she suspected it would remain that way. By now the handful of people working the dig site had either been rounded up or slaughtered as Arturo had. There was no reason for the assailants, whoever they were, to examine the cenote a second time unless they wanted to dredge the bottom for themselves.

She figured that wasn't too bloody likely, given the pile of artifacts that the team had already unearthed that were just sitting around in the research tent above.

Annja wasn't about to let the lack of a rope hinder her, either. Her colleagues were up above, friends who were clearly in trouble, and she'd go through hell and high water to get to them.

The walls of the cenote were formed from limestone and, thanks to the constant erosion of the water that had filled the hole, were pockmarked throughout, providing all sorts of hand- and footholds for those who knew how to use them.

Having done her fair share of rock climbing, Annja was one of those people.

She grabbed a hold and started climbing. She'd learned that those unfamiliar with the sport often tried to pull themselves upward using the strength of their arms alone. That causes lactic acid to quickly build up in their muscles, cramping them, and tiring the climber faster than necessary. Annja knew what was necessary. With more than a hundred feet of climbing to go, she had to be sure to conserve her energy, which meant using her hands primarily for balance and doing the majority of the work with her legs. She was careful where she put her hands and feet, knowing that the pockets of eroded rock might still be damp or even full of water. Without a rope, one slip could be fatal.

Slowly, carefully, she worked her way to the top.

Once there, she cautiously peeked over the lip of the cenote and then, not seeing anyone nearby, pulled herself up and onto solid ground.

As silent as a stalking cat, she rolled smoothly to her feet and slipped into the thick foliage of the nearby jungle. The sun had set during her assent of the sinkhole, something for which Annja was thankful. The darkness would provide additional cover for her as she moved through the dense undergrowth in the direction of the dig's main encampment.

3

She smelled him first. The thick odor of cheap cologne, unwashed human body and hand-rolled cigarettes clashed with the humid scent of the jungle around her and gave him away about half a moment before she blundered directly into him. Annja froze in place, waiting for her peripheral vision to pick him out in the gathering darkness.

He stood a few feet up the trail, his back to her. The rifle he carried was slung over his shoulder while his hands were busy in front of his body. The sound of liquid splashing in a thick stream against the broad leaves of the bushes in front of him reached her ears a second later and clued her in to what he was doing.

Taking a deep breath, she put her right hand into the otherwhere and drew her sword. Incredibly strong and unsurprisingly deadly, the ancient broadsword had once belonged to Joan of Arc, but when Annja had reunited the last of its pieces, it had become mysteriously bound to her in some kind of mystical fashion. She could summon it at will and release it back into the otherwhere when it was no longer needed. Reversing it in her grip so that the blade hung downward, she approached on silent feet. A quick snap of her wrist, the solid thunk of the pommel of her sword striking the back of the soldier's head, and then he was tumbling to the ground, his hands still on the zipper he'd been pulling shut when she'd struck.

Annja rolled him over, made sure he was unconscious and then took a good look.

The briefing they had received before arriving at the dig site had mentioned that members of a revolutionary group had been seen moving through the region, but Annja hadn't paid much attention to the warnings. In Mexico and most of Central America, insurgency was a way of life, and if they fell into a tizzy every single time a group was spotted by local villagers, nothing would ever get done.

Apparently she should have paid more attention this time.

The rebel soldier was dressed in a faded set of old fatigue pants and a dirty T-shirt. A new green cap with the emblem of his group emblazoned on it lay close to his unconscious form. He carried an assault rifle, an AK-47 to be exact, but unlike the rest of his uniform the weapon was new.

Someone, somewhere, was arming the troops.

She shrugged off the thought as soon as it came. It was not her problem and certainly not one she intended to get involved in. Right now, her only concern was rescuing the rest of her team from this guy's buddies.

Annja considered taking his weapon, knowing she might need a bit of firepower, but while she knew how to use it, she felt better with her sword in hand. In the end, she ejected the submachine gun's magazine and shoved it into the cargo pocket of her pants, then jammed the muzzle of the weapon into the mud at her feet, stuffing the barrel so that it couldn't be used again without being cleaned. She also took the time to peel off the man's shoelaces and used them to bind his hands and feet. Between the smack on the head and the bindings, he should be out of the fight for some time.

Satisfied, she moved off into the darkness again, slowly continuing to make her way toward the wide clearing where they had set up their main encampment a few weeks earlier.

The path ahead grew lighter, the glow coming from the portable lights strung up over the eating area outside the mess tent, and she knew she was close. As there were sure to be guards posted at the top of the pathway and she didn't want to blunder into another one unexpectedly, she decided to slide off the path into the thicker foliage and approach at an oblique angle.

When she came to the edge of the jungle, she stopped and peered out at the camp.

Their tents had been grouped haphazardly, without any real plan or design to how they had been set up. After all, this was an expedition, not a Boy Scout camp. Whenever someone new arrived, they just selected a patch of ground and set up their tent wherever they wanted. Portable lights had been strung up here and there on poles throughout the camp, as well. While they didn't light up the camp like broad daylight, they did do their share to banish the darkness around the most commonly used paths and in front of about half of the tents. From where she crouched Annja could see that she was to the right of the mess area and about halfway along the maze of tents.

She could also see several soldiers moving through the

camp; she counted four in all. They were stomping in and out of the tents, kicking aside piles of equipment and supplies, looking for anything of value. She could also hear someone yelling something in Spanish at the other end of the camp, where the larger mess tent and command center had been set up.

She couldn't see who it was. No matter. She'd find out soon enough.

First, though, she had to deal with the soldiers in front of her.

Annja waited until they were all either inside a tent or facing the other way, and then, when no one was looking, she left the cover of the trees behind and ran in a crouch to the nearest tent that hadn't been searched yet. Using her sword, she cut a long slit into the rear panel and then squatted at its edge, waiting.

It didn't take long.

The rebel came into the tent as she expected he would, head down, eagerly anticipating another iPod, cell phone or laptop computer to claim as his bounty. When he bent over to paw through a backpack someone had left open on the cot, Annja made her move. Slipping through the hole in the back of the tent she headed directly toward the soldier's unprotected back.

She had almost reached his side when he straightened and turned. Seeing her, his eyes opened wide in fear.

"*¡Madre de Dios!*" he whispered, frozen in place.

Annja could only imagine what she looked like to him with her hair, face and body covered in drying muck, and a sword almost as long as she was grasped in one hand, like some vengeful spirit come back from the grave to right some ancient wrong. She didn't give him a chance to make sense of what he was seeing, either, but rather jammed the point of her sword up under his chin and held a finger to her lips to indicate he should be silent.

"Give me your gun," she said in Spanish.

Stiff with fear, he complied.

"How many others are there?" she asked.

His voice trembled as he said, "Five plus the captain."

That meant she'd already taken care of the captain's only companion, since she'd counted four men looting the tents.

Too bad for them that the odds were in her favor.

"What are you doing here?" she asked.

The soldier shrugged.

Annja pushed the sword blade a bit harder and a thin trickle of blood ran down the man's neck in response. "Don't mess with me," she told him. "What are you here for?"

The soldier explained that they had stumbled upon the excavation while fleeing from the police. With no money and a need to resupply themselves with both food and ammunition, the captain decided that a quick raid was in order. If they discovered that the excavation had yielded gold or other precious artifacts, so much the better.

She could hear the other soldiers laughing nearby and knew she didn't have much time left. She was going to have to act and hope for the best.

"Give me your shirt and hat," she told her captive.

Once he had, she made him turn around and then struck him hard on the head with the butt of his own weapon.

Two down, four to go.

Releasing the sword back into the otherwhere, she pulled his shirt on over her own muddy T-shirt and shoved her hair up under the hat. The shirt was bulky and hung down to midthigh, which should help hide her shape and size from casual view. She only needed to pass for the other man for a few moments, just until she was close enough to carry out her plan. In the dark, and with the soldiers feeling secure that they were not in any danger, it just might work.

She left the man lying there unconscious and stepped out of the tent, the soldier's rifle slung over her shoulder and the hat pulled down low over her face.

The other soldiers were several tents away, a long stretch of darkness between them and her. They saw her emerge from the tent, but didn't think anything of it, her disguise apparently good enough at this distance to keep them from noticing anything was wrong.

The one in the middle turned to her, shouted for her to hurry up and gave a "come on" gesture with one hand.

Annja grunted something indistinguishable, waved to show she'd heard him and then held her breath.

This was the moment of truth. If they were going to notice something was wrong, it would most likely be now, while their attention was on her and they were addressing her directly.

The soldier hesitated.

Annja tensed.

The soldier turned back to his companions, apparently satisfied with her response.

They waited for her there in the center of the camp's main thoroughfare as she approached. The men laughed and joked among themselves, their attention on one another and not on her.

It proved to be a fatal mistake.

She considered simply gunning them down where they stood as she moved closer; after all, they'd certainly killed Arturo and probably several others at this point, as well. She didn't owe them anything. But the sound would easily carry across the camp and she wasn't ready yet to let the captain know that his pack of hired guns had been taken out of the equation. Instead, she kept her right hand down at her side, ready to snatch her sword out of the otherwhere the moment she needed it. Thanks to the fact that they were standing directly in a pool of light cast by one of the overhead lamps, Annja was able to approach quite close to them while remaining shrouded in shadow the entire time.

The man who'd spoken to her earlier turned as she approached, his eyes widening in surprise as she passed from shadow into light, revealing herself at last. His hand fumbled for the gun at his side as he pushed himself backward into the other two.

Annja called her sword to her and thrust forward in the same motion, skewering him where he stood.

By now the other two men had noticed she wasn't who they'd been expecting and the fact that they were in danger was just registering in their surprise-addled minds. Using the precious seconds that surprise had given her, Annja spun to her left, withdrawing her sword from the body of the man she'd stabbed while at the same time bringing her elbow around in a vicious arc that connected with the head of the man on the far right, dropping him senseless to the ground.

The man she'd stabbed dropped to his knees, his hands cupped across the savage wound in his gut.

As often happened whenever she was in a fight for her life, Annja's senses suddenly became hypersharp, giving the effect that she was moving incredibly fast in a world where time had suddenly slowed to a crawl. Out of the corner of her eye, she saw the third man had managed to get his hands around his gun and was bringing it up in her direction. Without stopping her momentum she planted her foot and continued her spin, the hand holding the sword coming up and down again, her weapon whistling through the air like the keening of a hungry ghost. The edge of the sword struck the man's arm just below his elbow.

The gun dropped into the dirt at his feet.

The soldier was opening his mouth to scream when Annja silenced him with one final blow of her sword.

Heart beating madly thanks to the adrenaline coursing through her system, Annja took a few deep breaths to get herself under control. She collected the soldiers' weapons and tossed them into the darkness. She stripped the belts from the bodies and used them to bind the hands and feet of the unconscious man, assuring that he wouldn't make a sudden appearance and cause her future difficulties.

When she was ready, she picked up her rifle once more and headed toward the mess area on the other side of camp. As she drew closer, the captain's voice came to her clearly.

"¿Donde esta el tesoro?"

None of the hostages answered him. Annja knew that the vast majority of those working the dig spoke Spanish and she was surprised that they seemed to be pretending otherwise, but she was glad they were. It meant there was still some fight in them and that was good. The sudden attack hadn't broken their spirit at least.

The captain tried again, this time in English.

"Where is the treasure?"

By now Annja had reached the edge of the wide area that served as the camp's main meeting place. Floodlights set up on the front of the mess tent lit the place up well, allowing her to get a good look at the rebel leader.

He was about her height, with that wiry look to him that told her not only would he be fast in a hand-to-hand fight, but that he'd have the strength to match his speed, as well. A wide scar started beneath his right eye and curled down to the edge of his mouth. Unlike the other soldiers, he was only armed with a handgun, a handgun that was currently pointed absently at the rest of the dig team who were kneeling in a semicircle in front of him. He did not appear to be happy with the cooperation he was getting, but he was clearly distracted, as well, glancing back repeatedly over his shoulder at the trailhead that led to the cenote.

Annja smiled grimly to see his unease.

Sorry, buddy, but there won't be any help from that direction.

She knew she was going to have to use the gun this time, for the sword would be far too conspicuous and there would be too many questions about it afterward. While it wasn't her preference, she'd handled guns before and shouldn't have any problems.

As the captain began shouting in anger at the captives, Annja checked to see that her weapon was ready to fire and then strode out of the darkness and into the light.

4

"Put down the gun!"

Annja stood just inside the circle of light, the automatic rifle in her hands pointed unerringly at the rebel commander standing in front of her.

He started in surprise at the sound of her voice and turned in her direction, the gun in his hand coming up slightly toward her.

Annja didn't wait to see what he was going to do with it, but stitched a row of bullets across the dirt at his feet.

"I said put down the gun," she said, "or I'll fill you full of holes."

It surely wasn't the first time the captain had had a weapon pointed at him and his sense of machismo wouldn't. let him surrender to a woman that easily, it seemed.

He didn't drop the weapon, but neither did he raise it any higher in her direction. Instead, he glanced behind her while trying to stall.

"You are making a mistake, *señorita*. A very big mistake."

Annja shook her head. "I don't think so. And you can stop looking over my shoulder. They aren't coming."

"Pardon?"

"Your troops. They aren't coming."

He scoffed, but after a moment or two more of silence, he frowned. As more time passed and help still didn't arrive, he began to realize that he was on his own.

Here it comes, Annja thought.

The rebel leader had been backed into a corner. He could either surrender to a woman, something his masculine pride objected to strongly, or he could try and fight his way out of his current predicament.

Annja had little doubt which option he was going to choose.

When he made his move, she was ready for him. He snapped his arm up toward her as he turned to the side, hoping to present a smaller target for her to shoot at while giving him enough time to kill her and thereby save himself.

Anticipating just such a move, Annja put two bullets into his upper chest before he could complete his turn.

An expression of surprise crossed his face and then he fell to the ground, dead on impact.

Silence covered the scene in its heavy embrace and then her companions were shouting her name and cheering. She dropped her weapon and moved to their sides, untying them and then directing those who were free to do the same for the rest.

Under Annja's supervision, the rebels were rounded up by the archaeologists and other camp staff, the hands and feet of those soldiers who were still alive tied securely with the ropes that they'd just taken off their own wrists. They were placed under the lights by the mess tent, where they could be watched until help could arrive. The dead were brought over, as well. Annja caught more than one of her dig mates watching her when they thought she wasn't looking—after they saw what had been done to the soldiers. Annja didn't care. She'd done what she'd had to given the circumstances. She'd spared lives when she'd been able to and so her conscience was clear.

When they were finished, everyone gathered in front of the mess tent, arguing about what they should do next. Annja had just managed to get everyone settled down so they could discuss things rationally when Evans, the cook, pointed back over Annja's shoulder and shouted, "Look!"

Annja turned to see multiple sets of headlights coming down the narrow dirt track that served as the only entrance to the camp. They were moving rapidly and it only took a few minutes before they were close enough to see the vehicles were American-made military Humvees painted in green camouflage.

As the trucks braked to a stop, armed soldiers in blue jumpsuits, black flack vests and helmets poured out and took up defensive positions around the camp while Annja stared openmouthed in surprise.

A short, muscular man in an officer's uniform climbed down from the passenger seat of the lead vehicle, looked at the rebel soldiers, all carefully bound and gagged, and then marched over to where Annja stood. He stared at her for a moment, his expression grim, and then said, "Who is in charge, please?" in heavily accented English.

Annja had no idea who these men were, what they were doing here, or even if they might be allied in some way with the rebels that she'd just defeated. Her hand curled ready to summon her sword, but she didn't draw it. Not until, at least. Not till she knew who they were or what they wanted.

Deciding her friends and teammates had had enough

for one night, Annja bit the bullet and answered his question. "I am," she replied.

His grim expression broke into a toothy smile. "Then my compliments to you, *señorita*. You and your people have saved me considerable time and energy in tracking down and detaining these dogs."

As he explained, the officer in question was Major Enrique Hernandez, of La Policia Mexicana, and he and his squad had been tracking this particular group of rebel soldiers for the past several days. Unfortunately they had lost them a few miles to the south of their present position. Hernandez had been trying to pick up the rebels' trail again when they had intercepted an emergency radio signal from the camp indicating it was under attack. The major explained that it had probably been just bad luck that the rebels had stumbled onto the excavation site, but their leaders weren't fools and the chance to add any artifacts that could draw good money on the black market had likely been too good to pass up.

Surprisingly, Hernandez didn't ask many questions about what had happened to the rebels or how a few archaeologists and graduate students had managed to overpower six soldiers armed with heavy weaponry. He seemed happy just to have the problem dealt with and in so final a manner. Perhaps he felt he was better off not knowing.

Either way, Annja wasn't going to complain. The last thing she wanted was more attention from the law enforcement community, in this country or any other. She'd certainly had her fair share of that lately.

As the major began ordering his men to secure the weapons and pick up the bodies, Annja excused herself and went looking for a hose. She could stand the stench of the muck she was covered in for only so long.

5

"They say that you single-handedly defeated the rebels. Is that true?"

The voice was male, with a clipped British accent, and decidedly unfamiliar to her.

Annja used one hand to shield her eyes from the glare of the floodlights and looked toward the speaker.

The newcomer was tall and good-looking, with dark curly hair and a five-o'clock shadow that somehow made him look more carefully groomed than if he had been simply clean shaven. His white shirt and tan suit had yet to pick up any of the telltale streaks of red dust that quickly covered anyone who had been on location more than a few minutes, which meant that he'd just arrived.

He stood in a relaxed, easygoing manner, but something about him still set her radar to tingling.

Ever since coming into possession of the magically restored sword that had once belonged to Joan of Arc, her life had been full of dangerous situations and even deadlier enemies. She'd been forced to fight for her life in more than a dozen places around the world, from the jungles of the Amazon to the sands of New Mexico, from the snows of Siberia to the waters of Indochina. She'd quickly learned to recognize the wolves moving among the sheep, and the man standing before her was definitely not one of the latter.

Given the close relationship between Mexico and the U.S., Annja pegged him for some kind of government adviser who had come in with the troops. Probably CIA or Department of Defense. It had to be something like that. His complete indifference to the police troops moving about the camp was a dead giveaway.

Having sized him up, she turned away, no longer interested.

"Yeah, well, you shouldn't believe everything you hear," she said dismissively, as she continued to hose herself down in an effort to get the blood and muck off her clothing. When she straightened back up, she found him still standing there, watching her, in turn.

"Can I help you with something?" she asked, with more than a bit of frustrated exasperation in her voice. The last thing she needed was some government flunky ogling her.

"That would depend. Are you, by chance, Annja Creed?"

Annja frowned. Aside from her producer, Doug Morrell, she hadn't told anyone where she was going when she'd left Brooklyn three weeks before. And while it wasn't unusual for fans of the television show she worked for—*Chasing History's Monsters*—to recognize her in public, it was strange to find a fan in the middle of the Mexican jungle at a dig site that only a handful of people were even aware of.

She used his words back at him. "That would depend. Who's asking?"

He chuckled. "Touché, Ms. Creed. Touché. Forgive me. My name is Mason Jones, though my friends call me Mason. I'm here with an invitation from my employer, John Davenport."

Annja wasn't certain if she'd heard him correctly.

"John Davenport?"

"Yes."

"*The* John Davenport?"

Jones cocked his head to one side and looked at her as if he were examining some fascinating new species of insect. "Is there some other John Davenport I should be aware of?"

"No. No, of course not," Annja said quickly, caught more than a little off balance by the way the situation was unfolding. So much for the government adviser theory. And Jones was right. There was only one John Davenport worth talking about. Davenport was to Britain what Gates was to America or Murdoch to Australia. All three were incredibly wealthy, but only Davenport had an active interest in ancient cultures and used his immense wealth to regularly sponsor major archaeological expeditions to all kinds of unusual locales.

Of course, none of them had the kind of wealth her mentor, Roux, or even his former protégé, Garin Braden, had acquired during their long existence, but that was neither here nor there. It wasn't actually a fair comparison for one thing. Both Roux and Garin were tied to the mysticism surrounding the sword of Joan of Arc, just as she was. She had met them both during that fateful excursion in the mountains of France, when she had been hunting the Beast of Gevaudan. She'd found the beast, but she also found something else—the final missing piece of Joan's sword, shattered by her English captors before they burned her at the stake. It was only later, after the sword had mysteriously reforged itself as if by magic, that she had discovered both men had been contemporaries of Joan. Roux had been one of Joan's protectors. Garin, in turn, had been his squire. Something mystical had happened when Joan's sword was shattered, something that had kept them from aging or dying for hundreds of years. Comparing Davenport's wealth, obtained over a single lifetime, to theirs was like comparing apples and watermelons. Still, the fact that Davenport even knew she existed was frankly astounding to Annja, never mind that he had sent someone to find her in the middle of nowhere.

With nothing else looming on the horizon, she had gladly accepted when the dig's director had come calling. Several weeks in the jungle unearthing the treasures of the past had sounded like just the thing to escape the hustle and bustle of Brooklyn and the pop culture version of archaeology she was often forced to serve up in the name of ratings or *Chasing History's Monsters*.

Now, it seemed, the world had come looking for her again.

"What can I do for Mr. Davenport?" Annja asked. She was suddenly acutely aware of how she must look—her hair still full of the muck from the bottom of the cenote and her T-shirt and pants now wet from the hose.

Jones reached inside his suit jacket and came out with a cream-colored envelope. He handed it to her. The envelope was sealed with a dollop of red wax, in the middle of which had been pressed the Davenport company logo. The seal was unbroken, but Annja didn't leave it that way for long. Inside was a note on a small white card. It was handwritten in a smooth, flowing script that spoke of the confidence inherent in the man who'd penned it.

Dear Ms. Creed,

It would please me greatly if you would accept my invitation to dinner this evening at my home outside Mexico City in order to discuss a particular business proposal. Mason is authorized to provide anything you require, including transportation to and from the estate, and I am willing to pay you a consulting fee of $5,000 just to hear me out, no strings attached. At the very least, you can be assured of having an excellent meal.

Sincerely,

John Davenport

Annja looked up from the note to find Mason waiting patiently for her answer.

She thought about it for less than a minute and then shrugged, "Sure. Why not?" she said.

AFTER CHECKING IN with the site coordinator to let him know that she would be leaving, Annja changed into clean clothing, gathered what little gear she had from her tent and returned to the main encampment to find Mason standing next to a newer model Land Rover. The black exterior seemed to soak up the tropical sun, but Annja had little doubt the air-conditioned interior would provide a cool refuge from the heat. Jones opened the passenger door for her, stowed her bag in back and then climbed in behind the wheel. Mexico City was at the other end of a three-hour drive down a poorly maintained dirt track and Annja settled in for the trip, only to be surprised when Mason pulled off the main drag onto a side road that amounted to little more than a goat trail.

"Mexico City is that way," Annja said, pointing back

in the direction they'd just come from, thinking he might have gotten turned around in the dense jungle.

Jones nodded. "You are correct, Ms. Creed," he said, glancing at her, his expression noncommittal. He turned his attention back to the road before him.

Annja gave him a moment to explain further, but when it was clear he wasn't going to do so, she asked, "Then why on earth are we going this way?"

"Because this is where I left the helicopter," he said.

"Oh," Annja replied.

They bounded over a few potholes, skirted a fallen tree trunk and emerged suddenly into a small clearing recently cut from the undergrowth.

In the middle of the clearing sat a Bell JetRanger helicopter, its sleek black frame looking like some kind of giant insect in the midst of that primeval landscape.

"Right. The helicopter. How silly of me," she said.

This time, Jones couldn't keep a straight face and actually grinned.

THE FLIGHT DIDN'T TAKE LONG and her companion turned out to be enjoyable company. They talked for a time and then Mason asked the one question that inevitably came up.

"How do you like working in television?"

Annja hesitated. "You've seen the show?" she asked cautiously, trying to feel him out to see what he thought. *Chasing History's Monsters* wasn't for everyone. The weekly show was focused around the exploration of legends, myths and the possible existence of strange creatures like the Loch Ness Monster and Sasquatch. Every episode featured two or three different stories, presented with a mix of facts and fiction. Being the scientist she was,

Annja's role usually involved shooting down the more outrageous claims, especially those of a supernatural sort. Her field of expertise was on the historical basis of even some of the most ridiculous stories and she tried to show how myths and legends grew out of factual events that were often distorted or misunderstood over time.

Of course, using hard science to prove that things like vampires and werewolves didn't exist only gave the true believers more reason to shout, "Cover-up!" and go on believing all the same.

Luckily, Mason wasn't one of those.

"I'm a regular fan," he said. "In fact, it was because of your work on the show that the boss decided to seek your advice."

"Oh," Annja said, thinking that one of the world's richest men watching her show on a regular basis was just a bit…weird. She couldn't quite wrap her head around it.

That little voice in the back of her head spoke up. Maybe he's watching it for some other reason, it said.

Almost as if he were reading her mind, Mason said, "Gotta tell ya, though. I don't care much for that other host. Kristen? Kathy?"

"Kristie. Kristie Chatham."

"Right. I mean, my Lord, could they hire a bigger bimbo? She can't even string three coherent sentences together and the wardrobe malfunctions became tiring after the first time or two. Do we really need one every other episode?"

Mason was banking the chopper, paying attention to the controls rather than looking her way, and so he missed the expression of shock on her face, shock that quickly turned to delight as he went on.

"Do they think every guy watching the show is a complete moron?"

Yes, Annja thought, but didn't say. She decided right then and there that she and Mason Jones were going to be very good friends.

"Tell me more," she said with a smile.

By the time he set the chopper down on the landing pad at Benito Juárez International Airport in Mexico City about forty minutes later, they were on a first-name basis.

A car was waiting for them when they disembarked, a uniformed chauffeur standing beside the open door.

Mason introduced Annja to the driver, whose name was José, and told her that José would take her to her hotel so that she could freshen up prior to her dinner with Davenport.

"What about you?" Annja asked.

Mason jerked his thumb over his shoulder at the helicopter behind them. "Someone has to put away the toys," he said.

Satisfied that she was in good hands and things were proceeding the way they were supposed to, something she had learned the hard way not to take for granted, she climbed into the air-conditioned vehicle and let José drive her to where she needed to go.

The hotel turned out to be the Four Seasons on the Paseo de la Reforma, or, as the locals called it, Reforma, just a few blocks from Chapultepec Park—the oldest national park in North America—as well as the National Museum of Anthropology and History. The hotel staff was expecting her, José obviously having called ahead, and she was quickly whisked away to a luxury suite on one of the hotel's upper floors. The porter who carried her bag upstairs and deposited it in the walk-in closet passed on the message that all gratuities had been taken care of and that the car would be back for her at six. He shut the doors softly as he exited the room, leaving Annja to take in her posh surroundings.

The suite consisted of a spacious living room area, complete with a wet bar, a flat-screen TV, a stereo and DVD player, all carefully arranged amid the couch and several armchairs. The bedroom contained a king-size bed and another television artfully mounted on the wall, as well as a walk-in closet and private dressing area. But it was the master bath, with its oversize soaking tub, that did it for her. Annja wasted no time in filling it with hot water and scented bath oil, then stripped off her dust-covered clothing and settled in to enjoy a long soak.

When she had scrubbed away the last of the dirt and grime of the jungle and her muscles had unknotted enough that she was again feeling human, she rose from the water and slipped into the thick terry-cloth robe the hotel provided its guests. She sat in the dressing area and brushed out her long hair, then, noting it was almost five-thirty, decided she had just enough time to get dressed for her meeting with Davenport.

But when she stepped into the closet to retrieve her bag, she found a selection of quality clothing of different colors and styles hanging on the racks.

She whistled long and low.

A peek confirmed her suspicions—all of them were in her size. How Davenport had known that was beyond her. While she appreciated the thought and attention he had obviously put into this meeting, it also made her feel uneasy. Just what did the man want? And why the show? She didn't know, but there was one way to find out.

She ran her fingers over the fabrics of the dresses hanging in the closet, admiring their cut and the feel of each garment, then turned away and pulled some clothes from her own bag. By the time the porter called up to tell her that her car was waiting, she was comfortably dressed in a pair of tan cargo pants, a white linen blouse and her sturdy hiking shoes. She wasn't here to play dress up for Davenport and she hoped her choice of clothing would convey that message without making her seem ungrateful. She added a native bead necklace that highlighted her amber-green eyes and decided it would have to do.

With a last glance in the mirror she headed for the elevator, her curiosity over being summoned to dinner by one of the richest men in the world nearly overwhelming her.

6

Davenport's note had said they would be meeting at his home, but Annja didn't expect that meant anything casual, so she wasn't surprised when they pulled up to an estate that looked as if it probably doubled the entire state of Rhode Island. A thick protective wall ran around the entire complex, and entrance to the property was gained through a tall iron gate, complete with a set of armed guards.

Inside it was like entering another world. Wide green lawns stretched out as far as the eye could see, with the grass and the endless variety of bushes and trees all carefully tended and landscaped. In the distance a group of horses grazed and Annja had no doubt that the bloodlines of those beasts were as pure as money could buy. The driveway twisted and turned, occasionally obscuring her view of the horses behind the trunks of age-old oaks, and then they rounded a corner and the house itself was revealed ahead of them, a vast sprawling structure in Saltillo tile and whitewashed stucco, complete with a flower-draped fountain in the center of the driveway.

As José brought the car to a halt, the door opened and Mason Jones appeared at the top of the steps in the company of an older gentleman with silver-gray hair and a long, narrow face. The severity of the man's features, however, was broken by the deep blue of his eyes and the playful smile that splashed across his face.

Annja recognized him at once.

John Davenport.

The two men descended the steps and waited for José to help her out of the vehicle. Mason performed the introductions.

"It's a pleasure to meet you," Annja said, extending her hand.

Davenport's smile seemed to grow wider, if that was at all possible, as he took her hand. "I assure you, lovely lady, the pleasure is all mine. Thank you for coming and welcome to my humble home."

Home, maybe, humble, no, Annja thought, but simply smiled at her host.

"I hope you like beef," Davenport said, as he turned and led her into the house. "I've had my chef prepare some fresh steaks from our organically fed Argentinian cattle. It is absolutely fabulous."

Dinner was excellent and through it all Davenport kept the conversation light and entertaining. It wasn't until well into the meal that Annja realized he would make an excellent interrogator. Davenport had subtly drawn her out on all manner of subjects, from her taste in music to the difficulties of working a dig in the midst of the jungle. She hadn't even been aware she'd been letting him direct the conversation for so long. Talking to him felt like the most natural thing in the world and Annja could see why he'd become as wealthy as he had. Anyone who spent five minutes in a room alone with him would come out feeling like they were old friends and it was simply human nature that friends wanted to help each other. She had little doubt that Davenport had built his empire on the strength of that personality.

Once the table was cleared and the servants had left the room, Davenport finally got down to business.

"Thank you for coming tonight," he said. "I'm sure you've been wondering why I've asked you here. The truth of the matter is that I could use some help with a special project, and after our conversation this evening I'm more convinced than ever that you're just the person to provide it."

Annja inclined her head graciously. "I'd be happy to help you in any way I can," she said honestly.

"Tell me. How familiar are you with Genghis Khan?"

Annja smiled. "Born in Mongolia in 1162. His given name was Temujin and he was named for a warrior slain by his father, one who exhibited bravery in that final confrontation. Declared himself ruler of the Mongol Empire in 1206 and died in 1227. In between, he created an empire four times larger than that of Alexander the Great, stretching from the Chinese coastline in the west to the Black Sea in the east, from the cold of the Arctic Circle in the north to the heat and humidity of India to the south. He was an innovator who assembled a nation out of a handful of warring tribes in perhaps one of the harshest locales on the face of the planet and held them together with nothing more than his iron vision and will. A man to be reckoned with in my view."

Davenport laughed. "I should have known better than to think I'd catch the host of *Chasing History's Monsters* without the facts at her fingertips." He took a sip of his wine and his voice took on a teasing quality. "Since you're the expert on monsters, tell me, was Genghis Khan the bloodthirsty conqueror that the media today has made him out to be? A man bent solely on rape, murder and mayhem?"

"Conqueror? Yes. Bloodthirsty? That depends on your viewpoint, I guess," Annja said, answering his question seriously. "Legend says that he once slaughtered an entire city—men, women, children and livestock—in retaliation for the death of his grandson. It also said that he made a habit of using the bodies of captured enemy soldiers to fill the siege trenches dug to keep his troops from reaching the walls of the cities he assaulted. But was that any different from what the Crusaders did at the siege of Jerusalem or at the slaughter at Béziers?"

"I guess not. But we don't generally think of the Crusaders as savage marauders hell-bent on ruining civilization," Davenport said.

"No, but perhaps we should. They did more damage and far less good than Genghis Khan did, and yet his people have come down through the ages being referred to as the Mongol horde. How's that for an epitaph?" Annja asked.

"Not one I'd choose for myself, that's for sure." Davenport paused as the servants came back into the room to serve coffee.

Accepting a cup, Annja inhaled the heady aroma and took a sip, then sighed in contentment. It was strong enough to knock your socks off, which was just the way she liked it.

Once the help had withdrawn, Davenport continued. "I'm considering putting together an expedition to find the Khan's lost tomb."

"Don't bother," Annja said, without even glancing up from her drink. Because she didn't do so, she missed the quick flicker of surprise that flashed across Davenport's face.

"Why not?" he asked.

"Because he more than likely didn't have one."

Davenport laughed, but when Annja glanced at him without joining in, he looked at her expression more closely. "You seem pretty sure of yourself."

"I am."

"Why is that?"

"Because, in the first place, the Mongol people didn't believe in tombs." Annja paused to gather her thoughts and to figure out the best way of passing on what she knew without seeming to preach at him. "Remember that the Mongols were a nomadic people, both before and after Genghis Khan united them as a single political body. They had few cities and those they did have were oriented toward storage of war booty rather than for any community-minded purpose."

Davenport nodded. "Go on."

"Because the Mongols moved from place to place, their religious beliefs evolved very much along similar lines. They considered the natural world to be full of spirits, much like the animists of feudal Japan. For instance, they were forbidden from bathing in rivers or streams because such places were considered the life blood of the earth itself and doing so would have been a horrible affront to the land.

"A Mongol warrior's greatest possession was his spirit banner. It was made by tying strands of hair from his best horses to the shaft of a spear. Whenever he made camp, the warrior would place the spirit banner outside the entrance to his tent to show his presence and to stand as a perpetual guardian. Over time, the union between the warrior and the banner became so strong that, upon the warrior's death, his soul was considered to reside in the banner and not the body."

"But Genghis Khan was not just any warrior," Davenport protested. "He was the spiritual father and warlord of the Mongol people. Just like people today, they would have wanted a place to remember him."

Annja shook her head. "They had one—the spirit banner. It rode with the Khan's descendants until 1647 when it was placed in the Shankh Monastery for safekeeping."

Davenport seemed fascinated with her story. "So you're saying the Mongol people didn't need a tomb because Genghis Khan's very soul rode alongside them wherever they went?"

While it wasn't a perfect explanation of Mongol religious beliefs, it was close enough that she nodded in agreement.

"Interesting," Davenport said, sitting back and watching her for a moment before continuing. "What if I told you that the legends were true, that the Mongols did build a secret tomb for their Great Khan? That they filled it with an amazingly diverse treasure trove, loot from the hundreds of cultures he conquered? And what if I said I had in my possession the journal of a man who had intimate details of the burial process itself, a journal that contained a map to the location of the tomb?"

Annja couldn't help but smile. "I'd say you'd better hire someone to authenticate the map and the writings pretty darn quick, because whatever you paid for it, it was too much. You've been had. Hell, I'd be happy to do it for you myself, just to prove to you the ridiculousness of the very idea."

Davenport smiled. "Good. Then that's settled," he said with a laugh. "You can start first thing in the morning."

Annja stared at him blankly for a moment, and then it dawned her that she had been neatly led right where Davenport had wanted her to go.

Well, she'd just have to take the job and show him how wrong he was. After what had happened she knew the dig was all but finished for the season; she'd simply give them a call and let them know she was going home early.

A map to the tomb of Genghis Khan? Ridiculous!

7

The next morning Annja rose shortly after sunrise and decided to get some exercise before she returned to Davenport's estate to view the artifact he claimed showed the way to Genghis Khan's tomb. Digging a pair of shorts and a T-shirt out of her bag, she threw on her sneakers and headed out to Chapultepec Park for a run.

Maybe it was the early hour, or possibly the anticipation of the work she was going to do that afternoon to prove Davenport wrong, but whatever the reason, Annja failed to spot the tail she picked up the moment she walked out of the hotel.

The man assigned to watch her was good; he stayed out of her visual area, sticking to the blind spots to the sides and the rear, and hung back enough that were she to stop suddenly he'd have plenty of time to react to the change of pace and act accordingly.

He needn't have worried, however, for the woman was too distracted to even notice him.

When she wandered into the park and began a series of stretches intended to loosen up her muscles for a run, the man knew it was now or never. He pulled a cell phone out of his pocket and dialed a number.

BACK IN THE LOBBY of the hotel, a second individual answered the call, listened briefly, then hung up and headed for the elevator.

It took the operative less than ten seconds to pick the lock on the woman's hotel room door and slip inside, closing the door gently behind him. He stood with his back to it for a moment, listening. His partner had said the woman was alone, but it still paid to be careful.

He hated these rush jobs; too little information meant too many potential ways that things could go wrong. You didn't argue with the boss, though. When he wanted something done, you did it, no questions asked. Simple as that. He'd seen what happened to people who questioned orders, and once was all it took to convince him never to do anything so foolish.

The suite was quiet; the only sounds were the faint hum of the air conditioner and the drip of a faucet that hadn't been turned off fully. Satisfied that the woman was staying alone and he wouldn't be interrupted, the operative threw caution to the wind and went to work, quickly and efficiently tossing the place, searching for the objects he'd been instructed to find.

He was an old hand at this kind of work and he took his time, methodically moving from room to room, mentally noting the position of every object before he moved it and putting it back in the exact same spot when he was finished. He'd come in like a ghost and he intended to go out again, as well, leaving nothing behind, not even the slightest clue, to indicate anything out of the ordinary had happened.

By the time his partner called, letting him know the woman had finished her run and was getting ready to leave the park, he had covered every square inch of the suite and was confident that he'd missed nothing.

The trouble was, he hadn't found what he was looking for, either.

Reluctantly, he withdrew his cell phone from the inside pocket of his jacket and dialed a number.

The phone rang several times before his employer's deep baritone voice came down the line.

"Yes?"

"They're not here."

"You're certain?"

The operative didn't need to be told what would happen to him if he turned out to be wrong; the implied threat in the man's tone was somehow more frightening than if he'd come right out and said something.

Swallowing hard to clear his throat, the operative said, "Yes. I'm certain."

He listened for a moment, nodding in agreement with what was said even though there was no one there to see him do it, and then lifted the business card he'd found among the woman's personal effects.

"Creed," he said into the phone in answer to his employer's question. "Annja. *A-n-n-j-a.* Annja Creed."

He listened for another moment and then closed the phone. There was no need to say goodbye; his employer had already hung up.

The operative took one last look around to make certain he hadn't left anything out of place and then slipped out of the room as quietly as he had entered.

ANNJA ENTERED HER HOTEL ROOM in a rush, knowing she had very little time left to get cleaned up before Davenport's car arrived to take her to the estate. She'd only gotten halfway across the living room, however, when she stopped abruptly, her senses screaming.

Someone had been in her room.

Nothing was disturbed; everything looked as if it was right where it had been when she'd left for her run half an hour earlier.

Yet she had the definite sense that someone had been there in her absence. Call it a gut hunch, a sixth sense, whatever. She knew it as surely as she knew her own name.

She stood still and listened, trying to determine if anyone was hiding in the bedroom just beyond, but all she could hear was the low hum of the air conditioner she'd left running earlier.

She reached out with her right hand and drew her sword out of the otherwhere. Having the weapon in hand made her feel more confident to face whoever might have invaded her space.

Cautiously, she walked forward and peeked around the door frame into the bedroom, ready to pull her head back at a moment's notice if there was anyone there.

The room was empty.

You're getting paranoid, she told herself. No one even knows you're in Mexico City.

Still, she checked the bathroom and the closets, just to be safe. When they turned out to be as empty as the bedroom, she at last allowed herself to relax and released the sword back into the otherwhere. Probably just the maid, she told herself, and turned her attention to getting out of her sweaty clothes and into something more suitable for a long afternoon of doing what she loved best.

MASON WAS WAITING when she arrived at the estate, and after a quick hello, he led her upstairs to a room on the second floor where Davenport was waiting. A long table stood in the center of the room, surrounded by a variety of scientific equipment. Annja glanced at them and then made a beeline for the glass case sitting in the middle of the table.

Inside was a small, leather-bound book, with yellowed pages and a cracked and faded cover.

"Is this it?" she asked, turning and acknowledging her employer for the first time since entering the room.

"And a good-morning to you, too, Annja," Davenport said with a laugh. "And yes, that is *it,* as you say. That little volume is going to lead us to the treasure of the centuries."

She smiled at his enthusiasm. "If it's authentic," she said. "What can you tell me about it?"

Davenport's tone became a bit more formal, as if he were reciting information he'd just learned and wanted to be sure to get it correct.

"In 1245, Pope Innocent IV, suspicious of the lingering power of the Mongols, sent a diplomatic party to the court of Guyuk, Genghis Khan's grandson, at Karakorum. Leading that party was a friar by the name of Giovanni di Plano Carpini."

Annja nodded. She was aware of Carpini's journey and the book he'd written upon his return, *The Story of the Mongols Whom We Call the Tartars.* It was one of the first European accounts of life in the Mongol Empire, and though it was later relegated to a secondary position when Marco Polo published the accounts of his own journey among the people of the steppes, it was still considered an important historical document.

"With Carpini went a priest by the name of Father

Michael Curran. Curran was a rising star, one of the Vatican's inner circle, if you will, and was there at the direct order of the pope himself."

"To do what?" Annja asked.

Davenport grinned. "Spy on the Mongols, of course. Remember, it had been less than twenty-five years since Genghis Khan's army had turned back at the Mohi River rather than continue his conquest of Hungary and the rest of Eastern Europe. I'm sure more than just the pope was wondering when, or if, Guyuk was going to try again."

"So this book—?"

"It is Curran's personal account of his time among the Mongols," Davenport said.

Annja frowned. "If Curran reported what he learned to the pope, why has the tomb remained undiscovered all this time?"

"That's just it. Curran never had the chance to tell anyone what he learned, least of all the pope. He never made it out of Mongolia," Davenport said.

Mason took up the story from there. "Apparently the group Curran was traveling with was attacked by a rival clan while deep within the Forbidden Zone, an area deep in the heart of the empire that the relatives of Genghis Khan had set aside forever as a monument to his glory. Curran managed to survive the attack itself, along with one other man. Badly wounded and left for dead, the two of them sought shelter in a mountain cave. That's where Curran learned the location of the Khan's tomb from his dying companion. Unfortunately for Curran, a winter storm trapped them in the cave for several weeks and he eventually succumbed from his wounds before he could make his way back to Karakorum." Mason gestured at the diary. "It's all in there—his impressions of Karakorum, his audience with Guyuk, the attack on the convoy, his ruminations as he lay dying all but alone in that cave."

Knowing that the little book in the case before her contained the last thoughts of a man who had died cold and in a place far from home made her view it with even more respect than she had before. Still, something about Mason's story bothered her.

"How do you know Curran's companion wasn't lying? That it wasn't all some fever dream brought on by his impending death?" she asked.

Out came the hallmark Davenport grin. "Actually, I don't. But nor do I have to prove that, at least not yet. All I need to know right now is whether or not the diary is the right age to actually be Curran's. Once we determine that, we can worry about the rest. First things first."

Annja thought about it for a moment. "Fair enough," she replied. "I guess that means I'd best get to work."

With the two men watching, Annja placed her backpack on the table next to the case and unzipped it. Inside were a digital SLR camera and a laptop computer. Both pieces of equipment had seen their fair share of adventures at her side and she'd come to rely on them in more ways than one.

She took out the laptop and started it up, then connected the camera to it. She fired off a few shots of the lab around her, just to test the connection. Satisfied that all was working the way it should, she put the camera down and turned back to her pack.

Annja fished out a pair of white cotton gloves from a side pocket of the bag and pulled them on. The soft material would protect the brittleness of the pages, as well as provide a barrier between them and her skin, keeping the damaging oil from her fingertips from doing the journal any harm. She might think it was a fake, but she'd treat it as authentic until she could prove otherwise. For the same reason, she laid out a wide piece of silk on the tabletop in front of her.

"May I?" she asked Davenport.

"Be my guest."

She opened the small brass clasp holding the case closed and lifted the lid. Reaching inside, she drew out the slim volume and set it down in the area she had prepared.

Just like that, she was lost in the work. She might be a minor television celebrity—and a fierce adventurer, thanks to Joan's sword—but that didn't mean she'd lost her love of archaeology and the mystery and suspense that came with it. Discovering a new artifact, tracing its lineage, verifying its authenticity—it still moved and inspired her in ways that few other things could. Her awareness of the other people in the room faded as she gave herself completely to the task in front of her.

Annja picked up the camera and used it to take a full-size color photo of every single page in the book. She did the same with the inside and outside cover pages, both front and back. The pictures were immediately downloaded on to the laptop and organized sequentially. This would allow her to view the entire work without the need to handle the book itself, eliminating the possibility, no matter how slim, of it being damaged in the process. It would also let her magnify various sections, something she couldn't do if she were working solely from the original.

Once she was finished, she put the camera away and replaced the journal in its protective case. Pulling up a chair, she settled in front of the laptop and began reading.

8

Annja was quickly engrossed in her work, so much so that she never even noticed when Davenport gestured to Mason and the two of them slipped out of the room behind her back.

The book had been handwritten in Latin in a thin, spidery script. The pages were faded and, in some cases, heavily stained, making it difficult to understand certain passages, but for a seven-hundred-year-old book it was remarkably well preserved.

She began to read.

The book was exactly what Davenport had claimed—the personal journal of a man who'd endured a long and arduous journey deep onto the Mongolian steppes on behalf of the church. Curran was an excellent writer and she soon found herself drawn into the story itself. She could sense the man's loneliness, could feel his determination to do the job right and return home. She even ached along with him when his only companion succumbed to his wounds and died in the middle of the night. Curran's death must have been sudden, for he hadn't made any reference to the coming end in his journal. One day he was writing about trying to dig himself out and then the next, nothing.

She read through the entire work once, start to finish, looking for glaring problems that would instantly tell her the document was a fake. When she didn't find any, she settled in for a more intricate examination.

The first thing she did was look for historical inaccuracies. She'd once examined a manuscript supposedly written by a Catholic priest who'd accompanied Vasco da Gama on his famous journey around the Cape of Good Hope. It had been an excellent forgery; the paper had passed the radiocarbon test, the text had been written in the dialect spoken in the area where the priest had supposedly lived at the time, even the ink had been correctly aged. The whole charade had only fallen apart when Annja reached the last page of the manuscript. The forger had added the words *Societus Iesu,* Latin for Society of Jesus, after the writer's signature. Apparently he hadn't done his homework on that little addition, for the Jesuits, a Catholic order founded by St. Ignatius of Loyola, wouldn't come into being until fifty years after the events portrayed in the manuscript.

The trouble was that not only were Curran's observations historically correct, as nearly as she could tell, such as the location of Guyuk's summer encampment and the establishment of trade with parts of China, but they contained many small details that the average forger more than likely wouldn't be aware of at all. Things like the stench that hung over the Mongol army at all times in the field due to their reluctance to bathe in rivers and streams, or the way Mongol horsemen would smear their exposed skin with yak grease to take the bite out of the winter wind on the high plains.

She stopped looking for historical errors after a few hours and turned instead to linguistic ones. Language grows and changes, just like any other organic element, and a good historian can also spot a forgery by the way certain words or phrases are used within a text.

Annja struck out there, too.

Her doubts about the authenticity of the manuscript were starting to take a beating in the face of what she was reading. So far, the manuscript had passed every test.

Knowing she'd been at it for hours, she got up and stretched a bit. She noticed a small serving tray had been left by the door at some point, and lifting the lid she discovered a plate of turkey sandwiches, complete with cranberry sauce and a bed of lettuce, along with a soft drink that was still icy cold. She gratefully dug in.

When she finished eating, she decided to give the text a rest and turn her attention to the map that had been hand drawn in the back of the journal.

She was in the midst of rereading the document for the sixth or seventh time when she saw a key piece of the puzzle. Several words on the page started with a funny little curlicue, as if the writer had left the pen on the page for a few seconds too long. At first, she thought it was just an artifact of the particular pen the author had used. Perhaps its point hadn't been cut properly and the ink had pooled where it shouldn't have. But then she began to notice that there wasn't a consistency to its appearance. On one page a word starting with the letter *T* would have the little curlicue, but two pages later the same word would not.

Curious, she went back to the beginning and began to flip through the images of each page, looking for the strange little mark. Her trained eye began to pick out a pattern to its occurrences, something a little less than random.

"That's interesting," she told the empty room around her.

Grabbing a piece of paper, she went back to the beginning of the text again, but this time she wrote down every word where the strange mark appeared. She listed them in a vertical column, one after another, until she had reached the end. Scanning down the list, she quickly noted that the words seemed to form sentences and so she rewrote them in horizontal lines instead, guessing where one sentence left off and another one began. When she was finished, she was left with several paragraphs of text.

Her eyes widened as she realized what they were.

9

They came over the wall like ghosts.

Unheard.

Unseen.

They didn't hesitate once they were on the ground on the other side but rather set off immediately for their objective, unconcerned with any of the defensive measures that had been put into place to prevent just the kind of thing they were attempting.

The mastiffs caught their scent within seconds of their appearance on this side of the wall. Trained to silently advance and render intruders immobile, the massive dogs moved through the darkness, intent on teaching their prey a lesson about trespassing where they were not wanted.

The lead man caught sight of the dogs as they came around the corner of the house. They were large, a good hundred and eighty pounds if an ounce, and they were coming on fast, but he kept his concentration on his objective, the south wing of the main house, and trusted his companions to handle their part of the job.

The dogs were quick, but the two men stationed in the trees outside the estate were quicker. Seconds after the dogs came into view, the sniper team went into operation, adjusting for distance, windage and the animals' oncoming speed, and then firing.

Two shots.

Two hits.

The tranquilizer darts took another few seconds to work, so the dogs had closed to within fifteen feet of the lead man before they faltered and then crashed to the ground, unconscious.

Ignoring them, the team raced on.

The intruders made it halfway across the lawn before the dogs' handlers came around the side of the house on their usual patrol route. The handlers had only just begun to process the fact that their charges were nowhere to be seen when the team in the trees fired again.

Unconscious, the handlers dropped into the grass before they even knew what hit them.

The motion sensors and floodlights came next. A swath of earth twenty feet in width had been seeded with pressure plates attached to a series of high-intensity lights that were intended to blind and disorient intruders who made it past the dogs. The specific section of the lawn containing the sensors looked no different than any other and an ordinary intruder would have been hard-pressed to get beyond it.

But as they had already demonstrated, this was no ordinary group of intruders.

The lead man never slowed. He charged into the designated area, his eyes on the wall that was getting closer with every step, confident that the sensors had been disarmed.

No sirens split the night.

No lights forced back the darkness.

The lead man reached the outside wall of the manor house. Unslinging the grapple gun from where he carried it across his back, he took aim and fired. The small steel hook shot upward, arced over the edge of the roof and embedded itself in the tiles high above. A sharp tug on the climbing rope attached to the hook confirmed its placement.

Hand over hand, the lead man and two others climbed to the roof, while the final two men in the team took up positions at the bottom of the rope, guarding the escape route for the others.

Once on the rooftop they followed the route that they had all committed to memory, moving from their initial entry point at the end of the south wing to a section of the roof above the main manor house. Their leader used the four chimneys to orient the team and then advanced to a spot midway along the roof's western edge.

At his signal, his two companions began pulling up the roofing tiles and stacking them to one side. When they had created a space large enough for a man to fit through, one of them stepped to the side. The lead man, who by now had assembled a portable cutting rig from parts removed from his pack, passed the rig to his waiting companion.

The item they had come for was less than fifteen feet away, separated from them by just a thin section of plaster and wood.

The leader glanced at his watch.

They were right on time.

He gave the signal for his teammate to start cutting.

ANNJA FOUND MASON and his employer in Davenport's study on the first floor. She wasted no time in getting to the point.

"Something about the journal has been bothering me since this morning and I've only just now figured out what it is. If Curran died in that cave, who found the journal and how did you come to be in possession of it?" she asked.

Mason glanced at Davenport and the other man nodded, giving permission for him to answer the question.

"I handle a variety of jobs for Mr. Davenport. One of those happens to be scouting out new business opportunities. I was in Mongolia recently with a geological team, looking for mineral deposits. While investigating a series of caves a few days outside of Karakorum, we stumbled upon the mummified remains of two men. The journal was on a shelf near one of the bodies."

"And so you took it?"

Mason shrugged. "I thought it might be important and taking it with me seemed the best way of preserving it."

Annja frowned. "But now that you've had time to examine its contents, surely you understand that the site, and anything it contains, could be of historic importance to the Mongolian people?"

Davenport stepped in. "Of course we do, Annja. But we also want credit for finding the site and permission to excavate it. That is why we intend to apply for the proper paperwork to sponsor an expedition to do just that in the spring." He spread his hands, as if to say, *Can't you see we're doing the right thing here?* "Determining the authenticity of the journal seemed an important step in that process."

Annja wasn't sure if that was the whole story or not, but she recognized that it was all she was going to get at the moment.

"Good enough," she said, with a shrug of her own that clearly said she wasn't going to make an issue of it. "Then

I guess it's okay to tell you…I think it's real." Annja couldn't keep the smile from spreading across her face as she admitted it.

Davenport let out a whoop of joy. "I knew it!" he shouted. "I just knew it."

Mason was up, shaking his employer's hand, congratulating him, the two of them laughing and talking, when Annja broke in again.

"I said I think the *journal* is real. Unfortunately, the map is not."

That brought both of them up short. Davenport's voice held a trace of steel as he asked, "What do you mean *the map is not?*"

Annja brought her laptop over to the table in front of the chairs where they'd been seated and turned it around to face them.

"Look," she said. "This is a full-scale image of the map from the back of the journal." The map appeared on the screen before them. "I cleaned it up some, but otherwise it is exactly the same. No image enhancements or anything like that."

The two men nodded to show they were following her.

"Now this," she said, calling up another image, "is a modern-day map of the same area. I've reduced it to scale to match the other one." The two maps appeared side by side.

Davenport glanced between them. "I don't see… Oh."

Annja grinned. "Yeah. Oh." She tapped the keyboard and they all watched as the two images slid over each other. Doing so allowed them to see that Curran, or whoever had drawn the map, had deliberately introduced errors into the positioning of many of the major landmarks. For instance, the Onon River had been moved slightly to the east while the Hentiyn Nuruu mountain range had been relocated a good distance to the south. The other errors were similar in nature; Annja had counted eleven in all.

Davenport stared at the map in confusion. "Why would he do that?"

Annja opened her mouth to reply but Mason beat her to the answer.

"He wanted to pass on the information but didn't want to make it easy in case it fell into the wrong hands. Remember, there's no way for anyone at that time to verify the map short of going there themselves. So a few subtle alterations and, voilà—the secret is safe."

Davenport frowned. "So the map's a fake? It won't lead us to the tomb?"

Annja smiled. "The map's authentic all right, in the sense that it is as old as we expected it to be, and more than likely penned by the individual we think penned it. The thing is, it just doesn't give accurate directions to the tomb. At least, not directly. The location of the tomb is in there, we just have to break the code to get it."

Davenport's eyes shone with curiosity. "Code?" he asked.

THE CUTTER SHUT OFF the torch and set it aside. He drew out a long-bladed combat knife. He used it to wedge up one side of the rectangle he'd cut in the roof, and then slid a gloved hand beneath it. A sharp tug broke the last remaining edge and the piece came free in his hand. He passed it to the others and then cautiously stuck his head down through the opening he'd created.

The work area was immediately below them, just as they'd been told it would be.

There was no need for instructions. The entry team had been briefed thoroughly before their departure and they all knew their own individual assignments. One man stayed behind to cover the roof while the leader and the last remaining team member lowered themselves through the hole they'd cut and dropped lightly to the floor below.

They were in!

"LET ME SHOW YOU." Annja closed out the maps and brought up several pages from the journal itself. She pointed out the strange addition to each letter that had caught her eye in the first place, then showed them how selecting only those words brought up another message hidden inside the text of the first.

Beneath the watchful gaze of the eternal blue heaven
The spirit of the warrior points the way

To where the blood of the world intertwines
And the voice in the earth has its say

The sixty brides rode sixty steeds
And now rest beneath the watchful eyes of those who came before

In their arms is the truth you seek
The way to all that was and more

Then climb to the place where Tengri and Gazan meet
It is there that the Batur makes his home

"What the heck is that?" Mason asked, bewildered.

"I'm not one hundred percent sure," Annja replied nonchalantly, "but if I had to guess, I'd say it is probably directions to the final resting place of Genghis Khan himself."

———————

10

Annja's announcement was met with renewed excitement from the two men.

"Do you think you can decipher it?" Mason asked.

Annja nodded. "I've worked through the first stanza already, I think. And I've got some ideas about the others. But understand, there's no way to be certain. We could get all the way there only to discover I was wrong about the first part, which would then call the rest of the solution into question, as well. It's a crapshoot."

She didn't miss the look that passed between the two men.

"Let's say, just for the sake of argument, that I can figure it out. What, then?" Annja asked.

Davenport laughed. "What, then? Why, we go after it, of course!" he said. "In fact, we'd better start making plans to do so now. The off-season is coming on quickly over there, so we'll have to wait until spring, of course, but that will give us time to get things organized and allow you a chance to work out the puzzle to your satisfaction before we leave the country. We'll need to get travel and dig permits from the Mongolian authorities, arrange for local guides and transportation, never mind choosing the right individuals to be a part of the dig team." He must have seen something in her face in reaction to that last statement, for he suddenly turned to her with a grin. "You are coming along, right?" he asked.

With a start, Annja realized she did want to go. Very badly, in fact. Working with the map and diary had fired her desire to follow this thing to the end, to see if there was any truth to the words Father Curran had so faithfully recorded all those years ago.

She'd been to a lot of places across the globe, but Mongolia wasn't one of them. And being able to take part in the search to uncover one of the world's greatest mysteries? It was the chance of a lifetime. Doing something like this was why she had become an archaeologist in the first place. There was no way she would pass it up.

Besides, she thought with a sly grin, she'd have her producer at *Chasing History's Monsters,* Doug Morrell, eating out of her hand for months if they pulled this one off.

"When do we leave?" she asked.

OUTSIDE IN THE GRASS, one of the dog handlers, Kyle Davis, stirred. He'd come into work that night as a last-minute replacement for a fellow employee who had gotten sick. Davis was a big man, not just tall but heavily muscled, as well; and, as chance, or perhaps fate, would have it, he outweighed the regularly scheduled guard by a good fifty pounds.

That meant the tranquilizer dose that had been prepared

for the original guard wasn't strong enough to keep Davis under for long. Certainly not long enough for the intruders to accomplish their goal.

He woke shortly after being shot.

Davis had been trained well. As he slowly came back to consciousness, he stayed where he was, lying facedown in the grass, and didn't try to sit up or attempt to discover what had happened. The details didn't matter; what mattered was letting the rest of the team know that they were under attack.

And he needed to do it without attracting undue attention to himself in case the enemy was out there, watching.

His arms had been flung out over his head when he fell and that proved to be an unexpected godsend. Moving just half an inch or so at a time, he slowly slid his right hand over to his left, until his fingers came in contact with the band of his watch. The military timepiece had a panic button built into its face. Pressing it sent a high-frequency signal to the main security station, letting the man on duty there know that something was amiss.

Davis searched for the button.

THE SPOTTER IN THE TREES scanned the grounds with his sighting scope, going through the motions just as he'd been taught in sniper school so many years before. Constant vigilance was his motto and it had never let him down.

Nor did it this time.

"Son of a—! Target! Sector B. From TRP 1, right 50, add 25."

His partner brought his weapon into position, repeating the location information back to the spotter as he did so.

"Roger. Movement on the ground. Second target from the left."

The shooter repeated the target designation and adjusted his grip on the stock of his weapon. Taking a deep breath he held it for a moment, made sure he was on-target, and then fired on the exhale. To an outside observer it would have seemed like one continuous motion, but to the sniper it felt disjointed and rushed.

He hadn't expected to have to use the weapon again once they'd taken down the guards, and it was only the fact that he made a habit of keeping his weapon loaded while in position that let him get the shot off at all.

The tranquilizer dart gun had been set aside just moments before and been replaced with his standard piece, a Parker Hale M85 rifle, and a sharp crack rang out over the estate as the gunman pulled the trigger.

The sniper's shot was true.

It struck Davis in the head, killing him instantly.

But the sniper had been about a quarter of a second too late. Davis had already found the panic button and mashed it down flat.

IN THE LIBRARY on the first floor, the celebration continued. Davenport cracked open a bottle of cognac and drinks were passed around.

"A toast, then," he said, raising his glass and waiting until the others followed suit. "To our expedition!"

"Here, here!" Annja and Mason replied with grins.

No sooner had they done so, however, than a loud siren began blaring throughout the house.

Annja cast a questioning look at her companions.

"We've got an intruder," Mason said, by way of reply, as he crossed the room and disappeared through the door.

Davenport and Annja quickly followed.

Out in the hallway they found Mason surrounded by a handful of hard-looking men who had apparently appeared out of thin air. Or at least it seemed that way to Annja, who up until now hadn't seen even a hint that a security team was present, never mind active.

"Sitrep," Mason said to the tall black man who was helping him slip into a ballistic vest.

"We've got a breach along the south wall. Davis's panic button went off just over sixty seconds ago. I tripped the alarm and assembled the team as per SOP."

"Good job, Jeffries. Any idea who or what we're up against?"

The other man shook his head. "The motion sensors never went off, which means the video feed wasn't activated. At this point, all we have is the lack of response from Katter and the active signal from Davis, which doesn't tell us a whole hell of a lot."

Mason turned to face Davenport. "Without knowing what we're facing, I have to suggest that you take cover in the secure room until this is over, sir."

The trusted friend had reverted back into the loyal employee, Annja noted. And it appeared that Davenport was more than willing to listen to him, too. She had long suspected that Mason was more than just Davenport's assistant and she felt some small sense of satisfaction that her hunch had proven correct.

One of the security team members stepped to Davenport's side, gun drawn and eyes on alert. "This way, sir," he said, indicating the hallway to the left.

Curious about what was going on, but not wanting to get in the way of what appeared to be a well-organized response, Annja chose to follow Davenport. Probably gets half a dozen death threats a week, considering how rich he is, she thought. Besides, if he was the target, at least she was there to protect him.

She was halfway down the hall when a sudden thought stopped her dead in her tracks.

The journal.

Whoever they are, they're after the journal, she was sure of it.

She turned it over once or twice in her head, testing it for accuracy, and finally decided that her hunch was right. They *were* after the journal. She didn't know how she knew it; she just did.

Turning, she charged back down the hall, headed for the staircase in the foyer that would take her to the second floor. She didn't know how someone could have learned of the journal, nor who might be after it. But that didn't matter. Right now all she cared about was imposing herself between the artifact and whoever it was that had come to claim it.

"Annja! Annja, wait!"

Davenport's calls echoed down the hallway after her, but she ignored them, intent on her objective. She hit the staircase and took the steps two at a time, her gaze directed above, watching for intruders, as she rapidly made her way to the top.

When she reached the second-floor landing, she flattened herself against the wall, settled into a crouch and peeked around the corner at knee height. If someone was there, she didn't want to stick her face right in their sights.

The hall was empty, however.

"Annja!"

She spun around to find Davenport coming up the steps, calling her name, his bodyguard a few steps behind and obviously not very happy about the current situation. Annja wasn't, either. She silenced him with a sharp wave of her hand and gestured for him to join her against the wall.

"What are you doing?" he asked in an urgent whisper, once he'd done what she'd asked. "Mason told us to get under cover."

"We need to check on Curran's diary."

Davenport processed that for a second. "You don't think…"

"Yeah, I do think. Now stay here and let me check things out." She turned to look at the bodyguard. "Make sure he listens, understand?"

The security agent nodded.

She straightened up and took a deep breath. Rounding the corner, she headed for the room at the end of the hall at a fast walk, doing her best to be as quiet as possible.

She'd made it about halfway there when the door at the end opened and a man clad in dark clothing stepped out. His back was partially turned as he listened to instructions given by someone still inside the room, but Annja could clearly see the automatic weapon he carried.

The closest door was behind her and to her left. He'd see her long before she could reverse course, get it open and slip inside.

There was nowhere else for her to go but forward.

Annja knew that at any second he was going to turn around and see her coming toward him down the hallway. If that happened she was as good as dead; it wouldn't take much to bring that weapon in line and gun her down in her tracks.

She had to reach him first.

All this flashed through her mind in the space of a

heartbeat and then she was rushing down the corridor toward the intruder as fast as she could go move. Picturing her sword in her mind, she reached into the other-where, wrapped her hand around its hilt and drew it forth.

Unfortunately for Annja, she didn't make it.

She was still a dozen or so steps away when the intruder closed the door and turned in her direction. His surprise at seeing someone charging down the hall toward him brandishing a sword didn't stop his training from taking over. The look of shock was still on his face when he swung his gun around and fired from the hip.

11

Faced with certain death, Annja did the only thing she could. Like a runner going for second base, she dropped into a slide, legs extended, sword held in a striking position, using her own momentum and the highly polished wooden floor to carry her closer to her target.

The move took her opponent by surprise and she slid under his line of fire, bullets streaming past over her head, and then she was up close, right there at his feet, surging to her knees, her sword thrust upward with all the momentum gained in her rush down the hall.

The gunman never stood a chance.

The blade caught him low in the gut, just under the edge of the Kevlar vest he was wearing, and rammed him back against the door, pinning him in place.

He stared at her in disbelief, looked down at the two feet of steel sticking out of his gut, then died without saying a word.

Rather than trying to pull her sword free, Annja simply released it into the otherwhere.

The gunman's body dropped to the floor with a heavy thud.

In the silence that followed, a voice called her name softly.

Annja turned.

The bullets had missed her, but that didn't mean that they hadn't found a target. John Davenport was kneeling in the middle of the hallway, cradling the badly wounded body of his security agent, the other man's neck stained a deep crimson hue.

Annja met Davenport's gaze. The slight shake of his head said it all; there was nothing they could do. The man in Davenport's arms sucked in a last breath, stared beseechingly at Annja and then joined his killer in death.

A loud crash from the other side of the door pulled Annja's gaze away from the duo.

Get the journal. At least make his death count for something, she thought.

She had to get inside that room.

As far as tactical situations go, it wasn't the best. She had no idea how many men were waiting for her on the other side of the door, nor how they were armed. She was going to have to trust that her instincts and her speed were going to be enough.

She pictured the room in her mind, noting the position of the furniture as it had stood when she'd been working there earlier, paying attention to what might provide adequate cover and what would not. When she was ready, she took a couple deep breaths to draw as much oxygen into her bloodstream as possible, drew back her right leg and kicked out with all her strength.

The door swung open. As it did she dove through the gap, tucking herself into a roll the second her hands touched the floor and letting her momentum carry her several feet to the left where a large island work area was built into the floor.

Gunfire filled the room, bullets chasing her across the floor and slamming into the island, sending chips of wood and metal flying, but the structure was thick enough to protect her and she made it through unscathed.

She peeked around the opposite side, looking for the gunman. The table where she'd worked all day was directly across from her and she could see the shattered remains of the glass case that had held the diary littering the floor at its base, but there was no sign of the intruder.

Nor was there any sign of the diary.

She scuttled over to the other side and peeked around that edge, ready to jerk her head back at the slightest sign of movement. The gunfire had come from somewhere. The door she'd come through was the only exit from the room and she knew that no one had gotten past her to go through it.

Where on earth did they go?

She heard a grunt from above and looked up just in time to see a dark-clad form disappear through a hole cut in the ceiling.

Annja stood, intending to chase after them, only to be forced to take cover on her knees behind the work area again as the intruder stuck his weapon back down through the hole and sprayed the room with a full clip of ammunition.

She waited several seconds after the firing stopped to be certain the shooter wasn't just changing clips. When the shooting failed to resume, she rose to her feet and raced over to the rope that still hung down through the hole.

She was betting that the intruders would be more concerned with getting out of there as quickly as possible and wouldn't have posted anyone to stand guard at the top. She grabbed the rope and shimmied up as quickly as she could, knowing that if she'd guessed wrong she was a sitting duck.

Luckily, she hadn't. When she poked her head out through the hole in the roof, she saw three figures running away from her across the rooftop, headed for the wing closest to the outer wall of the property.

Annja pulled herself onto the roof and gave chase.

MASON LED HIS MEN through the house and gathered them together in the underground garage, where they assembled into two squads, one to be led by him and the other to be led by his second in command, Jeffries. He'd chosen the garage as a staging area for two reasons. First, because it provided immediate access to the side of the estate where Katter and Davis were on duty and was therefore the closest point of egress to that location, and second, because of what it contained. There were two emergency evacuation vehicles standing ready at all times in the garage in case Davenport had to be taken to safety on a moment's notice, and Mason intended to put them to good use. The SUVs were armor plated and came equipped with reinforced steering, puncture-resistant tires and bulletproof glass throughout. They were adequate protection against just about anything short of a rocket-propelled grenade and would provide good cover while they crossed the estate grounds and tried to get a look at whoever it was that had breached their security.

The men climbed into the vehicles and Mason gave the signal to move out.

Lights from the outdoor floodlights that had been triggered by the alarm flooded into the garage as the gates were opened by remote from inside the vehicles, and then they were climbing the sloping driveway up to ground level, engines roaring.

They came under fire almost immediately. The bullets made odd thunking sounds as they impacted against the armored plate, but Mason ignored them, secure in that fact that the armor would hold up to the task. Still, the driver did what he could to avoid taking too many hits, throwing their vehicle into the evasive action pattern that he'd be taught to utilize, and Mason nodded his approval.

Given the fact that they were being fired upon, it didn't take a rocket scientist to figure out why Davis and Katter had dropped off the grid. The fact that he had two men down, condition unknown, bothered him, but Mason was too good a commander to give in to the urge to move right to their side. His first order of business was to protect Davenport and secure the property. His men would have to hold on until he could get to them.

Mason was glad that he had ordered Davenport into the panic room. Despite its comfortable furnishings, complete with a kitchenette and a minibar, Mason knew that the room was designed to withstand just about anything an enemy could throw at it. Blast-reinforced concrete, four feet thick, surrounded it on all sides; even with explosives at their disposal it would take an intruder quite some time to blow their way inside, and hopefully by then those hiding out would have used the secured lines inside to call for help.

With Davenport safe, Mason could concentrate fully on repelling the attack and securing the estate.

Katter and Davis had been assigned to patrol the east side of the property and when Davis's panic button went off, its GPS signal put him out in front of the house near the wall. An access road ran around the inside of the fence line, but time was of the essence now and the driver knew it. He cut directly across the front lawn, his tires tearing long furrows out of the grass. They'd worry about the landscaping later; right now they had to know just what they were dealing with.

Muzzle flashes could be seen along the wall and in the tree line just beyond, and Mason made note of their position, then relayed that information to those in the backseat. They would be in range in just another minute or two and he could feel his troops getting themselves ready, their desire to give back a little of what they were getting coming through in the set of their shoulders and the grim determination on their faces.

You picked the wrong team to screw with, Mason thought with a smile.

As they drew closer, their headlights picked up a dark shape on the grass and soon it resolved itself into a man's body. Mason pointed it out to the driver and snapped off a quick set of instructions. While he wouldn't go out of his way to check on his missing men, there was no sense in driving right by one of them if they could provide help without endangering their primary mission. The driver did as he was told, skewing the vehicle to a stop angled between the downed man in the grass and the line of fire coming from beyond the wall.

No sooner had the vehicle slammed to a stop than Mason was slipping out the door and rushing over to the unmoving man's side. Simultaneously, the men on the other side of the SUV opened the doors and crouched behind them, using them as cover as they returned fire at the enemy beyond the wall, giving Mason the time he needed to check on their companion.

Mason's men were all armed with HK MP-5 submachine guns, capable of spitting out 800 rounds of 10 mm ammunition per minute, and they hosed down the top of the wall and the trees behind it with deadly accuracy as Mason himself slid to a stop beside his wounded teammate.

The red hair told him right away that it was Katter. He reached for the man's neck and checked for a pulse. Thankfully he found one; strong and steady, too.

But when he went to remove his hand, it brushed up against something sticking out of Katter's neck.

Mason rolled the man over and let his head loll back, revealing the object sticking out of the side of Katter's throat, just below the ear.

Tranquilizer dart.

The sight of it froze him in place for a moment, his mind whirling with this new piece of data.

What on earth were they doing using a dart gun? he asked himself. And why switch from that to real firepower? It just didn't make sense.

Unless…

The gunfire was just a distraction. Something to keep he and his men occupied while the enemy went after something else.

Mason spun around, looking back at the house, and was just in time to see a group of figures running along the peak of the roof.

A moment later, the lithe figure of Annja Creed climbed out onto the roof after them and gave chase.

12

The roof was relatively flat, which made movement easier, but the tiles were worn smooth from years of summer rainstorms, and more than a few popped free beneath Annja's feet as she took off after the intruders. The crack of the tiles as they split and slid down the roof alerted the others to her pursuit. Annja saw the last man in the group glance back in her direction, but he didn't stop moving forward and neither did she.

Gunfire split the night air. Annja could see Mason and his men working their way across the lawn toward the south wall, using two large SUVs from the motor pool as cover. Return fire was coming at them from the tree line but so far it looked pretty ineffectual. Annja didn't know if that was a product of the enemy's weapon skills or just a ruse to suck the team in closer where more damage could be doled out. She was momentarily glad she wasn't on the ground with them.

The intruders had reached the edge of the roof and

were starting to make their descent by the time Annja reached the edge of the south wing. One of them looked back in her direction, saw that she had closed the distance between them and decided she'd come far enough.

He snatched up his gun and fired.

Annja's danger sense had gone off the moment she saw his hips begin to move and so she dove to the left, rolling across the tiles, as bullets stitched through air where she had been seconds before. By the time she scrambled back to her feet, two of the three intruders had already disappeared over the edge, headed for the ground below. As she watched, the last of the trio took hold of the rope and got into position for his own descent.

Annja knew she wouldn't reach them in time to prevent them from getting away.

The assault team leader must have realized it, too, for he gave her a jaunty smile and a wink before starting down the rope.

She put on a final burst of speed and then flung herself forward, her arms outstretched. As she struck the rooftop, her momentum carried her forward, her hand dipping over the edge as she sought to keep herself from hurtling over the side by dragging her feet behind her.

It worked. Just as her feet caught on the edge of one of the tiles behind her, stopping her slide, her hand bumped into something down beneath the lip of the roof and she snatched at it.

Gotcha!

She ended up with her head extended over the edge of the roof and, looking down, she saw that she'd caught the leader's wrist just as he'd been reaching for a new hold on the rope. His gun was slung over his shoulder and his other hand grasped the rope to keep from falling to the ground.

He was stuck.

Or so Annja thought.

As she struggled to pull him up toward her, however, he did something totally unexpected.

He let go of the rope.

Annja's arm nearly popped out of the socket from the sudden weight and she was forced to release her grip on the tiles beside her and grab his arm with both hands.

Now the only thing keeping them both from falling off the roof was the narrow lip of a tile under which she'd jammed the edge of one foot.

Grinning, her opponent dipped his free shoulder, causing his rifle to slide down into his hand.

Annja couldn't believe it. What was he going to do? Shoot her? If he did, he'd fall, which, when you thought about it, wasn't the smartest move. While the distance might not kill him, it would more than likely break both his legs and would certainly put a damper on his getaway attempt.

Apparently, he didn't see it like that. As she watched, he got a better grip on the butt of the weapon, stuck his finger on the trigger and swung the muzzle up in her direction.

Whatever his intent might have been, he never got the chance to carry it through. The sudden motion shifted their weight a fraction to one side, not more than an inch, maybe two, but that was enough to cause Annja's foot to pop free from the tile under which it had been braced.

Over the edge they went.

Thankfully, the long drop she'd been expecting never came. She tumbled only ten feet or so before crashing onto the balcony jutting out below them. Her opponent lost his weapon in the fall, but managed to land on his feet. He didn't give her time to recover but rather moved in immediately and delivered a violent kick to her midsection.

It hurt, but the sudden pain also had the effect of helping to clear her head, so that when he wound up to deliver another blow, she was able to respond.

She blocked the second kick with both hands, catching his foot in the process, twisting it savagely to one side in an attempt to throw him off balance.

Rather than toppling to the ground as she'd expected, the assault leader turned in the direction of her throw, twisting his body in midair and coming back at her head with the side of his other foot.

Annja had no choice but to let go as she leaned back to avoid the strike. As they separated, she scrambled to her feet and was ready when he waded in a second time, fists and feet flying.

They exchanged a flurry of blows, neither of them managing to land anything damaging, until he overextended himself on a spinning side kick and she was able to drop beneath it and sweep his feet out from under him.

As he fell to the ground, she sprung back to her feet and closed in, intending to force him to tell her where the journal was headed, but then he did the unexpected—again. Rather than getting to his feet, he placed both his hands flat on the ground and shoved his body upward and out, slamming his feet into her chest and sending her stumbling backward.

As her arms pinwheeled with an attempt to regain her balance, the backs of her knees struck the low railing running around the edge of the balcony and her momentum kept the rest of her body in motion.

Over the balcony's edge she went.

This time there was nothing between her and the ground.

13

When Annja came to, she found herself lying on the couch in the library where they'd been celebrating shortly before, an ice pack resting across the side of her face and head. The last thing she remembered was her opponent's feet striking her in the chest, knocking her backward and over the balcony railing. After that, there was nothing but darkness.

"You fell off the roof," a voice said, and she turned slightly to see Mason sitting in a chair a short distance away, watching her.

"Not my most graceful moment, apparently," she replied, wincing at the pain as she lifted herself into a sitting position. "Besides, it wasn't the roof, it was just the balcony." All told, she was in pretty good shape. A few bruises, a serious headache, but otherwise she was intact. "I'm guessing they got away?"

"Unfortunately, yes. My fault. I should have anticipated he would try something like this," Mason muttered.

Before she could ask what he meant, John Davenport came through the door, flanked by two of Mason's security team. Despite the fact that Davenport hadn't been the primary target, they were obviously not taking any chances. Annja thought it was a bit like trying to put the horses away after the barn had burned down, but then again, it wasn't her job and so she didn't say anything.

Davenport, it seemed, was far more concerned with her welfare than his own. He hurried over to her side.

"Are you all right?" he asked.

"I'm fine. Just sorry that I couldn't keep them from taking the journal."

He waved his hand in dismissal and turned to face Mason. "Was it Ransom?"

His security chief nodded. "The bastard even left you a note." He handed the other man a small white card, like those used as thank-you notes. Davenport read it and then passed it on to Annja for a look.

There was only a single sentence written on its face.

May the best man win—and we both know who that is.

Sounds like a real fun guy, Annja thought.

Mason went on with his report. "Katter is going to be okay; they hit him with enough trank to put down a rhino, but the doc says the worst of it will be the massive hangover he'll wake up with. Davis, unfortunately, is dead. We think they messed up his trank dose and had no other option but to take him out when they realized that he was going to warn us about the assault."

"And the enemy forces?" Davenport asked.

"Not sure. We found blood trails in the trees and evidence that we might have tagged one or two of them, but we can't be sure. They apparently had vehicles waiting for them a bit farther down the street and hightailed it out of here once they'd gotten what they came for."

"Which was the journal?" Davenport asked angrily.

"Yes, sir. Nothing else seems to be missing."

"That son of a bitch!"

Mason nodded. "My sentiments exactly. Though right about now I'm feeling the same way about you."

Davenport turned to him, surprise flowing across his face. "What?"

Mason shook his finger at his employer. "What were you told to do when the alarm sounded?"

"I—"

"Go to the safe room, right?"

Davenport struggled to find his voice. "But…Annja didn't…"

"This isn't about Annja," Mason said sharply, then turned to her and said, "No offense."

"None taken," she replied, still watching in fascination as this man chewed out Davenport, never mind the fact that not only was Davenport his employer but also the third richest man in the world, according to most sources.

"I told you to go to the safe room. I ordered Watkins to accompany you there and to keep you safe. By ignoring that order, you put not only his but your own life at risk."

"Well, yes, but I didn't think—"

"Exactly," Mason said, overriding him again. "You didn't think. And now Watkins is dead because of it."

Silence fell.

The two men stared at each other, with Annja looking back and forth between them as if watching a tennis match.

At last Davenport mustered his dignity, looked Mason

in the eye and said, "I'm sorry. You are entirely correct. It won't happen again."

"Damn right it won't," Mason muttered, but he turned away, his anger spent, and the tension slowly eased out of the room.

To help get things back on track, Annja stepped into the silence with a question she'd been wondering about since waking up.

"Okay," she said. "Time for somebody to bring me up to speed. Who is this guy, Ransom?"

Davenport sighed. "Trevor Ransom is a lowlife thug who happened to strike it rich during the dot-com boom of the 1990s. Unfortunately, he also happens to be my ex-business partner."

He went on to explain how the two of them had been involved in a series of commercial development projects early in their careers that had been extremely lucrative but that had also exposed Ransom's true nature. When Davenport had discovered that Ransom had been using substandard building materials and bilking the clients for the difference, he'd severed the relationship. Ransom, however, hadn't been happy with that result and the two had been bitter competitors ever since. They'd spent the past ten years fighting over everything from mineral rights in Siberia to a chain of grocery stores in Bird's Eye, Pennsylvania. More often than not, Davenport came out on top, which only served to fuel Ransom's rivalry.

Somehow, Ransom had learned about the journal and decided to take matters into his own hands.

Literally.

The information put a whole new light on what had happened to Annja that morning and provided one possible way for Ransom to have known about the journal.

She told them about the feeling she'd had that morning, that certain sense that someone had been in her room while she was out on her run. At the time, she'd written if off as just having been the hotel staff, but now she wasn't so sure. If Ransom's men had bugged her room, or even put a listening device on her clothing, all they would have had to do was eavesdrop on her conversations all day to discover what she and Davenport were up to.

Apparently Ransom hadn't wasted a moment in planning to secure the find for himself once he had known what it truly was.

"So what do we do now? Wait for the cops to get the journal back?" Annja asked.

Mason shook his head. "The cops are next to useless around here. Ransom bought them all off years ago. Why do you think we maintain our own security force? We'll just have to handle this problem ourselves."

Annja frowned. "You can't be serious. What are you going to do? Stage a raid of your own and try to take it back again?"

Davenport smiled, and this time there was definitely something predatory about it. "Actually, we don't need the journal at all. Ransom can have it, for all I care. We already have everything we need right here."

Annja must still have been groggy from her fall, for it took her a moment or two to figure out what he meant. Then her eyes lit up with understanding.

"We don't need the actual journal. We've got the whole thing imaged on my laptop!"

Mason nodded. "Right! And without that, Ransom will have to find and then translate the coded message buried in the text in order to avoid going on a wild-goose chase, which I don't think he's smart enough to do."

But they all decided that they weren't going to bet on it.

Afraid that Ransom might somehow uncover the secret of the journal if they waited several more months before setting out as originally planned, Davenport ordered the preparations to begin immediately. Annja would continue her examination of the code while Mason made all the necessary travel arrangements to get them overseas and in country. He would assemble the team on the other end and arrange for local support once they arrived on-site. The accelerated time frame meant they would be arriving in Mongolia at the tail end of autumn, necessitating that they travel fast and light if they hoped to achieve anything of value before winter set in.

There was a lot to get organized and little time to do it. Despite the exertion of the afternoon, their conversation went long into the night.

14

In a secure location on the other side of town, Trevor Ransom paced impatiently back and forth in front of the fireplace, waiting for his operative to arrive. The snatch-and-grab had gone smoothly enough, he'd heard; the loss of two of his men was a small price to pay for the artifact that they recovered from Davenport's estate, especially if it contained what he suspected it might. Hell, he'd gladly trade several more lives if that's what it took to secure what he was after. It was simply a question of economics—which side of the equation was more valuable—and he came down on the side of the artifact every single time. Men were expendable. The artifact was not.

He'd known Davenport was on to something, but he hadn't realized just how important until he'd discovered that his old partner had hired that Creed woman. His research had shown that despite her job working as the host of that ridiculous television show—*Monster Chaser, Monster Hunter,* whatever it was called—she'd been involved in some of the most astonishing finds in recent years and was regarded as one of the top up-and-coming authorities on the intersection of ancient legend and archaeological fact. Her presence in Davenport's home could only mean one thing—Davenport had found Curran's journal.

The bastard had actually achieved the goal he'd set all those years ago!

Which, of course, meant that Ransom had no choice but to take it from him.

There was a quiet knock on the door of his study.

"Come in," Ransom called out impatiently and turned to face the door as Santiago, the head of his security team, entered the room, a leather attaché case in one hand.

"We have it, sir," Santiago said, extending the case.

Ransom snatched it from Santiago's outstretched hand and moved immediately to his desk where he opened it and drew out the small, leather-bound book it contained. He felt a strange thrill of excitement course through him as he held the object of Davenport's decades-long obsession in his hands.

Ransom opened the journal and sat down at his desk, bending close to the page to be able to read the fine script. He knew his Italian was far from perfect, but it should be good enough to get the gist of what the journal contained. He would have the whole work translated later to be certain they hadn't missed anything vital but for now he'd just take a quick look for himself.

After a moment, he sat back and stared at Santiago in anger.

"Is this some kind of joke?"

Santiago stared at him, bewildered. "Is something wrong, sir?"

"Wrong? Of course there is something wrong, you bloody idiot! The freakin' thing is written in Latin."

"Sir?"

"The book, you fool, the book. Curran's journal is written in Latin!"

"I…see," Santiago said, though Ransom seriously doubted he did.

Unlike his former partner Davenport, Ransom hadn't gone to Oxford. He was a product of the streets and his own hard work, and there wasn't much use for Latin when you're struggling to expand your territory and keep the scum around you from taking what you had fought so hard to gain for yourself. The idiot should have known that…

Ransom took a deep breath and visibly calmed himself. It wasn't his lieutenant's fault. Santiago was a good man. He did what he was told without questioning everything, and that was hard to find in a man with his particular set of skills. No sense in taking it out on him.

He waved a hand at Santiago, indicating that he wanted to be alone, and the other man lost no time in removing himself from the room. When he was gone, Ransom picked up the phone and dialed his secretary in his office downtown.

"Marissa? I need you to find me someone who can translate Medieval Latin, late thirteenth century or so and I need them immediately. Standard nondisclosure agreement and the like. Call me when you have someone, please."

Hanging up, Ransom sat back and stared at the book on the desk in front of him.

"Just what secrets are you hiding?" he asked into the silence of the room, but of course there was no answer.

At least, not yet.

But there would be, he vowed, there would be.

Frustrated with how the day's events had turned out, Ransom got up and began to move about the room, pacing in order to try and burn off some of his nervous energy. He stopped in front of the unlit fireplace that dominated one wall of his office. There, on the mantelpiece, was a small framed picture.

It was a photograph of the two of them, he and Davenport, taken on the day they had signed their mutual partnership agreement. Things had gone pretty well until a day a few years later when Davenport had discovered his little side operation. Every instance of that conversation was etched indelibly on his memory.

THE DOOR TO HIS OFFICE slammed open and Davenport stalked in, the anger naked on his face for all to see.

"Just what the hell have you been doing, Ransom?" Davenport roared, over the protests of Ransom's executive assistant, who was still trying to prevent the other man from barging in on her boss.

Ransom spoke quietly into the phone, telling the individual on the other end that he had an emergency and would call him right back, and then hung up before Davenport could say anything else that might hamper the deal he'd been trying to close in Singapore.

Only when the phone was back in its cradle did he turn and address his assistant, his eyes never leaving Davenport's face.

"Thank you, Elizabeth. That will be all. Apparently my partner has something he wishes to discuss with me."

"You're damn right I do, you bastard. Just what on earth do you think you are doing? Trying to ruin us both?"

Ransom stared back at him with disdain, not bothering

to conceal his feelings now that the two of them were alone. He'd had enough of Davenport's self-righteous attitude over the past several months. "I'm making us money, you idiot. Or can't you see that?"

"Making us money? By using faulty workmanship and substandard building materials? Are you crazy?"

Ransom turned to the bar behind his desk and fixed himself a drink, stalling for time. How on earth had Davenport found out about that? And now that he had, just what was the best way to play it?

Davenport was visibly fuming when Ransom turned back to him, drink in hand. "Every single contractor I've utilized is licensed with the state in which they are operating and all of our materials purchases have met federal minimums," he said as way of answering the charge from his partner.

"Federal minimums?" Davenport asked incredulously. "I'm not talking about meeting specifications, you fool, I'm talking about people's lives! If you build these buildings with these materials, something will go wrong eventually."

Ransom waved his hand as if shooing away a minor issue. "Who gives a damn? If it happens, and I repeat, if, we'll already have sold the building by that point and it will be someone else's problem by then, not ours. In the meantime, we'll have pocketed the difference we save in using my selected materials over those you suggested. Isn't that why you brought me onboard in the first place, Davenport? To expand your operations?"

"Not in this way, I didn't." The older man said it calmly, his fury apparently having spent itself.

But what he said next surprised Ransom to the core.

"That's it. I'm dissolving our partnership immediately.

I'll not have my name and reputation associated with the likes of you for another moment longer."

Ransom stood there for a moment, stunned, and then he exploded. "What? You can't do that!"

"I just did, Ransom. You're done. Get the hell out of my building and don't show your face back here again."

Davenport stood his ground as Ransom came around the desk and stared up into his face, his fury evident. "Be ready for a fight, you jackass, because by this time tomorrow I'll have half a dozen lawsuits slapped on your back over this."

But the other man didn't even flinch. "Give it your best," he said with fire in his eyes. "Now get out, before I call security and have them throw you out."

RANSOM HAD LEFT WITHOUT further comment, but that hadn't been the end of the fight. It had simply moved on to a different battlefield after that. While their lawyers fought it out in court, he and Davenport had taken it to the arena they knew best, doing everything they could to ruin the other's business plans wherever and whenever possible.

Ransom stared at the photo of the two of them together for some time, and then smiled.

"I've got you this time, you arrogant ass. And when I discover the location of the tomb before you, the world will remember Trevor Ransom's name forever. You'll end up being nothing more than a footnote while I bask in all the glory."

15

It took a day to make all the preparations, but once completed they wasted no time in getting under way. The plan was to travel aboard Davenport's private jet to Moscow, at which point they would transfer to a local charter service that would fly them into Ulaanbaatar, the Mongolian capital. From there they would travel by convoy into the interior, following the directions Annja had decoded from Curran's hidden message.

After the raid, Mason had insisted that she either remain at the estate or, at the very least, change hotels and register under a different name. Annja had decided on the latter option. After doing so, she got a good night's sleep and was up early, ready for what the day would bring. She had a couple of hours before she had to meet Mason at the airport and she spent part of that time reviewing her analysis of Curran's hidden message. The entire expedition depended on a proper interpretation and she was feeling unusually concerned that she get it right.

After an hour's work, she still couldn't find anything wrong with her interpretation. Only one way to find out, she thought. If we don't find anything at that first location, we'll know we're way off. Simple as that.

Annja next turned her attention to a less interesting but equally necessary task—researching Trevor Ransom's background. If he was going to be interfering in their expedition, she wanted to know what he was capable of.

It didn't take her long to discover that he was capable of just about anything. By using a variety of online media databases, she was able to get a bird's-eye view of how the media had covered him over the past few years, and they certainly hadn't cast him in a favorable light. *Ruthless* was a word used fairly often. As was *uncaring. Vain, determined, arrogant, unkind* and *visionary* were all up there in the top ten, as well, the last from a Chicago columnist who'd reportedly been trying to curry favor for a job opening.

Ransom had flirted with legal trouble over half a dozen of his development projects, but nothing ever came from any of it. Witnesses disappeared or were bought off, documents vanished, a judge dismissed a case only to have his oceanfront property renovated by a subsidiary of a subsidiary of a subsidiary of one of Ransom's companies a year later.

The pattern was clear. Ransom usually got what he wanted and not always by the most ethical means. She'd only known Davenport a short time, but from what she knew of him she couldn't imagine him doing business with a man like that. Their rivalry certainly seemed real enough, though, and Annja decided it wouldn't hurt to watch her back during the next few weeks as the search got under way.

She put the laptop away and set about packing for the trip, laying her gear out on the bed first so that she could be sure she had everything she needed. While doing so,

Annja picked up the phone and dialed her producer at *Chasing History's Monsters,* Doug Morrell.

"Hi, Doug," she said when he answered.

Morrell, however, pretended not to know who was calling.

"Who is this?" he asked, suspiciously.

"You know damn well who it is, Doug."

"I know that it sounds like Annja Creed, but it can't be Annja because she's down in the Yucatán getting me this incredibly awesome story on Incan sacrifices to the moon god, right?"

Annja sighed. "It's Mexico, Doug. I'm in Mexico. You know, that big country right below Texas? And it was the Aztecs who sacrificed people to the sun god, not the Incas."

"Whatever. As long the special-effects department gets to reenact those sacrifices, I really don't care if they were carried out by aliens."

She heard him suck in a breath suddenly, the way he did when a brilliant idea occurred to him, and she knew whatever was coming next was not going to be good.

She was right.

"Wait a minute!" he cried. "That's it! We can do a story about how the Aztecs were visited by aliens who taught them…" His enthusiasm audibly deflated. "Damn!" he said. "Forget it. I just remembered that we did that one back in season two."

"Good thing, too," Annja said, with a laugh. "Because there's no way you were going to get me to do a story like that. Besides, I've got something better for you. I'm headed to Mongolia."

"Mongolia? Don't tell me you're finally going to do that story on the abominable snowman I've been begging you for?" His voice practically dripped with excitement.

"Not a chance, Doug. Besides, I said Mongolia, not Tibet."

"Mongolia, Tibet, whatever. I can never keep all those Chinese provinces apart."

Sometimes talking to Doug was an adventure in and of itself, Annja decided. Knowing it wasn't worth the time or the energy that would be needed to explain that Mongolia and Tibet were actually two separate countries, never mind the fact that they weren't part of China at all, Annja simply ignored the statement. Instead, she explained she was on the hunt for the lost tomb of Genghis Khan.

"Genghis Khan? Isn't he the guy who impaled all those Turks on stakes?

"No, that was Vlad Tepes."

"You're killing me here, Annja."

"I'm sure you'll survive," she said dryly. "Besides, did I mention the curse?"

She could almost hear him sitting up straighter. "Curse?"

Okay, so it wasn't really a curse, per se, but she knew she could spin it well enough that he wouldn't notice the difference. "Legend has it that anyone who lays eyes on the Khan's tomb will die quickly and violently. Just like the burial party."

She knew she'd hooked him when he came back with a breathless "What happened to the burial party?"

"They were ambushed after the burial and slaughtered to the last man. Sixty trained Mongol warriors, part of Genghis Khan's elite honor guard. And then those who did the deed paid the same price, so that no one would know just where the Khan was buried."

She told him about the journal and the clues it contained, but didn't mention anything about Davenport or the events at his villa in Mexico City. If she had, she'd never get Doug to pay for anything.

It turned out to be a good strategy. By the time she hung up, she had Doug's approval for the trip, which meant *Chasing History's Monsters* would pay her for the time she put in on the project provided she came home with enough of a story to let them stitch together a solid show about the leader of the Mongol horde and the terrible curse attached to his tomb.

Not too shabby, Annja thought. Now all she had to do was find the tomb. Piece of cake, right?

She finished packing and then caught a cab to the airport. She met Mason at the entrance to the private terminal and they walked out on the tarmac together to where the plane waited.

Davenport's private jet was a lushly appointed Boeing BBJ with several bedrooms, a fully stocked kitchen and bar and more than enough room for the three of them to stretch out and be comfortable on the long flight to Moscow.

Shortly after take off, Mason asked Annja if she'd had any luck with deciphering the message from Curran's journal.

Annja grinned. "It would be an awfully short trip if I haven't, now wouldn't it?" She dug her laptop out of her backpack, booted it up and then put the text of the hidden message she'd found in Curran's journal on the screen for everyone to see.

Beneath the watchful gaze of the eternal blue heaven
The spirit of the warrior points the way

To where the blood of the world intertwines
And the voice in the earth has its say

The sixty brides rode sixty steeds
And now rest between the watchful eyes of those
who came before

In their arms is the truth you seek
The way to all that was and more

Then climb to the place where Tengri and Gazan meet
It is there that the Batur makes his home

Mason looked at the screen and then back at Annja. "I'm glad this makes sense to you, because I have to admit, it's all gibberish to me."

"That makes two of us," Davenport said.

"It actually makes a lot of sense, once you look at it through the eyes of the Mongol warrior who dictated it to Curran, rather than through our own, twenty-first-century perspective," Annja said.

She pointed at the first set of phrases. "'Beneath the watchful gaze of the eternal blue heaven, the spirit of the warrior points the way.' Sounds like a bunch of foolishness to us but to a Mongol in the thirteenth century, that's almost as good as Mapquest.

"The eternal blue heaven is another name for their chief deity, Koke Mongke Tengri. The Mongolians had roughly ninety-nine *tengri,* or heavenly creatures, of which he was the highest, the creator of all things, visible and invisible.

"In essence, that entire first phrase is simply saying that their god sees all and that he knows where the Khan rests. It is the second phrase in the pair that is the important one and is our first real clue. Remember, the soul of a Mongol warrior did not exist inside the man's body, but in his *sulde.*"

"Explain that again," Mason said.

"His *sulde,* his spirit banner. The warrior would take

strands of hair from his best stallions and tie them around the shaft of his favorite spear, just below the blade. Each time he would make camp, he would stand the spear upright outside his *ger* or tent. The hair was tossed about by the almost constant wind on the steppes and in doing so it soaked up the power of the sun, the wind and the sky. This power from nature was then transferred to the owner of the *sulde,* driving him onward, influencing his dreams and helping him live out his destiny."

Annja looked at each of them to be certain they were following her explanation. "When a warrior died, it was said that he and his *sulde* had become so intertwined that his spirit remained forever in the strands of horsehair."

Mason frowned slightly, thinking it through. "So the first two lines of the message are telling us to find the *sulde* of Genghis Khan and that it will point us in the right direction."

"Right," Annja said, smiling as if at a star pupil.

But Davenport broke the moment with a very practical concern. "How on earth are we going to find a spear that has been missing for eight hundred years?"

"We don't have to," Annja replied, a smug expression on her face. "We only have to find a spear that's been missing for a little over seventy years. And I've got a hunch that it never actually went missing at all."

From the confused expressions on their faces, it was clear the others weren't following her logic.

"Genghis Khan had two different spirit banners, actually. One was made with the hairs from black horses, for wartime, and one made with hairs from white horses, for times of peace. The white one disappeared ages ago, but the black one was behlieved to be the repository of his soul and was cherished and protected by his descendants.

Until the mid 1930s, it was safely stored in the Shankh Monastery at the foot of the Shankh Mountains."

Davenport leaned back in his chair and looked at her thoughtfully. "What happened in the 1930s?"

Annja shrugged. "Communism. Stalin's thugs slaughtered more than thirty thousand Buddhist monks and destroyed almost every temple in the country inside of just a few years' time. Legend has it that the Khan's *sulde* was smuggled out of the monastery just before Stalin's troops arrived. It was supposedly hidden somewhere in Ulaanbaatar for a few years and then moved to another, more secret location. No one has seen it since."

"But you're confident that you can find it?" Mason eyed her with open skepticism.

She knew it sounded a bit egotistic, but that's exactly what she was. Confident. She'd given it a fair amount of thought and decided that the odds were in favor of her being right about the *sulde's* current location. That was good enough for her. But rather than answer him directly, she asked a question of her own.

"Tell me this. If you were going to hide something that important, where would you put it?"

"Hopefully in the last place anyone would think to look," he said.

Annja nodded. "Exactly! That is why our first stop is going to be Shankh. I don't think Genghis Khan's *sulde* ever left the monastery in the first place."

The other two digested that information for a few minutes and then Mason said, "Okay, let's say you are correct. We go to Shankh, convince the monks to give up the *sulde* or, at the very least, let us look at it. Then what?"

"We keep following the clues left to us by Father Curran." She pointed at the computer screen. "The second pairing of verses says we should search for the place 'where the blood of the world intertwines.'"

Davenport grunted. "Blood of the world?"

"Yes," Annja replied. "The blood of the world. To the Mongols everything has its own spirits, including the earth. Remember, the Mongols saw rivers and streams as being the lifeblood of the living, breathing world, which is why they never bathed in them."

Mason examined the verse more closely. "So all we have to do is find the intersection of the correct rivers and then 'the earth has its say.' What do you think that last bit is all about?"

This time, Annja didn't have a ready answer. "I'm not one hundred percent sure yet. I'm still working on that. I'm hoping that the discovery of the *sulde* will provide us with more information to decipher the rest of the clues. After all, the verse says it will point the way."

"All right. So we start our search at Shankh." Davenport turned to face Mason. "Is everything ready on the ground?"

Mason nodded. "We've got travel permits and search visas good for at least a month. I've hired local guides to help us negotiate the terrain and our gear has already been shipped to a warehouse in Ulaanbaatar where we will pick it up, along with our transportation. The rest of the team will meet us there on the ground."

They spent some time going over the maps, familiarizing themselves with what lay between the capital and their destination, and then decided to get some sleep.

Tomorrow was going to be a long day.

16

Despite the fact that Ransom didn't have a translation of the journal in hand by midafternoon of the next day, he knew that he had to get out in front if he wanted to ultimately beat Davenport to the prize. Time was of the essence and in a case like this just a few hours could make all the difference.

With that in mind, he ordered Santiago to go on ahead to their facility in Russia and begin the preparations they would need to carry out their own search for the tomb. Santiago was authorized to hire a team and to equip them as he saw fit. Transportation would have to be arranged, as well. In keeping with their usual way of doing things, disposable assets were to be used wherever possible, including the personnel. If they ended up having to cut and run, Ransom wanted no links back to his commercial operations.

A hastily contrived accident would take care of all their problems, should it come to that.

Confident that his man would handle things appropriately, Ransom went about making his own preparations for the journey. He called his executive assistant and had

her cancel all of his appointments for the next two weeks,
letting her know that he would be out of the country and
unavailable. He then had her book a first-class seat on the
next flight to Moscow. She had been trained well; she
didn't ask questions, she simply agreed to do what he
asked. And he knew that it would get done, right to the
letter of his instructions. Wouldn't it be nice if everyone
was so efficient? Ransom thought as he hung up the
phone.

THE FLIGHT WAS A BIT BUMPY but otherwise uneventful.
Santiago met Ransom upon landing and whisked him
away to a private facility they had on the outskirts of the
city. As they entered the grounds, Ransom reflected how
convenient it had been in the past several years to have a
place like this so close to all the turmoil, first in the Soviet
Union itself, then in places like Chechnya, Afghanistan
and the Middle East. There was money to be made in
turmoil, if you were willing and daring enough to go after
it.

Ransom had more than enough of both qualities.

Santiago brought him to the central hangar, where the
men selected to be a part of the assault force were gearing
up. Ransom ignored them; they were just tools, like any
other, and he didn't need to get acquainted with any of
them in order for the job to be carried out properly.

He was, however, interested in the transportation
Santiago had arranged. The Mil-8 Hip was a medium
twin-turbine transport helicopter that could double as a
gunship, one of the reasons he'd been attracted to it. The
fact that it was currently used by more than fifty countries
was the other. A quick paint scheme, a change of identifi-
cation, and the aircraft, like any of the rest of his fleet,

could disappear into the woodwork with a minimum of fuss. It was a useful trait, considering the kind of work he did in countries such as Somalia and Iraq.

The Mil-8 had a long, buslike body with a rounded nose and a glassed-in cockpit. This particular model had two fuel pods offset and mounted low on the body at the point just before it swept upward and tapered toward the rear. Santiago also had a Yakushev-Borzov Yak-B 12.7 mm remote-controlled Gatling gun mounted on the nose.

The aircraft stood eighteen feet off the deck and was more than six feet wide, with five rotors on the main shaft and three on the tail. The tricycle landing gear seemed almost too small to support the aircraft's massive weight, but Ransom knew from experience that it would do just fine.

The helicopter could climb at a rate of thirty feet per second and had a ceiling of just below fifteen thousand feet. The gunship's maximum range was just over two hundred miles; hence, the additional fuel pods. Santiago had already informed him that he was confident they could find additional fuel once in country, but Ransom believed in being prepared.

The plan was a simple one. Wait until they knew just where Davenport's group was headed, then swoop in before the other team could get under way and grab the prize right out from under their noses.

Oh, the revenge would be sweet, Ransom thought.

Satisfied with all he'd seen, he headed into the office to await the satellite call he was expecting.

17

They arrived in Moscow around 7:30 a.m. local time. Concerned with drawing too much attention by arriving in Ulaanbaatar in Davenport's private plane, and thereby tipping off Ransom's people that they were in country, Mason had arranged for them to enter the country like any other set of tourists aboard a commercial flight run by MIAT Mongolian Airlines. From there, they would meet up with the rest of their team, who were arriving separately, and continue overland by truck.

Their connecting flight into Mongolia, however, didn't leave until 11:00 a.m., so Mason let Annja and Davenport sleep in while he made certain their cargo was loaded aboard the proper flight. He roused them with plenty of time for them to get cleaned up and then they headed to the terminal to find their gate.

They made it with plenty of time to spare and ended up sitting around the waiting area with the rest of the passengers. Annja noted that Davenport actually seemed to be enjoying himself, and it took her a few minutes to realize that it was the sudden absence of attention that had put him in such a good mood. In just about every major industrial nation, Davenport was a recognized public figure and, more than likely, couldn't simply sit in an airport lounge without being noticed and possibly harassed. Here, in the small departure lounge devoted to Mongolia's national airline, he'd finally found some small sense of anonymity and was enjoying it.

The flight was uneventful and the flight attendants began their landing preparations for an on-time arrival. Annja had been assigned a window seat and she used the opportunity to get a look at their destination from the air.

It was the first time she'd seen Mongolia and she wasn't certain what to expect.

What she got was an industrial city of gray concrete-box buildings mixed with brightly colored shops and multistory modern commercial buildings. Factories belched smoke into the air while tent settlements filled with the traditional round tents known as *gers* lined the city all the way to the foot of the mountains in whose valley Ulaanbaatar rested.

The city was home to some 850,000 people, which wasn't many when one considered the population of New York or Chicago, but was frankly astounding when you found out it had somewhere in the neighborhood of 60,000 inhabitants less than eighty years ago. Its current population was, she knew, about a quarter of the country's total.

The plane banked, lining itself up with the runway, and Annja was treated to a surprising sight. There on the side of a nearby hill was a huge portrait of Genghis Khan himself, staring up at them, welcoming them to the capital city of the country that he had, for all effective purposes, brought into being.

Annja took his presence as a good omen and felt some of the tension she'd been experiencing since the attack on Davenport's estate ease. She knew that if anyone could find the Khan's tomb it was her and, as the plane finished its turn, hiding the Khan from her view, she told him silently that they would be seeing each other soon.

The pilot did a nice job of putting the plane down on the runway with little more than a slight bump, and when the team disembarked they found Jeffries, Mason's second in command, waiting for them at the gate. He led them through the terminal, out a side door and onto a section of the runway itself.

The air was cold but not unbearable. Annja knew it would be far worse once they got up into the mountains, and she was suddenly glad for the cold-weather gear that Mason had obtained for her before they left. Jeffries led them on foot about three hundred yards east, almost to the edge of the airport, where the rest of their team was waiting with all the gear in a private hangar Jeffries had rented upon his earlier arrival. Just beyond, Annja could see the edge of an outdoor bazaar perched right next to the airport, and she was wondering idly if she'd have time to wander through it before they got under way when Mason called the group together for a discussion inside the hangar.

The team consisted of eleven individuals divided into three vehicles. The lead vehicle would carry one of the local guides, Nambai, and three members of Mason's security team: Jeffries, D'Angelo and Kent. Annja, Mason and Davenport were assigned to the middle vehicle. The third truck would hold Cukhbaatar, their other local guide, and the final three security team members: Harris, Williams and Vale.

Annja was introduced to each of them one at a time by Mason. Some, like Jeffries and Kent, she'd met at the Davenport estate. The others passed in a blur of faces and names. She did her best to lock each of them in her memory—D'Angelo, the dark-skinned Italian with the quick smile; Williams and Harris, the near-identical Brits with the thick accents and stoic demeanor; the fun-loving Vale. She was most interested in Nambai and Cukhbaatar, their guides. Nambai was a grizzled man in his late sixties who Mason claimed had explored more of Mongolia than anyone else. He'd made multiple journeys into the Restricted Zone, even when it had been under Soviet control, and Annja knew he was going to be an invaluable member of the group. Cukhbaatar, whom everyone almost instantly started calling Chuck due to their difficulty in pronouncing his name properly, turned out to be Nambai's grandson, a strong young man in his early twenties.

Given what had happened at the Davenport estate, Annja wasn't surprised by the presence of the security-team members. Nor the fact that they would be traveling armed. What did surprise her was that she was the only one on the expedition, if you could call it that, with any formal archaeological training. She brought the issue up with Davenport.

"Think of this as a reconnaissance mission," he told her. "We're here to see if we can find the site in the first place. If we do, we'll bring in a full team and go over the place with a fine-tooth comb. But we have to find it first."

And we have to do it before Ransom does, Annja thought, but didn't say it aloud. There was no sense starting the obvious.

To that end, they had planned for quick movement and

light travel. Helicopters were considered but ultimately rejected because their movements could be tracked too easily and there was a chance they couldn't get the proper flight permits in time. Davenport wanted everything on the up-and-up. As a result, they went with four-wheel-drive vehicles instead.

The trucks were Russian UAZ-469s, four-wheel-drive vehicles that looked like shorter versions of the Jeep Cherokee. They each held four passengers, with racks on the roof to carry the gear. Annja hadn't been overwhelmed when she'd seen them, but Mason had assured her the simple design and lack of computerized parts made them the best vehicles for the steppes. Each of the trucks carried two spare tires and several cans of extra gasoline as added protection against their getting stranded far from civilization. They had enough food and water to keep them going for a week, if need be, though they fully expected to be able to trade with several of the nomadic communities they would pass through during their search. Each vehicle had a satellite phone so they could communicate with one another without stopping.

A large metal trunk had also been bolted to the inside of each of the vehicles and when Annja peeked inside one she found an assortment of weapons: several handguns, a few assault rifles that she recognized as being HK MP-5 submachine guns and the like. In the wake of Ransom's attack at the estate, Mason wasn't taking any chances.

Considering how quickly this had come together, Annja was impressed with the attention to detail. She was even more impressed with the way Mason made certain each and every member of their small team knew where they were headed and what the rendezvous points were should they become separated at any time en route to their initial destination at Shankh. It was clear Mason had led small-group operations before; all that military training and attitude were hard to hide, even after a number of years in the private sector. Mason led the team the way an officer would lead a squad of special-operations men on a mission in enemy territory and it showed.

"Where'd you serve?" she asked him,

He flicked a glance in her direction, then went back to watching as the extra gas was being strapped to the rear doors of the trucks. "Is it that obvious?" he asked.

Annja saw no reason to lie. "Yes."

Mason shrugged. "I was 22nd SAS Regiment." And then, in case she didn't know what that was, he added, "British Special Forces."

Annja was fully aware the SAS were some of the best trained and experienced Special Forces soldiers in the world. It made sense that if Davenport was going to hire someone to protect him, he would hire the best. Annja guessed that there had been more than one problem in the past; otherwise, he probably would have been content with any of the half dozen or so security agencies that were typically used by the rich and powerful. Going out and hiring a freelance former SAS soldier wasn't something that you did every day—or lightly.

She watched him for another few seconds, wondering where he had been and what he had done while in the service. Wondered what it was that had made him leave it for civilian life. She'd come to enjoy his company over the past few days and knew in other circumstances she might consider going beyond the working relationship they currently had between them.

Growing up in an orphanage, she'd never been very close with anyone. She'd had her share of romantic encounters, but they were always of the ships-passing-in-the-night kind; fun while they lasted, but then she was on to some new dig or assignments and there wasn't room in her life for both a relationship and her career.

Later, once she'd become the heir apparent to Joan's mystical sword, she hadn't felt it was fair to drag anyone into a long-term relationship. Not when trouble seemed to find her at the drop of a hat.

Still, Mason might be an interesting diversion for a while.

First things first, Annja, her conscience said and her brain agreed. Maybe there would be time for something else later. Right now, they had a tomb to find.

She turned away to tend to her own gear.

18

As the loading was being finalized and last-minute adjust-ments were made, the man who had been placed inside Davenport's operations more than three years earlier slipped away from the others. An outdoor bazaar was adjacent to the airport and he took advantage of the general noise and confusion to mask his passage as he threaded his way into its depths. If anyone was following him, he was certain to lose them in the maze of stalls and shouting merchants.

When he was satisfied that there was no one behind him, he stepped out of the main thoroughfare and into a side street. He took a small, satellite phone out of his pocket and dialed a number he knew by heart.

It took a moment for the phone to connect. When it did, he heard Trevor Ransom's deep voice come over the line.

"What do you have for me?"

"Shankh," the informant told him. "They're headed to Shankh."

"Very well. Call me if you learn anything further but do

not—I repeat, do not—jeopardize your position on the team."

"Understood."

The informant ended the call and pocketed the phone. Taking a deep breath, he stepped out of the alley and headed back the way he'd come.

TWO HOURS AFTER their arrival in Ulaanbaatar, the team was almost ready to head out. The trucks had been checked, the supplies divided and loaded on to the appropriate vehicles, and Annja had taken time to review the maps herself just in case something drastic went wrong.

But when it was time to leave, Mason wasn't anywhere to be found.

Davenport was just about ready to send out Williams and Harris to search for him when Mason wandered back inside the door of the hangar, something bright red held in each hand.

"Where'd you go? We've been looking for you," Annja asked as he walked toward her.

Mason grinned and tossed something underhanded in her direction. Annja caught it instinctively and looked down to see she was holding an ice-cold can of Coke.

"Last cold one for a while. After this, it's nothing but yak milk and warm water."

She had to admit, it certainly hit the spot.

Mason finished his own soda in one long swallow, tossed the can in a nearby trash barrel and then shouted so the rest of the team could hear. "All right. Enough lollygagging! Mount up! It's time to get this show on the road."

And, with that, they were off.

They quickly left the airport behind and headed west

on the main road out of Ulaanbaatar. Slush lined the roadside and here and there unseen potholes made the driving difficult, forcing them to go slower than planned. At first it seemed as if they would never leave the seemingly endless industrial areas and their thick, coal-fueled smog behind as they followed the track for the Transmongolian Railroad out of the city proper, but eventually the factories slipped behind them and they began to pass small villages and residential areas. Those of a more permanent status were farther back from the road, while the ones that were intended for a night, two at most, lined the immediate edges of the thoroughfare.

On either side of the road, large herds of sheep, goats and cows grazed idly, paying no attention to the cars moving past them, sometimes no more than half a dozen feet away. More than once they were forced to stop or maneuver around an animal that had decided the middle of the road looked like a great spot to stand.

The people they saw were friendly and seemed to be genuinely happy with their lot in life, at least as far as Annja could see. She knew the past few years had been hard for many of the locals. A harsh winter followed by a long drought had killed off a lot of livestock, and those who depended on the herds for their livelihood were still trying to recover what they had lost as a result.

A few hours into the drive, they left even the smaller towns behind and found themselves on the famed Mongolian steppes. High rolling hills covered by a carpet of dry grass stared back at them wherever they looked, an endless sea of tan stretching away in all directions. Even the road took on a brown cast as the pavement had run out long before and the path beneath them was reduced to a large track of hard-packed earth.

Annja knew it would look different in the springtime, full of color and life, but this late in the season only the occasional herd of wild horses, one of Mongolia's national treasures, broke up the sameness of it all.

With nothing to see and time to waste, Annja's thoughts returned to Mason. Seated in the passenger seat, she had plenty of time to watch him without being obvious about it. Her initial impression, that he was a good-looking man with a dangerous side, had certainly been confirmed during the past week, but she didn't have a problem with that. He drove surely, confidently, just as he did everything else. Competence and a clear understanding and acknowledgment of their own abilities were things she prized in a man. It was one of the reasons she was attracted to Garin, in an odd, unresolved way.

She had to admit that Mason's past intrigued her, which was something she wouldn't have expected. Maybe it was just the mystery and mystique that surrounded the famed SAS regiment or the similarity she found between that and her own unique journey as the bearer of Joan's sword. She wasn't sure; she just knew that she wanted to know more, to understand where he came from and what made him tick.

And when you want something, you usually get it, don't you? she thought to herself with a grin.

Mason must have caught her look for he turned to her and asked, "Something funny?"

"Just imagining you spending your life herding goats like those locals back there," she said lightly, hiding her true thoughts behind the emotional wall she'd learned to erect in the orphanage so many years ago. Don't get close to anyone for they might not be here in the morning was an old mantra that still gave her some comfort.

He laughed. "Me? A goatherd? You've got to be out of your mind." His gaze caught hers. "Then again, a man can be induced to do anything if the reasons are right."

Was he flirting with her? Maybe she hadn't hidden her thoughts as well as she thought she had.

"All I know is with the right clothes and some dirt in your hair, you'd fit right in!" she said.

They continued in that vein, bantering back and forth for a time until Davenport spoke up from the backseat.

"I don't get it," he said.

Annja and Mason stopped their teasing. "Get what?" Mason asked.

"Why in heaven's name anyone would want to live out here?" Davenport said with a frown. "I mean, just look at this place!"

Apparently he hadn't heard a word of their conversation, which struck both Annja and Mason as hysterical. They broke into gales of shared laughter, leaving a bewildered Davenport staring at them from the backseat.

"What? Did I say something funny?"

Annja and Mason laughed even harder.

19

A loud thrumming sound filled the air, causing the boy to look around nervously. He'd only come to the Shankh Monastery six months ago, on the eve of his eleventh birthday, but he'd heard enough stories of times past to know that the sound of helicopters in the morning air was not a good omen.

Hefting his water bucket, he hurried back along the path toward the main building, intent on telling the master. The thrumming sound grew louder as he drew closer and the boy felt his sense of inner peace begin to fray. A glance told him the brothers working in the field had heard it, too; they had stopped working and one or two were even pointing into the sky behind him.

The wind began to whip and churn at his feet, growing stronger and angrier by the moment, and the boy felt some great presence looming behind him. His heart leaped into his throat and all he wanted to do was run, but he knew if he did he'd end up dropping the water bucket and Master Daratuk would simply send him back out to fill it again. Instead, he turned around to look.

Immediately, he wished he hadn't.

A large black monster hung in the air behind him, gleaming in the morning sunlight, its bulbous eyes staring with unblinking intensity. Its hot breath washed over him like the tide and he could feel its growl of hunger all the way down to the core of his bones.

The water bucket crashed to the ground as the boy recoiled in shock.

Then the illusion washed away as the large military helicopter swung around so he could view it from nose to stern and then settled down right in the middle of the vegetable garden.

When the door on the side of the helicopter slid open and men armed with guns spilled out, the boy decided he'd seen enough.

The water bucket forgotten, he turned and ran for the main sanctuary.

RANSOM KICKED the flimsy wooden door open with one booted foot and strode inside the main hall, gun in hand. Behind him came Santiago and one of the local Mongolians that they had hired as an interpreter. Hundreds of candles lined the walls, casting a soft light across the room, allowing Ransom to see three rows of monks seated directly opposite the door, their orange robes a stark contrast against the dark wood and stone of the interior.

An older monk in brown robes sat cross-legged in front of the others. His expression was noncommittal, despite Ransom's angry entrance.

We'll see how long you keep that peaceful expression if I don't get what I want, Ransom thought with a grim smile. He knew he was two hours, maybe three at most, ahead of Davenport and his crew and he had no intention of wasting any more time than was necessary. This man was going to give him what he wanted, one way or another.

Ransom strode across the room and stopped directly in front of the older monk. "I've been told that you can provide me with information about the location of the tomb of Genghis Khan," he said.

The monk stared at Ransom's face for a long moment, then smiled. He rattled off something in Mongolian.

Ransom looked back over his shoulder at the thin-faced man who'd agreed to translate for him.

"He welcomes you and prays that the wisdom and grace of the Buddha will be with you all of your days."

Ransom grunted. So it was going to be like that, was it? He raised his arm slowly and put the barrel of his pistol directly against the gleaming skin of the older man's bald head. Still speaking in English, he said, "I won't ask you again. You have ten seconds to tell me what I want to know."

Ransom began to count. "One. Two."

The old monk closed his eyes and began talking in a slow, unhurried voice.

"What's he saying?" Ransom asked.

The translator hesitated.

Ransom was in no mood for disobedience. Without taking his eyes off the monk, he said over his shoulder, "I asked you what he was saying. If you prefer, I can shoot you instead."

That did the trick. The translator swallowed hard and finally found his voice. "He's praying, asking forgiveness for any sins he has committed and…"

But Ransom had heard enough. He considered the older man sitting in front of him for a moment, decided that threatening his life wasn't going to accomplish much and turned to face the three rows of younger monks sitting behind their leader.

As one they bent their heads over their hands, closed their eyes and began to speak in that same lilting tongue as their leader, no doubt praying for his safety, as well.

It's not his safety you should be worrying about, Ransom thought, and then shot the monk closest to him in the head.

Blood flew, staining the face and robe of the man sitting next to the unfortunate victim in a harsh spray of crimson, eliciting a sharp cry of surprise and fear as the echo of the gunshot bounced around the interior of the room.

"You can either tell me what I want to know, or I will continue to kill your people one by one until you do. Your choice."

The old man didn't move; he didn't say anything to Ransom, didn't acknowledge the death of one of his students, didn't do anything but sit there, head bowed, praying aloud, just like the others.

Ransom shot another monk.

This time, it seemed to take longer for the sound of the shot to stop echoing around the inside of the room, but the results were the same. The dying man splattered those around him in a shower of blood.

He shot three more monks, without learning anything more, before he grew tired of the game.

Turning to Santiago, he said, "Interrogate each and every one of them. If they know something about the tomb, I want to know it, as well. While you are doing that, have the rest of the men search the place. If it's here, I want it found."

He stalked back outdoors and over to the helicopter,

ignoring the sudden spate of gunfire occurring behind him. He climbed up into the copilot's seat and then made a call on his satellite phone.

Some seven thousand miles away the phone was answered on the first ring. "Yes, Mr. Ransom?"

"Do we have anything new with regard to the translation?"

He listened to the explanation, then asked, "And nothing with regard to the monastery? You're certain?"

"Yes, sir. I'm certain." There was no hesitation in her voice, no doubt. She was being a truthful as she could be.

"Very well. Keep me informed."

"Of course, sir."

He hung up the phone and leaned his head back against the seat behind him, his thoughts full of unanswered questions. Just what are you up to, Davenport? What had Annja Creed discovered in the text that his people could not? He looked through the windshield at the destruction his men were causing all around him. What did you expect to find here? He wondered.

He stayed like that, thinking, until Santiago came over fifteen minutes later to report that, despite his best efforts, the monks had not given up a single clue to the tomb's location.

Ransom nodded to show that he'd heard, but didn't answer right away. He spent a minute or two looking around him, trying to figure out what he had missed, but there wasn't anything obvious. So be it, he thought. At least I'll know that Davenport and his set of flunkies have no way of finding it.

"Burn it. I don't want anything left for Davenport to search through," he said.

"What about the monks?" Santiago asked

"Kill them all" was Ransom's disinterested reply.

20

The men in the lead vehicle saw the smoke first. Jeffries radioed the sighting back to Mason in the middle car, and seconds later the rest of them saw it, as well. It drifted up into the sky in a thick column, ominously dark against the clear blue. Knowing there was nothing else in that direction but the monastery left little doubt as to where it was coming from.

Someone had been there before them and it wasn't hard to guess who.

"Damn! How did he know?"

Annja didn't have to ask who Mason was referring to, but she thought it best not to jump to conclusions.

They drove closer, their hearts heavy in their chests, and found no relief from their fears when, fifteen minutes later, they were finally close enough to see what had happened.

A vast funeral pyre burned in the center of the compound, just in front of the steps leading to the main hall. The bodies of the monastery's former inhabitants could be seen in the midst of the vast flames, the occasional arm or leg jutting from the pile of wood and brush. Behind it, the once-beautiful buildings had been vandalized so badly that in some places they were hardly recognizable. Planks and beams had been torn down to make the pyre. The smoke it gave off had stained the vibrant colors—the brilliant reds, the stately gold, the mossy green—dark with soot.

The place looked dead. Nothing living moved in the ruins.

"Christ..." Davenport said, staring, appalled at the destruction in front of them, through the windshield of their vehicle.

"Wrong savior," Annja quipped sourly, but she knew exactly how he felt. Whoever had done this had intended to get results. As she opened her door and got out, the heavy stench of burning flesh and hair assaulted her nostrils. It was an unmistakable smell; once you've encountered it, you never forgot it, and Annja knew it would be implanted in her memory for years to come.

Whoever had done this was absolutely ruthless.

Mason and Davenport got out of the vehicle and came up to stand beside her.

"Think anyone made it out alive?" Mason asked.

"Only one way to find out," she replied.

Mason turned and signaled to his men in their trucks. The six security personnel quickly got out, drew their weapons and headed into the complex to search for survivors and any trace of whoever had done this.

Annja stood still and let the feel of the place wash over her. Since accepting the sword, and the adventures that came with it, her danger sense seemed to have heightened. Fear, pain and sorrow washed over her, but she didn't get a sense that the killers still lurked in the ruins.

She followed the others into the ruins of the monastery compound. The first few buildings they encountered were small outer buildings that looked as if they had been used as meditation chambers or meeting places. It was hard to tell exactly, since many of them had been torched and only the ruined shells remained. The larger, communal hall that served as the main meeting and meditation area still stood, though its walls were pockmarked with bullet holes and its door was partially smashed from its frame.

It was toward this that Annja headed.

She climbed the steps and went inside.

It took her eyes a moment to adjust to the dim light. Once they had, she could see that the building consisted of one large room with a raised dais at the far end. Candles had once lined the walls, it seemed, but were now scattered across the floor. Blood stained the polished wood flooring in various places and had even splashed across one of the Buddha statues that filled the corners of the room.

Annja walked to the center of the room, trying to piece together what had happened. The presence of so much blood told her that more than one lama had met his end in this room; the idea that blood had been shed in a place that devoted itself to serenity and higher value infuriated her almost as much as the death of the innocent monks did.

She walked over to one bloodstain and reached out to touch it with the tip of her finger. It was still tacky, which meant it wasn't too old. A few hours at best, was her guess, though she wasn't a trained forensic examiner and couldn't be certain.

"Ayyeeeeee!"

The shrill cry came from behind her and Annja whirled in response, her hand already reaching into the other-where for her sword.

A small, dark form hurtled at her from across the room. Annja's mind registered the details, which allowed her to react in time to avoid the sudden thrust of the knife as the boy closed in on her. Rather than slashing him with her sword, which had been her first intention, she left the weapon where it was and, instead, caught hold of his arm as the knife slid past her. She used his momentum against him, twisting back in the other direction and taking him with her in a perfectly executed judo throw.

His back hit the floor with an audible thud and Annja moved in quickly, kneeling on his chest and applying a wrist lock to maintain control of his knife hand.

A boy of no more than ten or twelve stared up at her from a face stained with soot and fresh tears. He struggled to free himself, but grimaced in pain when Annja applied a bit more pressure to his wrist.

"I'm not going to hurt you," Annja told him, but the scared expression on his face told her that he didn't understand.

She looked up to call for help, only to see Mason hurrying toward her from the front entrance with Nambai in tow.

"We heard a scream," he said. "Are you all right?"

"I'm fine. Rambo here decided I made a good target."

Mason looked down at the boy she still held securely in the wrist lock. "Does he speak English?"

Annja looked at the boy. "What's your name?"

The youth stared at her with anger in his eyes.

"Come on, we're not going to hurt you. We're here to help."

The boy said nothing.

Nambai stepped forward and spoke softly in Mongolian. The boy looked between them for a moment, then answered his countryman in a voice sharp with anger. The two talked for a few minutes more. The sound of a friendly voice speaking his language must have helped, for the boy quit struggling and Annja was able to let go of his arm and help him sit up.

Nambai turned to the others. "He says his name is Chingbak and he only recently came here as an apprentice to Master Daratuk."

"Ask him what happened here," Annja told Nambai.

The boy's reply was a bit longer this time.

"He says men came in a helicopter, questioned the lamas and then tore apart the buildings looking for something. When they didn't find it they questioned the lamas again, shooting them when they didn't like the answers."

"Is Master Daratuk dead?" Annja asked, watching the boy's eyes carefully while Nambai translated her question.

The split second hesitation before Chingbak nodded his head told her he was lying. Obviously, he didn't trust them, not after what he had seen the other strangers do.

"Tell him that if Master Daratuk isn't dead, we have a doctor and medicine with us, that we might be able to save his life if we get to him soon enough."

The boy stared at Annja after Nambai finished speaking, clearly weighing his options, then made up his mind. Getting to his feet, he led them off to one side of the compound, where he'd set up a makeshift shelter of partially burned timber and spare blankets. A solitary figure lay beneath it.

At first Annja thought the old monk was dead. He lay so still that it was almost impossible to see that he was breathing. The condition of his body didn't make it easy to look at him, either; the material of his once-brown robe seemed to have become part of his flesh, so badly was he burned. He moved his head slightly when she knelt beside him, however, and she knew he was hanging tentatively to life. Looking at the extent of his injuries, Annja was amazed that he could do so; she knew bigger and stronger men who would have succumbed to wounds like that.

She turned to call for the medical kit, but the Mason laid his hand on her shoulder and she understood the unspoken signal. As much as she hated to admit it to herself, there was nothing they could do for the old man, something Mason had understood immediately upon seeing his condition. The small medical kit in the truck wouldn't even come close to dealing with his visible wounds and they were more than two hundred miles from the nearest hospital. He would never live long enough to cross its threshold.

The boy must have seen something in her face for he turned away abruptly probably not wanting a woman to see his tears.

As Annja turned back to the old man on the ground before her, his hand came up suddenly, grabbing hers, and she could feel the hard tautness of the tendons in his palm where the fire had burned away his flesh. If the action caused him pain, he didn't give any sign of it. Instead, he pulled her downward toward his face.

Realizing what he wanted, Annja turned her head so that her ear came to rest less than a half inch from his lips when he stopped pulling. He began to whisper to her, in a strange, lilting, singsong voice, in a language she didn't understand.

But as he spoke, a picture began to form in her mind, an image of a long, slender object wrapped carefully in a red *tangka* which was tied shut with silk cords. She could see it there, hanging before her mind's eye, and as he continued to speak it began to grow more detailed, more solid, until she was almost convinced that she could reach out and take it from the thin air, just as she did with her sword.

Through it all, he never let go of her hand.

Eventually the monk's voice faded away into silence. Annja pulled her head back so she could see his face. He stared up at her with a surreal expression of peace and serenity on his face, given what he had just suffered through only a short while before, and then in clear and unaccented English, he said, "Go to the Buddha. Protect it."

His grip went slack and he died without another sound.

She let his hand slip out of her own and placed it gently on his chest.

"What was that all—" Mason started to say, but trailed off when she held up her hand in a gesture for silence.

She shook her head, as if trying to dislodge something from it, then stood and walked away.

Leaving the shelter and its grisly contents behind, she returned to the main hall and entered through the shattered front door. Once inside, she walked over to one of the four identical statues of the Buddha that stood in each corner of the room. This one had been defaced and riddled with bullets by Ransom's men, but they had apparently thought it was too heavy to move for it still stood upright in its intended location. As if in a daze, Annja reached out and twisted its left arm just so.

With a soft hiss, the statue tilted backward on the hinge built into the rear portion of its large, rectangular base, revealing the dark square of an opening beneath its ponderous bulk.

Annja grabbed one of the nearby candles and held it

over the opening, revealing the set of well-worn steps leading downward into darkness.

Without hesitation, she started down.

21

Behind her, Annja could hear Mason and Davenport scrambling to catch up. Mason was shouting for her to wait, that she didn't know what was down there, but she ignored him. After all, she did know, didn't she? The dying lama had shown her—somehow.

The stairs became a narrow corridor running directly ahead for another twenty feet before opening into a small room at the end. It wasn't much, just a ten-by-ten-square-foot room hewn out of the rock beneath the temple. A table made from a huge slab of marble stood against the back wall, as far from the door as possible. On it rested an ornate chest covered with gold and precious jewels that reflected the light from Annja's candle back at her in a thousand refracted patterns.

"Is that what we're looking for?" Davenport asked, his voice a hushed awe in the near darkness, as he stepped up next to her.

Annja nodded, not trusting herself to speak. As certain

as she'd been that Curran's journal had been authentic, she expected that her hunch as to the present location of the *sulde* would turn out to be, as well. She didn't have to look inside to know it was in there; she could almost feel it.

The chest was unlocked.

Inside was the object she'd seen in her vision; a long, slender package wrapped in red cloth and tied with strips of silk.

Annja lifted it out of the chest, laid it on the floor and carefully untied the silk strips that held the bundle closed. Silk was an amazing material, she thought. Even after all this time it was soft and supple, the way it was created to be, and Annja had no problem untying it.

The red wrapping turned out to be a gorgeous *tangka,* one of the traditional decorated banners that were so much a part of Mongol culture in the past. Its surface was covered with images of the gods and with the many symbols that stood for eternity, long life, good health and other positive omens. The vast majority of the *tangkas* had been destroyed by the Soviets in the 1930s when they had razed the Buddhist temples, Annja knew, and the archaeologist in her instantly noted that this was a magnificent specimen.

Inside the wrapping was a black *sulde.*

Annja felt the thrill of discovery course through her. She had been right! After being smuggled out of the monastery back in the 1930s, it must have been returned to its original hiding place once it had been deemed safe to do so. While the rest of the world was looking for it elsewhere, the *sulde* was right under their noses all along.

It was a brilliant strategy and it had worked like a charm. Apparently, no one else had suspected it until they had come along.

As she held the *sulde* up in the light, a slight breeze blew through the room, ruffling the long strands of horsehair that hung off the shaft of the spear just below the blade. For just a second she thought she heard the distant sounds of battle: the thunder of hooves on the plain, the clash of bodies, the shouts of the victors and the cries of the wounded. Then the room was still once more and all she heard was their breathing in the small chamber.

Apparently, Mason and Davenport hadn't noticed anything unusual, for they didn't react in any way other than with excitement over the find, and so Annja decided to keep what she had heard to herself. She'd become attuned to all sorts of strange things since taking up the sword and she'd learned that other people weren't always on the same wavelength. No sense in getting everyone worked up, she decided.

"I don't believe it! You did it, Annja!" Davenport cried.

"Okay," she said, grinning with excitement right along with Davenport. "We've found the *sulde*. Now what?"

The two men looked at her in surprise.

"What do you mean, now what?" Mason asked.

"What do we do with it now that we've got it?" she said.

"You don't know?"

Annja snorted. "It's not like it comes with instructions, Mason."

"'Beneath the watchful gaze of the eternal blue heaven, the spirit of the warrior points the way,'" Davenport said, repeating the first lines of the hidden message. "If the eternal blue heaven is the open sky above, and the spirit of the warrior is the *sulde,* as we've already decided, then according to Curran, the spear should point us toward the next clue, right?"

"Right," Annja agreed.

"So which direction was it facing when we took it out of the chest?"

Mason glanced at the chest, did some rough calculations based on where the room was situated with regard to the main hall above and then pointed off to one side, "East."

East? Annja thought. Back toward Ulaanbaatar? That didn't make sense.

She said so to the others. "Genghis was a nomad, through and through. The one city he did build, Karakorum, was built to house his overflowing treasury. His conquests had simply generated too much wealth for him to carry around. But he never spent time there to any great length and certainly didn't see it as vital to the running of his vast empire. Why would Ulaanbaatar, a city that didn't exist at all in his day, be any different? And why would his followers put his tomb in a place that was so far from what he considered home?"

It just didn't add up.

"What do you propose we do? Put the spear on the floor and spin it around, then head off in whatever direction it lands?" Mason asked.

Annja bit back the quick retort that sprang to her lips. "I just think we should look around a bit more. It has to be here somewhere. The lama wouldn't have sent us here if that wasn't case."

"Maybe he just wanted us to find and protect the *sulde*," Mason grumbled, but he started looking around like the other two, checking the walls, the floor, even the ceiling, for hiding places or secret passages.

When they struck out there, Davenport took the *sulde* and began going over it inch by inch, while the other two turned their attention to the platform itself and the chest the *sulde* had been stored in.

The two of them were searching the interior of the chest when Annja heard a soft click coming from Mason's end.

"Hold still!" she said sharply the second she heard it, and Mason, used to a lifetime of obeying urgent commands, froze immediately.

Annja had encountered quite a few booby traps while searching ancient ruins and the quiet snick she'd just heard sounded uncomfortably similar. She had a sudden vision of a blade flashing downward in the dark, of screams of pain echoing down the pitch-dark hallway through which they stumbled. She shook her head, dispatching the illusion. That had been another day, another time, and besides, she'd made it through. If she wanted to prevent something deadly from happening to Mason, she needed to focus on the here and now.

Mason's right hand was pressed against the inner surface of one end of the chest.

"What did you do?" she asked him.

Without moving his hands, he said, "Nothing. I just pushed against the interior wall, trying to see if it was solid."

Annja brought the candle closer and peered at the area behind Mason's hand. A small section of the chest wall had shifted backward the slightest bit, which must have been the sound she heard. With the candlelight, the outline of a small rectangular opening was revealed.

"Pull your hand away slowly," Annja said. She watched closely as he did so, ready to knock him out of the way if she saw any hint of movement from that section of the chest, but nothing shot out at them and Mason was able to remove his hand without incident.

Once he had, they could all see that he had inadvertently opened a small compartment built right into the side of the chest. Using the edge of his knife, Mason was able to slip the cover free, revealing the scrap of parchment that was hidden inside the cavity.

Very carefully, he fished it out and then handed it to Davenport.

"Why don't you do the honors," Mason said, and Annja nearly laughed aloud when she saw how excited the offer made their employer. He was like a giant kid turned loose in the candy store and, seeing his exuberant attitude, she understood what drove a man as wealthy as he to get his hands dirty, literally, on an expedition like this. She had to admit, that was one of the things she liked about him best, his desire to experience things for himself and not just through his employees.

Annja and Mason crowded around him so they could see as he unfolded the small piece of parchment.

The revelation, when it came, was a disappointment, however.

Annja had been hoping for another stanza or two in the puzzle, another set of clues that could help her narrow down the directions to bring them to the second destination necessary to find the tomb. Instead, all they got was a few wavy lines that looked like lightning falling from the sky; they started at the same point and then spread downward away from one another from there. Above them was a triangular shape that could have represented everything from the delta symbol to a visit by space aliens.

It looked pretty useless.

22

While Davenport puzzled over the meaning of the drawing, Annja and Mason finished searching the rest of the chest. That took another ten minutes and ultimately proved fruitless, so they turned their attention to the spear itself, looking for markings or any kind of writing that might help them.

They struck out there, as well, just as Davenport had moments before.

A glance at Mason's watch told them it would be dark soon, so they decided to wait until after their evening meal before making any decisions regarding what to do next. They placed the *sulde* back inside the *tangka* and wrapped it all up, then carried it with them back to the surface, closing the entrance to the secret chamber behind them and exiting the building.

Mason's men had managed to get the fire out and rescued what bodies they could while the others were underground. The heavy stench still hung over the area, as did a dark cloud of smoke, but there wasn't anything they could do about either, and so they did the best they could to ignore them.

There was considerable concern that whoever had done this might return and so the decision was made to continue up the road a bit before finding a place to camp for the night. Jeffries and his men hadn't found anyone else alive in the ruins and the boy had walked off in the wake of the old man's death.

Mason gave the orders and the teams quickly regrouped, loaded back into the vehicles and left the shattered remains of Shankh behind them as they drove toward the setting sun.

About ten miles farther up the road they found a nice spot in the lee of a small ridge to set up camp for the night. A cold wind was pushing down from the north at this point and the ridge would at least provide some shelter during the course of the night.

They had a quick dinner and then retired to their tents, one for each carload.

The excitement of the past few hours was still with them and so no one wanted to sleep. Davenport was making notes in his journal, chronicling the trip, while Annja stared absently at the map over Mason's shoulder as he tried to figure out their next course of action.

A sudden thought occurred to her. She stared at the map for a long moment, following the topographical lines to be certain, before turning to Davenport and asking him for the piece of parchment they'd found in the chest.

He saw the look in her eyes as he handed it over. "You've figured it out, haven't you?" he asked eagerly.

"Maybe. Not sure yet." She took the scrap of parchment from him and unfolded it, making sure she was remembering the design on it properly.

She was.

Mason was watching her now along with Davenport, so she reached out and took the topographical map he was holding. "May I?" she asked.

"Be my guest," he replied.

She laid it across her knee, then put the piece of parchment against it, comparing the two.

After a moment she looked up at her two companions and said, "I'm an idiot. It was right there in front of us the whole time." She pointed at the three wavy lines on the piece of parchment. "'To where the blood of the world intertwines, and the voice in the earth has its say.' Freakin' obvious," she said, grinning.

Apparently Mason didn't think so, for he stared at her as if she'd suddenly lost her mind.

"Obvious?" he said. "Riiiight."

She shook her head, frustrated with her slowness in not seeing it before. She hadn't expected Mason to catch it, but she should have seen it right away. "The Mongols were, at heart, animists. Everything had its own spirit, including the earth. Still with me?"

Mason nodded.

"A typical Mongol encampment stank to high heaven, which was one of the reasons the Europeans began calling them the Mongol horde, but that was because they didn't understand the cultural differences between the two societies.

"Unlike their European counterparts, Mongol warriors refused to bathe in rivers and streams. This wasn't because they liked being dirty, but because they considered such places to be holy. They saw the land beneath their feet as the body of the earth spirit, so to speak, which meant that the rivers and streams…"

"…would be the veins that carried its blood through its

body," Mason finished for her. "So, if that's the case, what's with the triangle-looking thing?"

Davenport answered that one. "It's a mountain. Or, at least, I think it's a mountain."

Annja nodded encouragingly. "That would be my guess, too. A mountain. Which means that all we have to do is find one that stands near the convergence of three rivers and we've found where the blood of the earth intertwines."

"Should be easy enough," Mason said, and the three of them huddled around the map.

Fifteen minutes later, they'd found several different possibilities and had only covered half of the map. Clearly they were missing something.

"How do we know which one is more likely than another?" Davenport wanted to know.

Mason thought about it for a moment. "Well, it would probably be one that was important to the Khan, wouldn't it? Someplace that held special meaning for him?"

They sat in silence for a few moments, thinking, until Annja suddenly exclaimed, "Khokh Lake!" and grabbed the map, looking it over as she explained. "Genghis Khan was named clan chief on the shores of Khokh Lake at the foot of Khara Jirgun Mountain. The Mongol name for it was the Blue Lake by Back-Heart-Shaped Mountain. Just about every single historical account we have about Genghis's life notes this as significant. That's got to be the place!"

But it wasn't.

Khokh Lake was fed by two rivers, not three.

That started them down a list of major events in the Khan's life, and it wasn't long before they figured it out. The boy who would later become the Khan of khans had been born along the Onon River, near the spot where the Onon, the Tuul and the Kerulen all began. Looming over them was the tallest mountain in the Hentiyn Nuruu range, Burkhan Khaldun, or God Mountain, as it was called.

Annja pointed to the spot on the map about three or four days' hard drive from where they were. "That's it. That's the place. It's got to be. That's where we'll find the next clue."

23

The night passed without incident. They broke camp with the rising sun and headed north toward the Hentiyn Nuruu mountain range. They kept their vehicles in the same formation, but now everyone paid more attention both to the traffic they passed on the road and to the clear sky above, looking for the helicopter Chingbak claimed Ransom had arrived in.

It wasn't long before they left the last remnants of civilization behind and headed into the heart of the Mongolian steppes. Annja had seen pictures of spring in the steppes: the vast green plains stretching as far as the eye can see, wildflowers and herds of wild horses occasionally breaking the ocean of green with a riot of color and motion, all framed by the clear blue sky above that just seemed to go on forever.

Unfortunately, they were just a few short weeks from winter at this point. Those endless green plains were now dull beige in color. The wildflowers were nowhere to be found and the horses had gone south for warmer pastures.

The blue sky was the same startling color, but even that seemed colder and harsher to Annja than it had in the photographs.

Just about midday they came upon an old chain-link fence stretching across the road and disappearing into the distance on either side. The gate had been forced at some time in the past; it lay bent and pulled to one side, the chain that once secured it now draped across the road.

A sign with Cyrillic letters, pockmarked with bullet holes, hung about five feet to the left of the gate.

"Restricted Zone," Mason read aloud. "Violators Will Be Shot."

They had reached the edge of the land Genghis Khan had called home.

Annja knew that after Genghis Khan was secretly buried in his homeland, his soldiers sealed off several hundred miles of pristine countryside. No one but members of the Khan's family could enter. A special group of soldiers was assigned to protect what would become known as the Ikh Khorig—the Great Taboo. Annja knew that even long after the Mongol Empire had collapsed and other cultures had invaded the area, the Mongol people had still prevented anyone from entering this sacred land.

When the Soviets arrived, there was concern that the Mongol people would use the memory of Genghis Khan as a rallying point for nationalism. To prevent this, they kept up the age-old habit of preventing entry into the region, even going so far as to stop referring to the area by its Mongol name and reclassifying it as the Highly Restricted Area, an innocuous bureaucratic designation if there ever was one. Not satisfied with that, they surrounded the Highly Restricted Area with another equally large buffer zone they named the Restricted Zone.

Neither roads nor bridges had been built anywhere within this zone during the Soviet era. With so many other issues occupying the Mongol people's attention, nothing had been built since the collapse of the Soviet Union.

It was going to be a different ride from here on out.

With a wave of his arm, Mason ordered the convoy to continue forward into the Great Taboo.

FROM HIS POSITION a few miles behind, Ransom sat and watched the blip on his tracking device that represented Davenport's convoy as they crossed into the Restricted Zone. He wondered exactly where they were headed. His team had struck out twice so far, first with the translation of the journal and then again at the monastery. Clearly, Davenport and his pet archaeologist knew something he did not.

But what?

He was growing more frustrated with each passing hour. Where were they getting their information?

His inside source was due to report in later that evening, so it was only a matter of time before Ransom would have a handle on where Davenport's team was headed. And once he had that, he could set up the next stage of his plan.

As if on cue, the rear door opened and Santiago slid into the seat beside him.

"Well?" Ransom asked.

"We're set. All we need is the cash to pay them off and they'll do whatever we ask them to do."

Ransom smiled and it wasn't a pleasant smile. "Good. And they know not to touch anything they find?"

Santiago nodded. "I made it quite clear."

"Excellent!"

Ransom turned back to the GPS monitoring device and watched the blip continue on its forward journey. "Let's see how Davenport deals with a little unexpected company, shall we?"

24

The trip became more surreal the deeper they went into the Restricted Zone. The Soviets might not have wasted their time building bridges or roads, but that didn't mean they shied away from building everything else. The first thing they encountered, less than half a mile from the boundary, was an abandoned tank base.

At least, that's what Annja assumed it to be, given the rusting hulks that sat still and silent off to each side of the road and the cluster of buildings they could see in the distance. The tanks looked as if they had been in the midst of maneuvers when the call had come for everyone to drop things where they were and walk off the set. It was an eerie feeling driving by those abandoned tanks; there was sense of fearful expectation about them, as if they were just waiting for the right stimulus to reawaken, to suddenly return to life and their deadly missions. Annja's imagination quickly went into overdrive as she imagined the turrets suddenly rotating in their direction, the squeal of steel on steel as long-unused ammo cases suddenly dropped a round into the firing mechanisms and…

That's enough of that, she told herself firmly as the tanks disappeared into the distance behind them.

That was just the beginning of the weirdness, however.

They passed a long stretch of flat country filled with craters and strewn with the wreckage of trucks, tanks and what seemed to be the partial remains of aircraft. Any interest in examining them was quickly stifled when un-exploded artillery shells were found in a nearby crater. Collapsed buildings and complexes also showed up regularly along their route, lounging empty and all but forgotten among the waving grasslands.

More than once they were forced to detour around large pools of stagnant water mixed with unidentifiable chemicals that shimmered in the sunlight like Christmas lights. Far more often than not the banks of such oases were lined with the decaying carcasses of animals that had crept down to the water's edge for a drink and never managed to leave. Even the air seemed to be against them, with strange smelling vapors rising from the cracked and cratered landscape as they drove farther and farther from civilization.

They had been driving for eight long hours when Mason called a halt. It would be dark soon and he wanted to have camp set up while they could still see. A quick conference with the other drivers resulted in the choice of a suitable location. The tents were pulled out and set up while two of Mason's men set about making dinner for the rest of the team.

The food was good and the coffee afterward even better. Annja found that she enjoyed Mason's company and the two of them stayed up much later than the others, swapping stories. Annja talked about the various expeditions she'd been on and what it was like working on a popular cable show, while Mason filled her in on all the craziness that came with being the personal bodyguard to one of the world's richest men. By the time they were both ready to call it an evening, it was close to midnight.

Mason banked the fire, ensuring that there would be hot coals to restart it in the morning and they both retired to their tent.

Annja, however, was unable to sleep. She'd had too many cups of coffee after riding in the truck all day and nature called. She really didn't want to go outside in the cold, but sharing the tent with two men didn't leave her any other option.

Trying to be as quiet as possible so that she didn't wake her companions, she dug around in her pack until she located the packet of tissues she'd set aside for just such an event and then, flashlight in hand, stepped out into the night air.

The moon had yet to rise and the camp was shrouded in darkness, but she refrained from turning on the flashlight as she didn't want to call attention to herself should anyone still be awake. She figured she'd get beyond the ring of trucks at the edge of camp and then switch it on.

The dying embers of the fire gave her enough light to see by and so she crossed past its remains, headed for the trucks parked just beyond.

In the darkness on the other side of the vehicles, a horse snickered softly.

Annja froze.

A horse? Way the heck out here?

She waited, her pulse raising and her ears straining, trying to decide if she'd heard what she thought she'd heard or if she'd simply been imagining it.

A few seconds passed and right when she had just about decided it must have been something else, a light chuffing sound reached her ears, as if a large animal had just blown air out of its nostrils.

This time it came from directly behind her.

Annja lowered herself into a crouch and quietly transferred the flashlight to her left hand. The hair on the back of her neck was standing upright and adrenaline flushed her system as she realized that the camp was more than likely surrounded.

Whoever they were, they weren't here to welcome her team to the neighborhood.

While Annja was trying to figure out what to do, the decision was taken out of her hands.

A huge form came rushing out of the darkness ahead of her, moving so quickly it was upon her almost before she knew it was there. Only her heightened reflexes saved her as she dove quickly to one side, the club swung in her direction by the horse's rider missing her by scant inches.

She hit the ground, rolled and came back up on her feet, drawing her sword from the otherwhere as she did so. "Mason!" she shouted, hoping to give the others some warning before they were run down in their tents. She could sense other large shapes moving out there in the darkness, but right then she needed to concentrate on the rider in front of her as he was reigning in his mount and turning around for another try at her.

Good, she thought, turning her body slightly to one side, using it to shield her sword from the rider's sight. Come and get some…

The rider did just that. He shouted in what Annja recognized as Mongolian, dug his heels into the flanks of his horse and tried to run her down.

Annja stood her ground, waiting until the last possible second as the massive beast bore down on her position. When he was less than half a dozen feet away, she stepped to one side and brought up her left hand, simultaneously flicking the switch on the flashlight she held and shining it in the rider's face, hoping to blind him.

It worked better than she expected. The rider threw up a hand, trying to shield his eyes from the light and unintentionally pulled back on the reins. His horse reared up on its hind legs, threatening to throw him off its back, and as it crashed back down to the ground Annja took advantage of the distraction to move up and inside the rider's swing.

His club passed harmlessly over her head and Annja responded in kind, thrusting upward with her sword.

Unlike the rider, Annja didn't miss.

Her thrust caught him square in the gut and the forward momentum from his horse almost tore her sword from her grasp as it bolted away from this new threat. If she hadn't killed him with her first thrust, the resulting damage caused when she hauled her sword free certainly did the job. Annja wasn't waiting around to find out, however; there were more attackers still to deal with.

No sooner had she turned to see if her shout had roused the others than two more men ran out of the darkness. The one on the right held a curved sword similar to a scimitar and the one on the left was carrying a tire iron. Neither of them seemed happy to see her still standing.

Sorry to disappoint you, boys, she thought, and then took the fight to them, closing with the one carrying the blade. She made sure to keep his body between her and his partner, preventing the other man from closing with her at the same time.

A loud pop sounded and suddenly the scene around her was lit as if by daylight. Someone must have shot off a flare. She could see the faces of the men in front of her now, hard Mongol faces with even harder expressions. Their eyes told her everything she needed to know; these men were intent on killing her and taking what was hers. So be it, she thought, now the gloves come off.

She traded several blows with her opponents, still maneuvering to keep the two of them in front of her where she could see them both. The Mongol's sword was lighter than her own, but shorter, as well, which actually gave her the advantage. He'd obviously used the weapon in the past; he slashed and cut with an easy familiarity. But Annja had trained extensively with her sword since she'd acquired it and she used it as if it were an extension of her body. Very quickly her opponent tired of the exchange and that's when he made his fatal mistake, taking a half second too long to recover from a thrust that disturbed his center of gravity.

Annja recognized his error and was moving toward him before he had a chance to do anything about it, knocking his sword to the ground with her own. She followed that up with a snap kick to his leg, viciously smashing his knee in the wrong direction. As he toppled toward her she swung her other hand, striking him in the temple with the flashlight.

Down he went.

Now that his partner was no longer in the way, the second man suddenly rushed toward Annja. Luckily, she'd caught sight of him as the first man dropped to the ground and she was already responding. As her body twisted to the right in the follow-through of her strike, she planted the foot she'd just kicked with firmly on the ground and spun on it, bringing her sword up and around her body in a downward swing that brought to bear all the momentum of her moving form. The edge of the blade caught her new assailant in the collarbone and kept going, cutting him diagonally from shoulder to hip.

Gunfire sounded from behind her and she instinctively threw herself to the ground, scrambling to find cover but finding only the body of her dead assailant to hide behind.

Another volley of gunfire sounded, this time nowhere near her, and then she heard Mason's voice calling her name above the din.

"I'm here!" she shouted in return and then cautiously poked her head up to look around.

Mason and his men stood in a loose circle in front of her tent with Davenport in their center, guarding him quite literally with their bodies. Between her and the rest of the team were the bodies of almost a dozen Mongol men and two of the horses they had ridden on. They were all dead, the majority gunned down in midassault by Mason's men as they had reacted to Annja's warning cry and rose to defend their employer. Annja herself had accounted for three of them, including the one she'd struck with the flashlight.

It had been close. If she hadn't needed to use the bathroom, things might have turned out rather differently, Annja realized.

Mason rushed over to her, anxious for her safety, and as he came toward her, Annja made sure to release her sword, letting it vanish. She didn't want the hassle of explaining how she had suddenly come into possession of a medieval broadsword; if asked, she'd say she had disarmed her opponent and used his weapon against him.

Suddenly exhausted, she climbed to her feet in time to meet Mason.

"Are you all right?" he asked. Without waiting for an answer he took hold of her upper arms and turned her body this way and that, looking for injuries.

His concern surprised her. Was there more here than just an expedition leader worried about one of his people? It also made her a little uncomfortable. He must have sensed it, too, for he abruptly let her go with a smile.

Unfortunately, not everyone had escaped unscathed. Both Harris and D'Angelo had been wounded and needed medical attention. Kent did what he could with the medical kits they had in the vehicles, but he told Mason he wasn't sure if they could continue the journey, given the extent of their injuries. If their conditions grew any worse in the next twenty-four to forty-eight hours, he recommended that they return to Ulaanbaatar where they could be treated properly.

While Mason was talking to Kent, the others had stoked the fire back into a roaring blaze to provide some warmth and then turned the trucks around so that the headlights were pointed into their camp, giving them the light they needed to conduct a search as they sought to understand who had attacked them and why.

Jeffries and Williams dragged the bodies into a line near the fire, then Annja and Mason went over them one at a time under Davenport's watchful gaze. While they did that, Jeffries, Vale and Williams did a quick canvass of the area around the camp, just to be certain there weren't any more attackers lingering in the perimeter.

Their assailants had all been Mongol men, locals it seemed. Their clothes were mostly handmade and had been repaired more than once. Their weapons were traditional, as well: clubs and hatchets and scimitars. But the money in their pockets was new and, more telling, it was foreign. American dollars, crisp and shiny, as out of place as a whale in a jewelry shop.

Putting it all together, they came up with what would have been considered a paltry sum back home.

"A hundred bucks!" Mason raged. "They were willing to kill us for a hundred lousy bucks?"

"It must have been Ransom," Annja said.

"But how?" Mason wanted to know. "How is that bastard tracking us so effectively? How does he know where we are all the time?"

The same thought occurred to them both.

"The trucks!" they said in unison.

It took them almost two hours, but they finally found the transponders hidden in a crevice in the well of the spare tire in each of the vehicles. One-by-one they were carefully removed and laid out beside one another on a folding table Davenport had taken from their tent.

They were small, rugged units, designed for use in harsh environments, and they probably would have gone undetected if it hadn't been for the failed attack and the recognition that someone else besides the bandits themselves were behind the assault.

Annja wanted to destroy them at once, but Mason overruled her. He called Jeffries and ordered him to see if he could round up any of the horses the bandits had been riding.

He borrowed a piece of paper from Annja and tore it into three long strips. He quickly wrote something on each, then wrapped them around the listening devices. By that time Jeffries was back with the horses and Mason dropped one of his little packages into the saddlebags on each horse. For the time being, the horses were tied to the front grilles of the vehicles to keep the animals from roaming during the night.

Mason intended to make good use of them come morning.

25

After untying the horses and letting the animals roam where they wanted, they continued on, making their slow way across the shattered landscape. Hopefully it would take Ransom a while to discover the ruse and by then they would be well on their way to their next destination.

They hadn't made much distance by midday and any hopes of making up the time lost quickly disappeared when the road petered out shortly thereafter. One minute it was there, the next it disappeared from beneath their wheels and they discovered that they had reached the limit of human expansion, at least in this day and age. As a result, their pace slowed even more.

On the bright side, they began to see returning signs of life in the landscape around them as they left the road farther and farther behind. First it was just the occasional small bush, hardy little plants that could withstand the climate of the polluted area to the south. Then bushes and grasses began to show up with more regularity—scrub, rye, sage grass and the like—until the land ahead of them became carpeted in vegetation.

Midafternoon brought them to a wide-open plain on which a massive herd of gazelle grazed. They scattered as the trucks moved among them, and at one point Mason sped up alongside the racing beasts, clocking their speed at just under thirty-five miles an hour. Shots rang out from the vehicle behind them and Annja knew that they were going to have fresh meat for dinner that evening.

As the herd raced ahead, Mason brought the truck over a gentle rise and there ahead of them loomed the Hentiyn Nuruu Mountains, tall snowcapped peaks that rose in a ragged line that stretched out toward the horizon. In their midst was one that was larger and more prominent than the rest: Burkhan Khaldun—God Mountain.

Mason let the truck roll to a stop and Annja climbed out for a moment. There weren't too many westerners who had the opportunity to see what she was seeing and she took her time, savoring the view. Somewhere, amid those peaks and valleys, the greatest warrior the world had ever seen had been laid to rest more than eight centuries before. And she was determined to find him.

It was at that point that they ran into a problem with their local guides. Up until then Nambai and, by extension, his grandson had been keeping them on track, even after the road had stopped and they had been forced to cut across country. But now, with the mountains looming ahead of them, Nambai had a change of heart.

He refused to take his grandson any farther into the heart of the Ikh Khorig.

When questioned, he mumbled something about a dream he'd had the night before in which the spirits told him that none of them would return alive from such a trip.

He was willing to risk his own life, and those of the foreigners who had paid him, but he would not risk the life of his daughter's child.

Neither talk nor threats could change his mind. Even Cukhbaatar's pleading didn't work. The man clearly believed what he had seen was an omen and nothing was going to alter that fact.

Mason paced in frustration, venting his anger on anyone who got too close. Turning back wasn't an option. They had come too far to have to backtrack and then retrace their route. Ransom was sure to get ahead of them if they were forced to do so and that was simply unacceptable.

But Mason couldn't leave the young man there to await their return, either. Recent events had clearly shown that those on their tail were willing to kill to stop them from reaching their goal, and Cukhbaatar would be a prime target for them.

Finally he stopped pacing and pulled Kent to one side. "How are our wounded doing?" he asked.

Kent glanced over at the truck where the two men were resting. "Harris is doing okay. The knife wound he took to the shoulder seems to be responding decently to the sulfa powder and it hasn't started bleeding again, which is a good sign. D'Angelo, on the other hand, is a mess."

"Can he go on?"

The other man shook his head. "Not if you want him to have use of that leg for the rest of his life. That hatchet must have been dirty as hell because I can't get a hold on the infection and I'm afraid it's going to spread. If it does, he'll wind up losing the leg before we make it back to civilization."

"All right. Thanks," Mason said, clapping the other

man on the shoulder to let him know that it wasn't his fault that the news wasn't good. Things go wrong sometimes on an op; that's just the way it goes.

D'Angelo's medical condition made Mason's decision easier, though. Because Kent was trained as a medic, Mason ordered him to take one of the trucks and accompany Harris, D'Angelo and Cukhbaatar back to the city. In the meantime, the rest of them would continue on in the other two vehicles. That would give the wounded men the medical care they needed and satisfy Mason's obligation to Nambai, all in one fell swoop. It was the best he could do under the circumstances.

They divvied up the supplies, making sure both groups had what was needed to continue on their way. Farewells were exchanged, and with a last, parting wave Kent and his crew piled into their truck and headed back toward Ulaanbaatar and civilization.

The rest of the group continued on. Mason, Davenport, Annja and Nambai were in the lead truck now, with Jeffries, Williams and Vale bringing up the rear in the other, the carcass of the antelope Vale had managed to bring down tied to the roof.

As the day grew longer they left the plains behind and, after passing through a region of rolling hills, began to climb through a series of interconnected alpine valleys. They were slowly gaining in elevation as they went and the air took on a bit of a chill, causing several of them to break out warmer clothing. Near the end of the day they came upon a pristine mountain lake and despite the bone-chilling temperature of the water, they all took the opportunity to take a quick dip and wash up. The men went first, laughing and roughhousing the whole time, and then Annja took a turn, with Mason standing guard.

Afterward, they hung out their freshly washed clothes to dry and enjoyed antelope steaks and fresh fish that night for dinner as the sun dipped over the horizon.

It was almost enough to make Annja forget what they had been through the previous evening.

Almost.

26

Ransom paced back and forth in the large Quonset hut he was using as his temporary headquarters, his irritation growing as the clock ticked onward. Turning to where Santiago sat in front of their communications equipment, he asked, "Any word from our new friends?"

Warily, Santiago shook his head.

"What the hell is keeping them?"

"I don't know. Maybe they're still mopping things up."

"All right, give them another hour."

But when they hadn't reported in at the end of that time, Ransom's patience had worn thin; he'd finally had enough. "I'm tired of waiting around for someone else to do our work for us. Do we still have them on the trackers?"

Wordlessly, Santiago spun the laptop that was sitting on the table in front of him in Ransom's direction, so that his boss could see the display. Three bright red dots marked the location of the three vehicles against a sea of green lighting.

Near as Ransom could tell, they hadn't moved much

since the night before. There they were, still clustered near one another in the same general place.

"How fast can the chopper be ready?"

"Five minutes, sir," Santiago replied, a hint of anticipation in his reply.

Without taking his eyes off the screen, Ransom said, "Let's pay them a visit."

Santiago pumped his fist in the air in agreement.

Ten minutes later they were airborne and headed toward the rendezvous with their unsuspecting enemies. The chopper could cover the territory much faster and more efficiently than the trucks Davenport's men were using and so it didn't take long to get into position.

Ransom held the laptop containing the tracking software on his lap, providing instructions to the pilot, while Santiago cradled his rifle in his arms, making certain the weapon was ready for action when he needed it.

No more screwing around, Ransom thought.

It didn't take long for their targets to grow closer on the screen and Ransom turned to be sure Santiago understood what he wanted.

"Remember what I said."

Santiago's eyes shone with excitement. "Yes, sir. Quick clean shots. Minimum damage to the vehicles if at all possible but collateral damage to the occupants is acceptable, even preferred, regardless of whether it is the tribesmen we hired or Davenport's team."

That's what he liked about his lieutenant. You didn't have to spell everything out for him. He had initiative in spades.

The targets were less than a mile out and Ransom gave the signal for the pilot to take it lower. He didn't want to give them any more warning than was necessary.

The pilot took the chopper down low, and behind him

Ransom felt Santiago slide open the side door and ready himself for what was to come.

Screw you, Davenport, Ransom thought. Time for this little game to come to an end.

He thought back to that day when Davenport had discovered his activities on the building project. The fool should have been happy that he'd found contractors willing to use the cheaper materials that he'd had shipped in when no one was looking. If they had finished the building the way he had planned, they would have saved eleven million dollars in construction costs alone, never mind what he could have done with the interior. So what if the structural engineers had claimed the building wouldn't hold together long-term; he'd have found another inspection firm who would have said the exact opposite. All that mattered was the money they were making.

But Davenport hadn't agreed. Ransom had been humiliated and now he intended to return the favor. He'd be known worldwide as the man who found the lost tomb of Genghis Khan, and Davenport would be buried in a shallow grave in the middle of east nowhere, right where he belonged.

A glance at the trackers showed their targets should be just over the next rise. Anticipation surged in his veins.

"Get ready!" he shouted to Santiago, and the other man gave him the thumbs-up.

Like an avenging angel—one of darkness, at least—the helicopter crested the ridge and Ransom looked through the windscreen, searching for the trucks on which the bugs had been planted back in Ulaanbaatar.

At first, all he could see was brown scrub grass. Then the herd of wild horses that had been grazing on it burst into motion, surging left and right as they sought to escape the thunder of the mechanical bird above them.

"Where are the trucks?" Santiago shouted.

Ransom didn't know. Confused, he looked down at the tracker, noting that it showed all three of them almost directly below the helicopter.

"They should be down there," he replied, pointing at the screen with his finger.

But all they saw was horses.

Ransom peered carefully down into the herd below him, looking for a sign, something to confirm what he suddenly suspected, something that would prove—

There!

A horse split off from the herd, the saddle on its back now clearly visible, the blip on the screen representing the tracking bug sliding away to the left just like the animal below them.

Enraged, Ransom clambered in the back, grabbed the rifle from a bewildered Santiago and began firing at the galloping beast. It took him a couple of tries, but eventually one of his shots went true and the horse toppled forward to lie still in the grass.

The pilot was ordered to land and Ransom got out, Santiago at his heels.

The horse was still alive, though just barely, when they reached it. Ransom didn't care; all he wanted was to prove his suspicions were correct. Ignoring the animal's labored breathing, he dug around in its saddlebags until he found a folded piece of paper in which his tracking transponder had been placed.

Drawn on the inside of the scrap of paper was a smiley face.

Ransom screamed in fury at the sight.

Without another word he turned and stalked back to where the helicopter was waiting.

That was it, he thought. That was the last time Davenport or his minions were going to get the better of him. By the time this was over, their bodies would lie rotting beneath the Mongolian sun.

He intended to make certain of it, if it was the last thing he did.

27

As the sun crept over the horizon it found Kent already up and about, preparing a quick breakfast of powdered eggs with Cukhbaatar's help. They had driven well into the night, not stopping until they had backtracked most of the way out of the Restricted Zone. The entire place gave Kent the creeps and he wanted to be rid of it as quickly as possible. He figured the tank base they had passed the day before was only another mile or two up the road, which meant they would be back on the steppes by midmorning at the latest.

When he'd finally decided to call it quits for the night, he'd simply pulled over, turned off the lights and gone to sleep in the driver's seat, the other three men already snoring away in the back.

He handed two plates to Cukhbaatar, one for him and one for Harris, and then shoveled his own share of the lukewarm eggs into his mouth before taking a plate over to D'Angelo. The wounded man could barely eat, the infection in his leg filling him with fever and threatening to overwhelm his immune system if he didn't reach a hospital soon.

"Hang in there, man," Kent said, partially to himself, as he dosed D'Angelo up with another round of antibiotics and painkillers. He was starting to see the wisdom in Mason's decision to send them back.

A few moments later they got under way once more.

The first hour passed without incident and Kent was almost ready to cheer when they drove past the abandoned tank base right about the time he'd expected them to do so. The edge of the Restricted Zone wasn't too far ahead.

Unfortunately, things weren't going to be that easy.

It was Harris who saw it first. A quick glance, it was nothing more than a dark speck framed against the clouds in the distance. But something about the way it moved bothered him and so he kept his eyes on it.

A few moments later he was glad he had, for as he watched, it changed course slightly. Calculating quickly in his head, he could see that it had just moved from a parallel course to one that would intersect with their own in short order. His unease grew like a monstrous tendril deep in his gut.

That's no eagle, a voice in the back of his head told him.

He snatched the pair of binoculars out of the case he wore on his belt and brought them up to his face.

Under the high-power magnification of the military-quality glasses, the dark speck suddenly resolved itself into the bulbous front end of a Soviet-made helicopter. A Gatling gun was mounted just beneath the cockpit and what looked like rocket pods or fuel tanks hung from the body of the aircraft.

"Contact!" he shouted, so loudly that Kent flinched and nearly drove them into a ditch.

"What the hell, Harris?" Kent swore, but the other man quickly cut him off.

"We've got a military helicopter, exact model unknown, coming directly for us at two o'clock!"

Even as he said it he was pulling out his rifle and rolling down his window. While they had no evidence that the helicopter meant them any harm, none of them could forget the description the boy at the monastery had given of the men with guns who had arrived in the helicopter and killed everyone in sight. This far out in the middle of nowhere, chances were better than good that the men in the helicopter worked for Ransom and that meant they were *not* going to be friendly.

Harris knew it was crazy, thinking that he could cause any kind of significant damage to an armored chopper with just an assault rifle, but then again, stranger things had happened before. The Afghan mujahideen had fought the Soviet army to a standstill with weapons older than the one he now carried, hadn't they? So at least it was possible, right?

He did his best not to think about how many Afghans the Soviets had killed in the process.

"I see it," Kent said.

Harris's only answer was to rack the slide on his rifle. With Kent behind the wheel and D'Angelo unconscious from his injuries, it was going to be up to him to defend them if it came down to it.

Up front, Kent ordered Cukhbaatar to get down on the floor of the car beneath the dash, hoping the heaviness of the engine block would give the youth some protection. Then he began scanning the landscape, looking for somewhere that might provide them some measure of protection.

There wasn't much.

Most of the land in front of them was the same flat,

rock-strewn landscape that they'd been driving through for the past several hours. Off in the distance he could see a few small rises, but it was going to take several long minutes to reach them.

Kent drove grimly on.

To their surprise, the chopper roared overhead, giving no indication that it cared about them at all.

ABOARD THE CHOPPER five hundred feet above, Santiago keyed the mike and informed Ransom that the vehicle below them was, indeed, from Davenport's group.

"Good. Try to take them alive," Ransom replied. "They might know where Davenport is headed."

Santiago gave directions to the pilot and the chopper swung about, angling downward and headed for a position to the side of the moving vehicle.

HARRIS WAS WATCHING the helicopter through the rear window and as it swung back in their direction, he said, "They're turning about!"

In the front of the truck, Kent swore loudly.

There was no doubt about it now. Whoever was in that chopper wanted something from them and it didn't take a genius for them to guess what it might be.

Kent's hands tightened on the wheel and his foot pushed down harder on the accelerator as he gave in to the instinct to run. But his mind kept returning to the same essential question.

Where, exactly, were they going to go?

THE CHOPPER TOOK UP POSITION to one side of the fleeing vehicle. Santiago reached for the minigun controls, a grin a mile wide splashed across his face.

"Let's see what they think about this," he said happily and triggered the weapon.

The minigun on the front end of the Mil-8 threw a line of 12 mm slugs across the truck's path.

"LOOK OUT!"

The machine-gun fire cut across the road in front of them, forcing Kent to spin the wheel to the left to avoid it, bouncing off the narrow track they had been following and striking out overland, heading for the rocky outcroppings he'd spotted earlier.

There was no way they were going to outrun the helicopter. That much was obvious. Nor did he think that the truck could withstand repeat attacks, not with that chain gun mounted on the front of the chopper.

That left them only one option.

They were going to have to fight it out.

SANTIAGO LAUGHED ALOUD as the truck carrying Davenport's men abruptly left the road and headed overland. Go on and run, he thought. You won't get far, that's for sure.

"Well?" Ransom asked.

Santiago shook his head. "They aren't stopping, sir."

"Then make them stop."

"Roger that."

Santiago turned to the gun controls once more.

THE HELICOPTER MOVED AROUND in front of the truck and hovered a short ways off, the chain gun sending another stream of slugs ripping through the air toward them.

Kent spun the wheel to the right this time, avoiding the majority of the gunfire. Still, more than a few slugs impacted against the side of the vehicle and stitched a line along the roof, shattering the window and sending small bits of glass flying through the interior. Sunlight streamed in through the new holes and the smell of cordite filled the car.

"Everyone all right?" Kent shouted over the sound of the wind now whistling through the frame.

"I'm good, I'm good." Harris had a few small cuts on his arms and face from the flying glass, but that was nothing given what could have happened. He checked D'Angelo and breathed easier when he saw that their companion had escaped unscathed. A long stream of Mongolian came from the floor of the front seat, which both Kent and Harris took to mean Cukhbaatar was all right, as well.

"Where are they?" Kent asked, his eyes on the uneven terrain ahead of them, not daring to look away as he fought to keep them from inadvertently driving into a ditch or other obstacle.

"Left side," Harris replied.

Kent saw Harris's form suddenly fill his rearview mirror as the big man crossed to the other side of the vehicle, leaning over their wounded comrade.

"What are you doing?" he asked.

"Teaching them a lesson in predator-prey dynamics."

As the helicopter came back into view, Harris stuck the muzzle of his automatic rifle out the remains of the window and held the trigger down.

The stuttering roar of his weapon filled the car, drowning out his battle cry.

BULLETS BOUNCED OFF the armored cockpit of the helicopter, causing the pilot to swerve up and out of the line of fire before they could do any damage. The Mil-8 had been built to withstand much more firepower than what was currently being thrown at it, but when they had the sky to themselves, why take chances?

Santiago told the pilot to get behind the moving vehicle and keep moving from side to side as he sent stream after stream of 12 mm slugs in their direction.

He was enjoying this.

AND SO IT WENT.

The chopper would make an attack run, Kent would do his best to avoid it and a little more of their vehicle would be obliterated as a result. By the fourth or fifth pass—Kent wasn't certain which it was as he'd already lost count— things were going from bad to worse inside the truck. Both he and Harris had minor gunshot wounds; he from a ricochet that carved a furrow past his left ear and Harris from a round that had gone straight through his foot. D'Angelo, on the other hand, was dead. A line of slugs had stitched their way along that side of the vehicle and his body had jittered with the impacts while his blood had splashed over the other two men and the boy indiscriminately.

Kent estimated that they'd lost about fifteen percent of their engine power and a loud clanking noise was coming from under the hood somewhere. The rear tire on the passenger side had been shot out, as well, and they were now rolling along on what was left of the tread and rim.

The terrain wasn't helping them, either. All of the wild maneuvering Kent was doing was kicking up great clouds of dirt and dust, obscuring their view of both the road ahead of them and of the helicopter behind.

Then Harris leaned forward and said possibly the only thing that could make matters worse.

"That's it. We're out of ammunition."

Short of throwing their guns at their attackers, they now had no way of firing back.

DESPITE SANTIAGO'S OBVIOUS enjoyment playing with the fleeing vehicle, eventually Ransom had enough. It was clear at this point that there was no way they were going to stop, and even if they did, they obviously weren't going to give up without a fight.

It was time to be done with this and continue their hunt for Davenport and the rest of his men. Every minute they spent here meant the others were getting farther away.

Ransom passed the order to Santiago to end it.

AS KENT THREW THE VEHICLE into another series of wild maneuvers, all thoughts of driving into a ditch forgotten as he sought to avoid getting hammered by the helicopter's chain gun, he lost sight of the chopper.

"Where did he go?" Kent shouted.

"I don't know!" Harris was frantically moving from window to window, trying to see through the haze of dust and smoke, searching vainly for their attacker but unable to find him, either.

"Well, find him, for heaven's sake! Before he finds us."

But it was already too late.

The helicopter popped up from behind a small rise to their left, hovering just a few feet off the ground, the rotors clearing the dust like a giant broom, giving them a clear view of their quarry. The gunner would have to be blind in order to miss, and unfortunately for the men in the truck, he was not.

The Gatling gun sang out and hundreds of slugs tore into the vehicle, shredding metal, plastic and human flesh on contact.

The truck continued forward for another few seconds before a stray slug punctured the fuel tanks and an explosion ripped through its frame, sending what was left of the vehicle bouncing end over end across the rocky landscape.

There was no way anyone could have survived the strike, but Ransom wanted to be certain so the gunner sent another round of slugs pulsing into the burning wreck.

When no one emerged after several long moments, Ransom gave the signal for them to move out, a smile of satisfaction on his face.

Behind them, the wreck burned brightly in the early morning sunlight.

28

Unaware of what was happening to their comrades, Davenport and the rest of the team awoke the next morning to find a thin coating of snow covering everything in sight. It was less than half an inch deep, barely worth worrying about and certain to melt before the morning was over, but for Annja it was a reminder that their time here was limited. Winter was coming, and once it arrived, it would mean the end of their search for six long months or more.

They were going to get one shot at this and that was it.

Better make it count.

They broke camp quickly and got under way, the knowledge that they were close to their destination spurring them on. In the light of day they were able to see that the density of the forest on the far side of the valley was not going to allow them to continue with the trucks, so supplies were transferred to backpacks that had been brought along for just such an eventuality and the group continued on foot. If all went according to plan, they would return to the trucks after finding the "voice in the earth" and figure out their next move from there.

They hiked upward into the trees for a couple of hours, taking a brief rest along the way to gulp down a cold lunch and rejuvenate their systems.

It was shortly after that that they emerged into a clearing about a third of the way up the mountain and were given the first chance they'd had to see what lay ahead of them since taking to the trees earlier that morning.

"There," Nambai said, pointing at a near-vertical wall of dark stone that loomed above the trees surrounding it a short distance away.

"The birthplace of the river is at the foot of that mountain."

He went on to explain how he had come here several years before, hunting eagle chicks to sell in the market in the city, and had seen where the river bubbled up from the base of the mountain, as well as where it diverged into three separate waterways shortly thereafter.

"How much farther is it?" Davenport asked, breathing a bit heavier than usual due to the exertion.

"Not far," the Mongolian said with a smile.

Apparently "not far" in Mongolian translated to "far enough that you'll want to strangle your guide for lying to you" in English. They climbed upward through the dense tree cover, using saplings to pull themselves forward when the trail, or lack thereof, became too steep.

Just when Annja's legs started screaming for release, the group emerged from the trees to see the river rushing past them perpendicular to their line of travel. Upriver to their left, the sheer face of the cliff wall rose from the forest floor like some looming giant, ready to squash them at the slightest provocation.

Nambai led them in that direction without comment.

Once they were close enough, they could all see that a raging torrent spilled out from under the base of that mammoth wall, bubbling up from somewhere deep beneath their feet. A few hundred yards downstream it split into three distinct rivers—the Onon, the Tuul and the Kerulen. They all had their common origins in that single waterway surging past their feet.

Davenport gathered the group around him and gave them their instructions. "All right, this is it. This is the place we've been looking for. I want you all to spread out and start looking around. We're searching for something referred to as the 'voice in the earth,' but that's all I can tell you about it, so look for anything unusual, any sign of human habitation, that kind of thing, okay?"

The rest of the team nodded their understanding, then split up and began covering the surrounding area. Wanting a little time to herself to think, Annja strode off on her own before anyone else could volunteer to accompany her.

She had to admit that she was surprised by the beauty of the place. After the drab colors of the plains and the scorched damage of the Restricted Zone, the green of the forest and the bright blue color of the river at their feet was a welcome change. As she walked along the riverbank she was able to relax for the first time in days, to just let go and enjoy where she was, even if it was for only a few minutes. The trees around her swayed in a gentle breeze that had kicked up shortly after they had arrived and though it made things a little colder, the air seemed fresher, the smells richer because of it.

She watched fish dart back and forth beneath the surface of the water, listened to the cries of the birds in the trees, but after half an hour without finding anything, she gave up and returned to their starting place at the base of the cliff.

Annja found a relatively flat rock to stretch out on and sat down, letting the afternoon sunlight warm her as she went back over everything in her mind. The answer was there somewhere; she knew it. She just had to ask the right questions in order to get the right answers.

She must have dozed off a little in the peace of the moment, for something intruded on her consciousness and she jerked upright, suddenly aware of how quiet the forest around her had become.

"Mason?" she called softly. "Mr. Davenport?"

There was no answer.

The air held an expectant feeling, ripe with tension, as if the forest around were holding its breath, waiting for something to happen.

And she was all alone.

She reached out into the otherwhere, made sure she could get to her sword if she needed it. It was there as it always was, waiting for her touch to bring it to life, but she didn't draw it just yet. There would be time for that.

She waited.

Listened.

She was just about to call out for her companions a second time when, as if on cue, a deep, groaning cry burst up from the ground nearby.

She jumped in surprise, her skin rising in goose bumps, the sound just the right timbre to cause the hair across her body to stand on end.

The noise came again almost immediately but this time it was gentler, quieter, and somehow she knew it would continue getting softer until she wouldn't be able to hear it at all.

She had to find its source before that happened.

Annja scrambled back to the point where the water

surged up from beneath the cliff face, her gaze flashing frantically about, her ears straining.

Come on, come on, she thought, just one more time.

She caught movement out of the corner of her eye but she dared not turn away, dared not miss the opportunity, for who knew when it would come again.

"Annja!" she heard Davenport call, but still she didn't turn.

One more time. Please.

The voice obliged her.

It came again, much more softly, but this time she was ready for it, standing as she was directly in front of the wall when the sound issued from it a third and final time. She saw that it came from a small hole about the size of her fist, a hole that was at shoulder height and, lucky for her, on her side of the stream.

"Did you hear that?" Davenport asked, as he and Mason rushed over to her side. Williams and Kent weren't too far behind.

Annja barely heard the question. Guided by some inner sense she couldn't define, she watched as if from afar as she put her hand inside the hole and pushed.

A deep grinding sound came from somewhere within the wall in front of them and a section of the stone a few feet away rolled slowly to one side, revealing an opening large enough for several of them to fit through at once.

Annja started toward it, but Mason stopped her with a hand on her arm. "Hang on a second. We do this the smart way."

He pulled a pair of high-intensity flashlights out of his pack, keeping one for himself and handing the other to her.

Together, they stepped as one through the opening.

29

The door opened up into some kind of antechamber, complete with benches around the perimeter and niches in the wall for storing items.

There was a door directly across from the one they'd entered and even in the dim light of their flashlights they could see that it led down a short tunnel and opened into a large space just beyond. A sconce holding a torch hung on either side of the door and they paused a moment to light them, noting from the dust and cobwebs that neither torch had been lit in many years, ages even.

The torchlight flickered off the stone and sent their shadows chasing after them as they continued. Their footfalls sounded louder than normal in the narrow confines and deep silence of the place. Annja felt the thrill of discovery coursing through her. It was what she loved about archaeology—the suspense, the anticipation, the wonder, of what they might find and what they might learn.

Satisfied that there wasn't anything immediately threatening inside the chamber, Mason called out to Davenport and had him join them. After all, this was his expedition. Jeffries and Nambai came in, as well, leaving Williams and Vale to guard the entrance and to watch for any sign that Ransom might be on to them again.

Once the others were inside, Annja and Mason continued on. They quickly found that the short hallway opened into another room, though this one was much larger than the first; they could see darkness pooling out beyond the edge of their torchlight, indicating there was more to uncover. But they barely paid any attention to that fact as soon they got a glimpse of what had been drawn across the floor in the center of the room.

It was a map.

It had been painted on the floor and was partially obscured by years of dust and dirt, but it was clearly recognizable as such. With specific instructions from Annja, everyone got down on their hands and knees and gently brushed the loose debris off the painting, exposing it all for perhaps the first time in centuries. Once they were finished, they stood back to examine what they had uncovered.

Not the handiest thing to use in finding your way around, was Annja's first thought. Maps needed to be portable in order to be useful and this was anything but. Still, you didn't create a map of this size and then hide it away from the rest of the world if there wasn't a point to it. There was a reason it was here and she just had to discover what that was.

Like many ancient maps, this one was more a general representation of the surrounding area than a scale drawing. In some ways, that made it easier to read. The blue line that split in three and stretched down toward the bottom of the map obviously represented the three rivers. The round circle with the three squiggles running out of it near the source of the river must represent the voice in the earth. And the tall peak rising above the others could only be Burkhan Khaldun—God Mountain.

The entire map had been produced at a huge scale, so that you literally had to walk from one side of the chamber to the other in order to see it all.

Annja was still doing just that, working her way slowly from the lower section of the map, which represented the area they had traveled through the day before, toward the summit of God Mountain, the most likely place for Genghis Khan's tomb to be located. She was determined not to miss anything significant.

There was a shout of excitement from the far side of the room.

"Annja!" Davenport yelled. "Come quickly!"

He was standing roughly two thirds of the way up the slope of the large black triangle that represented Burkhan Khaldun and waving to her frantically.

So much for meticulousness, she thought and headed over to see what the commotion was about.

A symbol had been drawn on the map—a crude sketch of a woman riding a horse—and next to it were words in a fine flowing script that looked to be Mongolian. Annja couldn't decipher it, but it turned out Nambai could.

"The sixty…I think that translates as brides…rode sixty horses and now sleep under the, um, not sure what that word is…eyes of those who came before," he said.

Before he could move on to the second set of verses, both Annja and Mason spoke up, translating it from memory. "'In their arms is the truth you seek, the way to all that was and more.'"

It was an exact match to the hidden message Annja had uncovered in Curran's journal!

Nambai looked at the script, then nodded. "That's right. How did you know?"

"It's a long story," Mason replied and went on to explain about the message hidden in Curran's journal.

While he did that, Annja squatted down, letting her fingers trace the outline of the symbol on the map, wonder running through her veins as she realized that they were one step closer to their goal. The symbol put the Tomb of the Virgins on the south slope of Burkhan Khaldun, which couldn't be more than a day's hike north of their current position. They were so close!

Her musings were interrupted by Mason. "You'd have to ask Annja," he said.

She looked up at him. "Ask me what?"

"Nambai wants to know what the whole 'brides and steeds' thing means."

"Right."

The playful gleam in Mason's eyes told her that he wanted to know, as well, but he wasn't going to admit that when he had someone else to play the innocent. She threw him a blatantly fake smile, to let him know that he wasn't fooling anyone, least of all her.

"Well, the theory I'm running with at the moment ties the riddle back to the things we know about the Khan's burial." She stood, brushed off her hands on the legs of her jeans. "When Genghis died, he was in China with his army. Not wanting to bury his body among his enemies, his generals had it transported back to his homeland with an honor guard of sixty warriors. The guard traveled ahead of the funeral train, so in essence they could be said to have 'come before' Genghis. Once the procession reached the place in the Great Taboo where they intended to bury him, the entire honor guard was slaughtered down to the last man."

"That's what they get for volunteering," Mason remarked, but Annja ignored him. She noted that she had Davenport's and Jeffries's attention now, as well.

"Along with the honor guard, sixty virgins and sixty of the finest horses were sacrificed to provide the Khan with a harem and a herd for all eternity. Legend states that they were all buried together in a magnificent tomb, commonly referred to as the Tomb of the Virgins, but its exact location has always been a mystery because those who did the burying were themselves slaughtered to keep the secret safe."

"If I'm right, the phrase 'the way to all that was and more' means that we'll find the next clue inside that tomb."

She pointed to the symbol of the woman on horseback that graced the map at Davenport's feet. "And that tells us where to find it. Come on, I'll show you."

She led them all back outside and pointed up at the looming peak of Burkhan Khaldun. The mountain was far higher than the rest of those around it, making it easy to locate, and even from here they could see the deep snow that covered most of its face.

"That's where we'll find the Tomb of the Virgins, and, ultimately, where we'll find Genghis Khan's final resting place."

30

The horseman hidden in the trees higher on the ridgeline above the river watched the intruders enter the Chamber of the Winds and felt anger grow in his heart. The chamber was sacred; how dare they defile it with their presence!

He'd been following the group ever since they'd entered the Ikh Khorig, just as he'd been ordered to do, but this was the first time since they'd come into the forbidden territory that they'd done something so unexpected that he wasn't certain how to respond. He'd been told to watch, but not interfere; yet surely that didn't include sitting back and allowing them to do this, did it?

He wasn't certain and it was that uncertainty that stayed his hand. That and the guns the intruders carried openly.

He chose to wait and watch, to see if he could determine what they wanted, so that when he reported back he wouldn't look like a fool.

The watcher was still there when the intruders emerged

from the chamber almost an hour later and pointed north, toward the looming peak of Burkhan Khaldun.

That decided it for him.

It was time to tell the Voice of the Wolf.

31

Darkness came early, thanks to the looming cliff face at their backs and the high trees surrounding them, so while there were a few hours of daylight left, it was all but useless as night began to settle in around them. Rather than try and blunder about in the dark, the decision was made to stay right where they were and use the antechamber for that night's camp. This had the added benefit of keeping them under cover should Ransom use that chopper of his to do a night flyover in search of their position, something Mason saw as fairly likely.

The extra meat they'd cooked the previous night was passed around and eaten cold, but no one complained. They were happy to be out of the tents for a change, and the closeness of the rock around them locked in their body heat, creating a comfortable, if cramped, little haven for the evening.

A watch was set up, with Mason, Williams, Jeffries, and Vale taking three-hour shifts, in that order. Each man was to position himself a short distance downriver in the hope that the extra time they would gain with an advance warning might be enough for the others to escape into the nearby woods if it became necessary.

After dinner, Annja wandered over to where Mason was setting up his bedroll, getting everything ready before he went on watch.

"Do you think Ransom is still looking for us?" she asked.

Mason nodded. "Without a doubt. He's like a dog with a bone. The guy never gives up. He either gets what he wants or he destroys it so no one else can have it."

The stench of burning flesh rose in her memory and she shook it off with an effort. Ransom had certainly shown he was willing to destroy things to keep Davenport from finding the tomb before he did. It made her uneasy to think Ransom was out there somewhere, plotting how to get back into the game.

"Do you think we've lost him?"

Mason must have heard something in her voice, for he stopped what he was doing and looked over at her, studying her face as if trying to memorize it. "Do you know something I don't?" he asked.

She shook her head. She didn't know anything; she just had an uneasy feeling that something wasn't right. They'd missed something and she wasn't sure what. The feeling nagged at her, but she couldn't put her finger on it.

"We've lost him for the time being, but I don't expect for it to stay that way for long. He'll find us again eventually. Best I can do at this point is keep us moving at a steady pace and hope we get there before he does."

He looked around at the rest of his charges as they prepared to bed down for the night, and then looked back at Annja. "I think we're okay for tonight. Why don't you get some rest and we can talk about it later?"

"All right." She began to lay out her own bedroll, all the while wondering what it was they were missing.

THE INFORMANT WAITED an hour into his turn at watch before deciding the time was right. He moved off into the shadow of a large outcropping of rock and took the satellite phone from the concealed pocket inside his jacket. He dialed Ransom's number and waited for the other man to answer.

He didn't wait long.

"Where the hell have you been?" Ransom nearly shouted after answering the call.

The informant wasn't intimidated in the slightest. "I'm right where I'm supposed to be. Stuck like glue on your target, the one you seem to be having trouble dealing with." He'd worked with Ransom too long to be worried about the man's threats. He knew he was the megalomaniac's only hope of tracking down the tomb before Davenport did, and that was a far more important task than teaching him a lesson. Still, he'd have to watch his back later and he made a mental note to be sure to do so. Once his usefulness ended, he'd become excess baggage, and Ransom would try and get rid of him as expeditiously as possible.

There was a pause and then the other man said, "What do you have for me?"

The informant took out a pocket GPS device and honed in on their exact position. He relayed the coordinates to Ransom and then filled him in on what they had uncovered in the map chamber earlier that afternoon.

Ransom listened patiently, asked a few questions that the informant answered the best he could, and then dropped the bomb the man on-site wasn't expecting. "It's time to use the package."

Tactically, it wasn't the best move, the informant thought, but he wasn't the one calling the shots. If he had been, then things would have gone very differently. If the boss wanted him to use the package, he'd use the package. It would be up to the boss to figure out what to do from there.

"Use the package? If that's what you want," he said.

"You still have it with you, correct?"

The informant didn't grace that comment with an answer. Of course he still had it with him; he hadn't let it out of his sight since the night he'd received it.

Ransom continued. "Use it tonight. Get it in the water, then call us in the morning and we'll bring the chopper in."

"Very well. In the water it is, then."

With that the informant hung up, slipped the phone back in his jacket and returned to his position on the rock overlooking the lower section of the river.

Sitting there, he idly fingered the smooth packet of powder that he carried in the same pocket as his phone. Just a pinch in each water jug would be enough. With everyone carrying their own water supply, now that they had left the trucks behind, actually pulling it off was going to take some planning.

No matter, he'd get it done. After all, that's what they paid him for, wasn't it?

ANNJA'S HEARING HAD ALWAYS been good and in the silent surroundings it was even better. Hidden as she was among the thick vegetation that surrounded the rocky outcropping they had selected as their watch station, she was able to hear most of the conversation going on above her. Or, at least, this end of the conversation and she could guess at some of the rest of it due to the responses she was hearing. The longer she listened, the more incensed she got. She wanted to eliminate the threat to the group right then and there, had gone so far as to draw her sword and begin to edge her way around the rock, looking for a way up, when the comments about the package and water stopped her.

Something told her to watch and wait, to catch him in the act so that it wouldn't be his word against hers.

Maybe then the others would believe her.

She released her sword and quietly made her way back upriver to their camp.

Along the way, one thought kept playing over and over again in her mind.

Of all people, why did it have to be him?

32

The smell of frying antelope brought her out of her sleep the next morning. Mason, rolling up his bedroll just a few feet away, greeted her with a smile and a cheerful good-morning.

Annja turned away with just a quick nod, not trusting herself to speak, and went to splash some water on her face and get a plate of food. Antelope strips weren't as good as bacon, but they were a lot better than the powdered eggs she'd been eating for the past few days. She wolfed them down, knowing she'd need the protein for the day's events.

After breakfast, Annja found reasons to avoid Mason as she packed up, but always made sure she was close enough to hear what he had to say. When he ordered Jeffries to help him fill everyone's water carriers from the river outside, she knew that was her call to action. She made sure no one was looking in her direction and then slipped out ahead of them.

She made her way downstream a short distance to the clear pool where they had been gathering their water since they'd arrived. A thick pine tree extended over the spot and its lower branches were easily accessible. She grabbed one and pulled herself up into the tree, finding a spot where she could see what was taking place below her but that was also shielded enough to keep her from being seen.

Satisfied with her position, she settled in to wait.

It didn't take long.

He came down the trail alone, the canteens he was supposed to fill slung on a rope over his shoulder. He squatted down at the edge of the water, removed the containers from the rope, and began to fill them one at a time. He stood them up next to one another in a line behind him, and by the time he was done he had more than a dozen containers lined up on the riverbank.

Annja tensed, knowing that this was it. If something was going to happen, it would happen now.

He straightened and then carefully looked around, no doubt making certain that he was alone.

If the circumstances hadn't been so dire, she might have laughed at the sight. No one ever looks up, she thought with a slim smile of satisfaction.

He reached into the inside of his coat and removed a paper packet, like the kind old-fashioned druggists gave their powdered medication in. Opening it, he moved toward the first bottle in line.

That's my cue, Annja thought.

She let go of the branch that she'd been holding on to and dropped lightly to the ground. Drawing her sword, she came up silently behind him and touched the point of her weapon to the back of his neck.

Before she could say anything, the sound of a gun being chambered came from almost directly behind her.

"Don't move, Annja," Mason said.

She didn't.

He moved into her peripheral vision on her left side, far enough away that she couldn't easily swing the sword and reach him, yet close enough to keep her from rushing for cover and escaping.

In front of her, Jeffries tensed, as if considering making a run for it himself, and she applied a little more pressure down the length of the sword, letting him know that it was a bad idea.

A very bad idea indeed.

"Someone want to tell me what's going on here?" Mason asked in a soft but deadly tone.

Annja kept her sword hand steady and her eyes on Jeffries. If he was going to try something, it would be while Mason's attention was on her.

"He's working for Ransom," she said.

"Jeffries?"

"I don't know what she's talking about, boss," the other man replied. "I came down here to fill the water bottles, just like you said."

Annja resisted the urge to skewer him where he stood. She wouldn't convince Mason of anything by doing so and might end up getting shot herself. That would leave the rest of the group in danger.

"Ask him what the packet in his hand is for," Annja said.

Mason moved out from behind her and around to the side where he could see both Annja and Jeffries. He had his pistol in his hand and he kept it pointed in their general direction.

"Show me," he said to Jeffries.

Jeffries slowly lifted his arms out to his sides and opened his hands.

They were empty.

"He's got it on him somewhere. Search him," Annja said. She could hear the anger leaking into her voice.

Jeffries sensed Mason's hesitation and went on the offensive. "For heaven's sakes, boss. Will you get this crazy bi—"

"I'd watch that mouth if I were you!" Annja shouted. She twisted the sword back and forth in her hand to make sure he got it the point.

Mason lowered his gun slightly. "Look, Annja. I don't know what's going on here, but…"

"I've already told you what's going on. He's working for Ransom and he intended to do something to our water supply."

Mason shook his head. "This expedition is getting to all of us. Ease off, okay?"

"Not a chance. Not until you search him."

Jeffries was quiet, biding his time. Annja knew she had only seconds left to convince Mason that she was telling the truth. He'd worked with Jeffries for years. Considered him a friend. It was his word against hers and right now she wasn't coming out on top. She needed something…

The phone!

Jeffries had made calls with a satellite phone and had put it in his jacket. The same jacket he was wearing right now.

"There's a satellite phone in the inside pocket of his jacket, Mason. If you check the last number dialed you'll see that it goes right to Ransom."

Please don't have deleted your list of calls, she thought.

If Jeffries handed over his phone without a problem, she was dead in the water.

But he didn't. Instead, he started protesting harder, calling her a liar, saying the whole thing was absurd and she'd better let him go or else.

Annja could see the wheels turning in Mason's eyes. Thou dost protest too much…

Mason stepped toward Jeffries. "I'm going to reach inside your jacket. Might as well get this over with so that there aren't any issues later."

"If you must," Jeffries said, the disgust that Mason wasn't taking his word evident in his tone.

As Mason stepped closer, Jeffries made his move.

He lunged forward and to one side, taking him out of easy reach of Annja's sword and directly into Mason, who had made the fatal mistake of not keeping his gun on his former comrade. As Annja watched, Jeffries barreled into Mason, trapping the gun between their bodies. Jeffries' elbow came around in a vicious arc that connected with Mason's jaw, sending him to the ground as Jeffries charged past, headed for the river.

Annja rushed after him.

She scooped up Mason's gun as she went by, then, hearing a splash that told her Jeffries had gone into the river, angled to the left in an effort to cut him off, knowing the current would quickly take him out of reach if she didn't do so in time.

Detouring around a large outcropping of rock that blocked her path to the river, Annja reached the water's edge just in time to see Jeffries rushing past her. He was in the middle of the river, stroking hard, hoping to get away.

Annja wasn't prepared to let him do that.

She raised the gun and fired off several shots in rapid succession.

At least one struck Jeffries, possibly two. The impact drove him under and he stayed down for several long minutes.

Annja ran along the riverbank, gun extended, ready to fire again, when he broke the surface, but as it turned out she didn't need to. When Jeffries popped back up, he was facedown in the water and no longer moving. She watched his body roll in the current and disappear out of sight downriver.

Mason was waiting for her when she returned upstream.

"How did you know?" he asked, as she handed his weapon back to him.

"I've been wondering how Ransom knew where we were going all the time. Bugging our trucks is one thing, but someone had to plant those bugs and that required an inside man."

"Ransom could have hired someone from the rental-car company to do it."

Annja shook her head. "I didn't think so, because he would have to be certain it had been installed by someone who knew what they were doing and not some local yokel."

"But how did you know he was going to try and do something to our water supply?"

"I overheard him making a call last night. It sounded suspicious, so I've been watching him ever since."

Mason shook his head. "I can't believe I didn't see through his act. I must be—"

He was interrupted by the ringing of a telephone.

They looked at each other and then sprang into action, both of them searching around frantically for the source, hoping to find it before it stopped ringing. Mason spotted the black casing of the dropped cell phone first and snatched it up. He answered the call, then hit the speakerphone button so Annja could listen in.

"Is it done?" the caller asked.

The voice was unfamiliar to Annja, but she could guess who it was. Judging by what Mason said next, she was right.

"You mean are we dead yet? Not even close!"

"Jeffries?"

"Mason Jones. Your faith in Jeffries is misplaced. We're all still alive and he's dead. So help me God, if I catch you anywhere near us again I'll gut you myself. Do you understand me?"

Mason's voice rose in intensity as he went on, until he was shouting into the phone in anger.

Ransom shouted right back. "You'll never make it out of Mongolia alive. That tomb is mine!"

"You just try it, Ransom. 'Cause when you do, I'll see to it that you wake up in hell!"

He stabbed his thumb down on the disconnect button and then tossed the phone into the river.

"Come on. We've got to tell the others," he said.

They gathered the water bottles and headed back to camp.

IN THE COURTYARD of the abandoned Soviet base where he had ordered his pilot to land a half hour before, Ransom turned to his communications specialist in the back of the helicopter. "Did we get it?"

The other man did not disappoint.

"Yes, sir. I used Keyhole 5 to lock it in within a ten-yard radius." The technician pointed at the laptop screen resting on his knees that was showing a topographical satellite map of the surrounding landscape. "They are right here, sir," the technician said, using his finger to circle the spot on the map. "It's the same location that Jeffries called in from last night. As of now, they haven't moved on. And even if they do, they won't get far."

Ransom stared at the point on the map near the base of Burkhan Khaldun, where his man's finger currently rested. The helicopter would get them that far, but if Davenport and his team went any farther up the mountain they would have to follow them on foot.

That was just as well.

Ransom preferred his killing to be up close and personal.

33

Once the rest of the group was informed of Jeffries's treachery, the decision was made to get under way as swiftly as possible. They had no idea just how much information the insider had relayed to Ransom, so the farther they got from their position the better off they were likely to be. The group packed up quickly. They sealed off the entrance to the map chamber by tripping the hidden lever in the same way Annja had opened it, and headed out.

That morning's travel was the hardest yet. Their route took them higher into the mountains, along narrow trails that Nambai said were made by argali, the wild mountain sheep whose curved horns were prized for their supposed magical properties. Annja secretly hoped they wouldn't run into one, for they were known to be fiercely territorial.

The air grew colder as they climbed higher and Annja found herself wishing for the warmer temperatures of the steppes. While they didn't encounter any argali, they did see their fair share of rodents, squirrels and pikas. Nambai told them how the pikas, which were part of the rabbit family, were also known as whistling hares due to the high-pitched sound they made when threatened, and then proceeded to demonstrate by cornering a few of them against the trunk of a downed tree. He was right; the little things screeched like banshees. The fresh meat they'd have for dinner that night would more than make up for it, though.

The forest grew thicker as they climbed. The trees rose around them like silent guardians, watchful and aware. Mixed through the evergreens were patches of white birch, bringing flashes of white to all that green, and heightening the sense that they weren't alone, that out there among the trunks some ancient guardian was keeping score, and Annja almost expected one to come strolling out of the shadows between the deeper trunks.

Annja waited until she and Mason had dropped back a bit behind the others and then asked, "You okay?"

"Compared to what we used to do in the SAS, this is a Sunday walk in the park," he replied, without looking at her.

The lack of eye contact said it all. He was avoiding the real question.

"Not what I meant at all and you know it," she said quietly.

Mason stopped and turned to face her.

"You're right. I do know what you meant. But what, exactly, do you want me to say?"

She shrugged. "I don't know. I just thought you might need to get some of it off your chest."

Mason looked away. "I knew the guy for almost ten years, Annja. He was part of my squad in the regiment. He saved my life half a dozen times and I returned the favor just as often. I'm having a hard time believing any of it really happened, to tell you the truth."

Annja could feel her anger creeping up. "But it did happen," she said firmly.

"Oh, I know. I'm not doubting that at all. But what I can't figure out is why he would do something like that. What would motivate him to sell us, or rather me, out like that?"

Now it was Annja's turn to look away. The shiny look in Mason's eyes told her just how deep the knife had cut. "People do things we don't understand all the time. It's not our place to figure it out. We have a hard enough time just living with the consequences."

"Ain't that the truth," he muttered, and the dark cloud that had been hanging over them moments before seemed to break up and move on.

Their conversation turned to lighter things as they hustled to catch up with the others.

In the early afternoon they found their first indication that they were not alone. They emerged from a particularly thick copse of trees to find Nambai standing in the middle of a trail cutting its way northward through the forest.

In the middle of the trail were fresh horse tracks.

"What do you think?" Mason asked their guide as he stood frowning down at the tracks.

"Not good," he said, as he lifted his gaze to the trees around them. "Could be the Darkhats." The name fell from his lips like a curse and sent him off into a half-whispered ramble in Mongolian.

Annja had been around the wiry old guy long enough to recognize that he was saying a prayer, no doubt to ward off evil and keep his enemies far, far away.

"What are you talking about?" Mason asked. 'Who, or what, are the Darkhats?"

Nambai remained silent, refusing to say anything more, so Annja answered for him.

"Legends say that after Genghis Khan's body was returned from China and hidden away forever from the sight of man, a small group of warriors were designated to keep watch over the Great Khan's tomb for all time. When one died, the duty fell to his son and that man's son and so on down through the centuries. Anyone brave, or foolish, enough to enter the Great Taboo in search of the tomb would be punished by death. The warriors were known as the Darkhats, though where the name comes from seems to have been lost in antiquity."

Mason scoffed. "And people still believe this stuff?"

Annja watched Nambai, who hadn't taken his eyes off the woods around them, and said simply, "Yes. Some people do."

Mason gave their guide an odd look and then moved off to talk with his employer.

After some discussion between the two of them, the decision was made to follow the trail they had found, horse tracks or not. It was easier than winding their way through the trees and would require less hacking at the undergrowth, which had the added benefit of conserving their strength for when they might actually need it.

The trail was wide enough to manage two horses riding abreast, and to Annja it indicated the presence of much more than just a solitary horseman. But despite keeping a careful watch, she didn't see any evidence that they were being followed. Nor did she find any indications that anyone else was out in the primeval forest with them.

Until they came to the burial ground.

RANSOM AND HIS MEN were airborne by midmorning, with Santiago acting as gunner-copilot and Ransom sitting in the back just behind the pilot. In the loading area behind him, ten of the men Santiago had recruited for the job were strapped into the crew seats on either side of the hull, ready to be deployed at a moment's notice once they hit the ground.

With the GPS coordinates to guide them, it wouldn't take them long to catch up with Davenport and his team.

If Ransom thought the morning's firefight had put him in a good mood, his feelings positively soared when they discovered the remainder of Davenport's convoy parked just outside the forest that covered the approach to the slopes of Burkhan Khaldun.

The pilot landed nearby and Santiago got out with several of his men to search the vehicles. They returned to the helicopter fifteen minutes later, and as the pilot took them back up, Santiago reported what they had found.

"Engines are cold, which means they've probably been here overnight, just as Jeffries said. Looks like they took their gear and headed off into the woods over there," he said, pointing down to a narrow path just beyond the parked vehicles that could easily be seen from the air.

"There was some blood on one of the seats, so at least one of them has been injured recently. That's about it."

Ransom nodded and sat back to think, watching the scenery pass by beneath the aircraft without actually seeing it.

The bloodstains gave a possible explanation for why the team had separated; it was likely that one of them had needed serious medical attention and Mason Jones had been stupid enough to split his forces in two while his enemy was nipping at his heels. It also meant that there would be fewer of Davenport's team to contend with when Ransom and his men caught up, giving them the numerical advantage, which was just fine with him.

It took them another fifteen minutes to cover the ground that Davenport and his team had taken hours to climb the day before. Still, when the pilot put the helicopter down in a small clearing not far from where the GPS coordinates said Jeffries had made his call, Ransom was happy enough to get out and stretch his legs.

Santiago had the men fan out, sending them up the mountain in search of the map room that Jeffries had mentioned in his call the night before.

Ten minutes later two of his men radioed in. They had found Jeffries.

He'd been in the water for at least six hours and his flesh had taken on the bloated look so common in drowning victims. Though, from where Ransom stood on the bank, he could see the bullet wounds in the man's back that had been the true cause of death.

Apparently Davenport's security chief, Mason Jones, must have stumbled on to the truth about Jeffries, and in the confrontation the traitor had paid the ultimate price.

Ransom didn't much care; Mason had saved him some trouble, actually. It was simply one less loose end he'd have to deal with later.

He told his men to drop the body back into the river and turned away in disinterest before the current had carried it out of sight.

He had more important things to be worrying about, like where on earth Davenport had gone?

Ransom snapped at his men, ordering them to pick up the search and find the trail. Driven by his anger and

Santiago's constant bullying, it didn't take them much longer to locate the trail Davenport and his team had used to climb higher into the mountains.

The trail wasn't all that old and Ransom felt the thrill of the hunt course through his system. He knew his prey was close and if he played his cards right he might even catch up to them before nightfall. Then he would see just what Davenport was made of.

With hunger in his eyes, Ransom ordered the ground team to start following Davenport's team on foot, while he and Santiago returned to the air to provide aerial recon and additional firepower if it came to that.

As he took to the sky once more, Ransom stared down at his men as they disappeared into the forest ahead of them.

Time's almost up, Davenport, he thought with satisfaction.

Time's almost up.

ONE MINUTE DAVENPORT'S PARTY was deep in the forest and then next the trees suddenly fell back on all sides as the trail led them right into the midst of a sunlit clearing. Three other trails could be seen emerging from the forest and ending at other locations around the clearing. But the group paid the trails little mind at this point, for the small hill that rose before them, carpeted with a thick sheen of green grass, had them all entranced.

Atop the hill stood twelve spirit banners, the horsehair attached to their shafts stirring in the slight breeze.

A hush fell over the group.

It was a scene out of a time long since passed and Annja found herself wondering just how long the *sulde* had stood there in stark relief against the eternal blue sky above, soaking up the spirit of the place.

She was entranced by the sight, so much that she didn't hear Nambai's shout until the second or third time.

He was pointing up over the hill, through the break in the trees caused by the clearing, to where the cliff face of the rising mountain behind it could be seen.

A cave entrance was visible a few hundred feet up the sheer cliff and what looked like two *sulde* stood guard on either side of the entrance.

Annja felt her heart go into overdrive.

The tomb of Genghis Khan. That had to be it!

Everyone was talking and shouting at once, excitement spilling through the group like wildfire, and it took Mason a few minutes to get them all calmed down.

The horse tracks in the dirt were forgotten.

They skirted the ceremonial hill, only to find the entrance of a fourth and fifth trail very close to each other directly on the other side. Mason sent Vale and Williams along the right-hand path, telling them to go down a short way and then report back, while he and Nambai did the same on the left. When everyone returned, Vale described a canyon over which stretched a rope bridge that appeared to be in disuse; many of the wooden slats were missing from the flooring and the ropes themselves seemed brittle and worn.

On the other hand, the trail Mason and Nambai had followed led to the base of the cliff they had seen from the clearing. The decision was an easy one.

A few minutes later, they all stood staring up at the cave mouth roughly one hundred feet above them. The cliff face leading up to it was almost vertical, with no obvious means of ascent short of climbing it like a spider on a wall.

"This is going to be fun," Mason muttered under his breath.

Annja laughed. "Come on, now. Don't tell me you are afraid of heights?" she said.

Mason did his best to ignore her, which Annja found even funnier.

Williams, the most experienced climber in the group, was pulling wrapped coils of rope out of his pack when Annja moved to join him and offer assistance. They discussed the route they intended to take and the gear they were going to use to protect the route on the way up. Once they were both satisfied, they got under way, with Annja leading and setting the protection and Williams belaying her.

The climb itself went very quickly.

There was no ledge to speak of in front of the cave entrance so Annja was forced to enter the cave mouth in order to find a place to set the anchors for the rope. The sunlight coming in from outside illuminated the first ten or so feet of the tunnel, allowing her to see what she was doing and secure the rope properly so that the others could make the climb up to the cavern. She could also see that the tunnel continued deep into the mountainside. As she turned back toward the entrance she discovered a group of torches piled on the floor to the left side of the entrance.

Annja leaned out of the cave mouth and waved to the others below, indicating it was okay for them to use the rope to climb up. While she waited for them, she lit one of the torches and moved a short distance down the tunnel, her excitement almost palpable in the narrow confines of the passage.

As it turned out, there was only so far she could go.

About forty feet in, she discovered two massive wooden doors blocking the passage, each one reinforced with several bands of iron that ran horizontally across them. Annja guessed that they probably weighed several hundred pounds each. By the light of her torch she could see that the stone on either side of the doors had been carved with excruciating detail, reminding Annja of any number of the Buddhist temples they had passed during their trip across the country—especially the one at Shankh. The carvings were obviously old but, protected from the harsh Mongolian winds in the depths of the tunnel, they stood out in stark relief.

The doors looked as if they had stood undisturbed for centuries.

Provided you ignored the footprints that led up to the doors. Clearly, someone had been here before them, Annja realized.

Recently, too, by the look of it.

OUTSIDE AT THE BASE of the cliff, Mason stood on belay, waiting for Davenport to be hauled up by the others who were already in the cave mouth above. Davenport had never climbed before, and given that he was one of the world's wealthiest men, no one dared take a chance at letting him do so now. Mason had helped him get into a harness and then had secured the ropes to the hooks on the harness using carabiners. When everything was ready, Mason gave the signal and Williams and Vale began to pull the rope up hand over hand.

Once Davenport was safely at the top, the rope was dropped back down and Mason tied himself off just as he'd been shown. After that it was simply a matter of watching where he put his hands and feet as he climbed up the wall. Despite Annja's jeering earlier, he'd done his fair share of climbing and rappelling in the service, so he wasn't bad at it. He just didn't like it, that was all.

Partway up the wall a faint sound at the edge of his hearing caught his attention. Mason made sure his feet and hands were firmly planted and secured, then turned slightly to look back over his shoulder at the mountain splayed out below them.

The view was phenomenal, giving him a good look down the forested mountainside they had just spent several hours climbing earlier that afternoon. The trees were a vibrant green from this height and he could even see the blue waters of the Onon, the Tuul and the Kerulen rivers as they spread out from the spot where they had camped the night before.

He waited but the sound didn't come again.

He returned to his climb, finishing the last few dozen yards and then helping Vale coil the rope behind them. There was no sense giving anyone else any clues as to where they had gone, but they left the rope anchored and set so that they could deploy it quickly when it was time to go back down.

Vale lit a torch of his own and disappeared down the tunnel after the others, but Mason stopped for a moment and looked out at the valley below for another moment, his ears straining.

Nothing.

He shrugged, deciding that what he'd heard earlier had only been his imagination, and set off down the tunnel.

But as he did so, the sound he'd heard earlier followed him in his mind.

It was the sound of a distant helicopter.

WHEN THE REST OF THE GROUP caught up with Annja there was more than one gasp of surprise at the sight of the doors ahead of her.

"What now?" Mason asked, eyeing the closed doors as if all the demons from hell lurked behind them.

Maybe he dislikes being underground as much as he dislikes heights, Annja thought.

"I say we go in and have a look around," she replied, not giving voice to her musings. Teasing him about his fear of heights was enough for one day, she decided.

"And how do you expect to do that?" Mason asked. "Last time I looked our gear list didn't include any C-4 explosives."

Annja didn't reply, just reached out with one hand and gave a gentle push.

The door on the right swung open without a sound.

"How the hell?" Mason said, then shook his head at his own lack of insight.

One set of footsteps led up to the doors. One set of footsteps led away. Obviously, it hadn't taken more than a single individual to open the doors previously, so it stood to reason that they could do it, too.

Torch in hand, Annja stepped inside.

34

The tunnel continued on the other side for a short distance and then opened up into a wide chamber hewn from the living rock.

Stunned at what she was seeing, Annja slowly moved into the space.

Every square inch of the walls had been covered with painted images of Mongol life in bright, vibrant colors. Most, if not all of them, focused on a dark-haired boy and showed him in various scenes of everyday life. He could be seen milking goats in the early morning sunlight. He was helping herd the flocks on the wide steppes. He was fishing in the dark waters of a broad lake, and he was learning to ride one of the short, stout horses the Mongols used for warfare.

She moved around the room, taking it all in, as the others followed behind her. From the similarities in the paintings it seemed they had all been done by the same hand. She didn't want to think of the time and energy involved in creating such a huge and moving masterpiece.

Davenport's awed voice drifted across the room. "The figure in these paintings? Is it who I think it is?"

Annja nodded. "If I had to guess, I'd say yes. We're most likely looking at scenes from the early life of Temujin, the child who would grow up to become Genghis Khan."

The paintings alone were an incredible find. There were no written records of the Khan's life that could be traced to being contemporaneous to his lifetime. The only surviving account in existence, a text known as *The Secret History of the Mongols,* was written by an anonymous author on behalf of the royal family sometime after his death. It was likely full of as much myth as it was fact. But these—if they proved to be authentic—would be of incalculable value in understanding the early life of one of history's most enigmatic figures. The archaeologist in Annja was nearly breathless with discovery.

"Hey! There's a door here," Vale said from across the room and suddenly everyone was rushing to his side, including Annja.

He was right. A particularly bright painting of the young Mongol warrior learning to fire his bow concealed a door set into the rear of the chamber. It was much smaller and far less grandiose than the doors they'd just passed through, but it appeared to be the only way out of the chamber.

It opened easily at their touch, revealing another passageway like the one through which they had first entered. Leaving the painted chamber behind, they headed off down the tunnel.

The tunnel was wide enough to allow them to walk two abreast and Annja had Mason join her up front, he on the right and she on the left. She was surprised by the quality of the air as they moved deeper into the tunnel. She'd been expecting it to be dusty and stagnant, and yet it was almost the exact opposite, crisp and cool. There must be another opening at the other end, she thought, allowing the air to move about.

She was about to mention her thought to Mason when the ground beneath her feet suddenly gave way and she dropped like a stone.

Annja let go of her torch and instinctively lunged forward as she fell. Her fingers hit and then caught the edge of the floor on the far side of the trap. Her body slammed chest first into the wall and for a moment she thought the motion would jar her fingers loose from their precarious perch, but she managed to hang on.

When the sound of crumbling rock and earth quieted, she could hear Davenport and the others calling through the cloud of dust that had been kicked up by the collapse of the floor.

"Here!" she called, coughing a bit until the air settled again.

"Whatever you do, don't let go. And don't look down." Mason's voice was very close.

And full of fear.

She turned her head slightly and saw a gaping hole where the floor used to be. Mason was nearby, balanced on a small ledge against the left-hand side of the corridor. He stood on his toes, the ledge beneath his feet no more than an inch or so in width, with his body flattened against the wall for balance and his arms outstretched on either side.

Of course, telling her not to look down resulted in her doing just that, her curiosity getting the better of her. A gaping chasm dropped away into the darkness beneath her feet. The bottom was too far away to be seen, if there was one at all.

"Stupid, stupid, stupid!" she muttered to herself. She'd been so caught up in what they were uncovering that she'd let down her guard. She should have realized that the tomb would be rigged; she was only surprised that they'd made it as far as they had without any problems.

She shifted her position slightly, getting her feet in contact with the wall in front of her and using her toes as leverage wherever she could find purchase against the rock. She pushed and hauled herself free one inch at a time.

Once she had pulled herself out, she caught her breath and waved to the others across the gap. "I'm fine," she called out, before turning her attention to Mason.

He was standing on that tiny ledge, less than three feet from the other side. If he jumped, he was almost certain to make it. With Annja there to catch him, he should have no trouble at all.

As she watched, the muscles in his left leg began to shake. He couldn't hold his position for much longer.

She explained her plan to him.

"You've got to get off that ledge while you still have the strength to do so. Just push off the wall in this direction. It's not far. Less than three feet or so. I should be able to grab you easily."

"No."

His voice was flat, a sure sign that fear had taken control.

"Come on, Mason. All you have to do is fall sideways."

"I said no."

Perhaps it was her use of the word *fall*. She wasn't sure. But Mason's sudden attempt to push his body through the wall he was leaning against let her know she wasn't helping the situation much.

She tried a different tack.

"What are you going to do? Stay there all afternoon?"

"Yep."

But the ledge where he was standing had different ideas. The small lip of stone where his left foot rested suddenly gave way, dropping into the gulf below him.

"Mason!"

Annja's shout echoed off the stone around them but Mason wasn't listening. He was too busy working to find purchase for his foot to avoid falling into the gaping chasm himself.

After a second of scrambling that felt like a lifetime, he managed to get his foot back on solid ground.

"That whole ledge is going to go soon," Annja pleaded. "You've *got* to jump."

Annja thought he was going to argue with her again, but the sudden shift of stone beneath his feet for a second time prompted him into action.

Pushing off the wall with both hands, he threw himself toward Annja.

She caught him with open arms and the two of them slammed to the ground.

"Thank you," he told her, his face only inches from hers. His body covered most of her own as a result of their fall and she could feel herself wanting to maintain their closeness.

"Don't mention it," she said with a smile.

The sound of clapping reached them from the other side of the tunnel and they climbed to their feet amid hooting and cheering from Williams and Vale. They stood on the other side of the now-obvious tiger trap, next to a quite visibly annoyed Davenport.

"How the hell are we supposed to get over there now?" the millionaire asked, gesturing at the twenty-foot-wide gap that separated the two groups.

Several ideas were floated out but most of them seemed impractical or excessively time-consuming. Knowing that Ransom was actively hunting for them made every wasted moment seem precious and they didn't want to do anything that might significantly slow their progress. In the end, it was decided that Vale, Williams, Davenport and Nambai would work to construct a bridge across the gap while Mason and Annja continued on without them.

No one was thrilled with the idea, least of all Davenport, who was crushed with the thought that the pit might keep him from being in the advance party that would be the first to lay eyes on Genghis Khan's resting place. Still, like any good leader, he recognized what needed to be done and ordered the others to make it happen.

New torches to replace the ones they had lost when the trap was triggered were tossed across the gap and, with their companions' shouted warnings to be careful echoing off the stone around them, Annja and Mason continued on.

They passed through the door at the other end of the corridor and into another room similar to the first, except in this chamber the paintings depicted scenes of conquest from Genghis Khan's long military career. There were paintings of the seasons of intertribal warfare, as Temujin united the steppes peoples into a cooperative nation. There were paintings of his alliance with the Uighurs and of the marriage of the Khan's daughter to the Uighur khan. The taking of Beijing and the defeat of the Jin Dynasty occupied one entire wall, showing its importance by the artist. One particularly brutal painting showed the city of Nishapur just after its people had revolted against Mongol rule and killed the husband of the Khan's daughter. In retribution, the daughter asked that everyone within the city limits be killed, and the Khan acquiesced to her wishes.

"Nice guy," Mason said, turning away from some of the more brutal images.

Annja couldn't say much. Her years of working with ancient cultures had given her a bit of distance on her perspective. And after all, the twentieth century really hadn't been that much different than the thirteenth, she said to herself. Genghis Khan had twenty years or so of warfare. We had World War I, World War II, Korea, Vietnam, the Six Day War, the Falklands, the revolutions in Nicaragua, El Salvador, Colombia, tribal warfare in places like Somalia and Darfur; she could go on for hours. In eight hundred years only one thing was certain—the veneer of civilization wasn't so thick, after all.

They noticed there was a door at the far end of this gallery, just like the one before, and beyond, another short tunnel with a third door at the far end.

Having been fooled once, they didn't take any chances this time. Mason used the stock of his weapon to test the way ahead, banging it against the stone hard enough to be certain it was going to hold their weight before they stepped forward and tested the next area.

In that fashion, they crossed the entire length of the passageway and finally stood in front of the door. The light from their torches fell on a bas-relief carving above the lintel displaying the face of a Mongolian warrior. His eyes seemed to gaze down at them in judgment. So strong was the illusion that Annja half expected it to open its mouth and ask what they wanted.

Beneath the figure was a set of Mongolian letters carved on an ivory disk about two feet in diameter, the white of the ivory contrasting sharply with the dark stone in which it was set.

"What do you think that's for?" Mason asked.

Annja shook her head; she didn't know. She eyed it suspiciously and then turned and looked at the empty corridor behind them. An uneasy feeling was building in her stomach.

After the collapsing tunnel trap, this passage had been too easy.

She'd missed something.

She turned back to see Mason reaching for the door, intending to push it open.

Warnings ran through her head. "No! Wait!" she cried.

But she was too late.

BACK IN THE TUNNEL behind them, the others quickly worked out a plan. Because they had the most climbing experience, Vale and Williams were given the task of rappelling back down the cliff and cutting down three to four reasonably straight trees that could be used to bridge the gap. Davenport and Nambai would use their position to play guard during the process, alerting the others if there was any sign of Ransom or his men. After stripping the branches off the trunks, Williams and Vale would drag the trees over to the base of the cliff where Davenport and Nambai would haul them up into the tunnel with the extra climbing ropes they still carried in their packs.

With the four of them together again in the tunnel, they would push the trunks across the gap, then bind them together to create a makeshift bridge.

They knew there was a considerable amount of work ahead of them, but after coming this far, none of them, Nambai included, wanted to miss out on the final discovery.

Selecting the trees was the easy part, as the area below the cave mouth was full of reasonably straight conifer trees. With only small camp hatchets available for use, it took the two men some time to cut down the trunks and trim off the branches. Once they had, they carried them to the base of the cliff and tied one of the climbing ropes to each end of the first log.

At the signal from Williams, Davenport and Nambai hauled each log up the side of the cliff and set them down inside the cave mouth.

Once all four logs had been brought up, Vale and Williams rejoined the others inside the cave.

The foursome took a short break, eating some food and drinking a lot of water to replenish what they had sweated out during their efforts. In the midst of their meal a sudden booming sound reverberated through the cavern.

The same thought went through all of their minds.

Another trap!

Their meal forgotten, they jumped to their feet and began pushing the logs out over the gap, working as quickly as possible to complete the bridge and go to the aide of their companions.

MASON'S HAND PUSHED against the door, but it didn't open as expected. Instead, it sank several inches into its frame and then stopped.

"What the heck?" Mason said, more to himself to Annja.

Annja wasn't listening to him, however. She'd already turned to face the corridor behind them, every muscle tensed as she waited for whatever was coming.

And come it did.

A low grinding sound filled the corridor and the bottom

edges of the left- and right-hand walls fell backward, revealing a long, narrow opening running the length of the passageway.

Water began to pour out of those openings with a loud rushing roar, and in less than a minute both Annja and Mason were standing ankle-deep in freezing-cold water as more flooded into the room by the second.

"The other door!" Annja shouted above the din.

They rushed for the entrance they'd passed through previously, their feet splashing through the water that was rapidly flooding the passageway around them.

Before they had even gone halfway down the tunnel a stone slab slid down from a hidden recess in the ceiling and blocked the door.

Mason continued running and threw himself at the barrier. Maybe he was hoping he could shatter it or something; Annja didn't know. What was clear was the water was still rising, up to midcalf now, and it would probably continue to do so until it reached the ceiling.

If they were still here at that point, they would be beyond caring.

Mason tried again, slamming himself against the stone wall, but it had as much effect as a mosquito would to an elephant.

He looked back at her, his expression clearly letting her know his efforts were futile.

They weren't getting out that way, that was for sure.

Annja spun around, taking in everything in the corridor, looking for the solution, the way out. Her gaze fell on the carving of the Khan and the ivory wheel beneath it. Her rudimentary knowledge of the Uighur script, which was used to write the Mongolian tongue, told her that the arrangement of letters on the wheel translated into gibberish.

Why put a series of letters there if they didn't actually spell anything? she wondered.

"Come on!" she shouted over the roaring of the water, and took off back down the length of the corridor without waiting to see if Mason was following.

Reaching the door at the other end, she discovered that despite her height she could not reach the ivory wheel. Mason had already figured out her quandary, however, and bent over so that she could climb up on his back. From there, he leaned against the door, using it for support while she clambered all the way up until she was standing on his shoulders and found herself directly opposite the disk. This close she could see that there was a small arrow just below the image of the Khan, pointing down at the disk.

"I don't know what you're doing, but whatever it is, you'd better hurry," he shouted up to her. In that short time since the flooding had started, the water had already risen over Mason's knees.

Despite having hung there for centuries, it only took a gentle push to get the disk moving. Working quickly, Annja spun the disk like a combination lock, lining up each letter in the name *Temujin* with the arrow below the carving.

She looked down, noting that the water was now up to the middle of Mason's chest, and said, "Try the door."

With his hands already against it to help in holding Annja up, all Mason had to do was push.

Nothing happened.

BY LAYING THE TREE TRUNKS on the floor one at a time and pushing from behind, they were able to slide each of them across the gap without too much difficulty. The rope in Davenport's pack was sacrificed and cut into shorter strips, which were then used to tie the ends of the logs together in an effort to keep them from sliding away from one another.

Vale volunteered to make the crossing first and he did so by shimmying across the makeshift bridge while seated on the logs with a leg hanging down on either side. His position spread his weight out as much as possible and helped keep the logs from separating beneath him by trapping them between his thighs.

Once he was across, he took several strips of rope he'd carried over with him and used those to bind the other end of the logs together.

With a man holding down either side of their makeshift bridge, the others followed Vale's example and crossed to the far side as quickly as possible.

Nambai was the last one to cross and the older man did it with more panache than any of his younger colleagues. Standing and walking across as though it was something he did every day of the week, he strolled along the narrow causeway with a gaping void to either side that would have given a mountain goat second thoughts.

Fresh lit torches in hand, they hurried after their colleagues, afraid that they might already be too late.

They passed through the first room and into the short tunnel beyond, only to find that the door at the other end of the tunnel was blocked by a large slab of stone.

Pushing against it got them nowhere and it was clear from the size of the stone that attempting to lift it, particularly without the proper tools to give them leverage, would be an act of futility.

A roaring noise could be heard on the other side, and once Davenport thought he heard Annja's voice, but it was too hard to tell for sure. They banged on the stone, shouted at those they believed to be on the other side, but to no avail.

If Mason and Annja were on the other side, they were trapped good and proper.

"TRY IT AGAIN!" Annja shouted down to Mason.

He gave the door another shove.

Still nothing.

Annja swore. What had she missed? Was she using the device incorrectly? Did she need to spin the disk in only one direction? Clockwise? Counterclockwise? Did she have the right password?

She tried the Khan's given name twice more, moving the disk only clockwise the first time and then, when that failed, trying the same thing in the other direction.

It still didn't work.

"Annja?"

She looked down and saw that the water was almost up to Mason's chin.

"Better hurry," he said, looking up at her, a strange calmness in his gaze.

She turned back to the disk. She needed a different password. That had to be it.

But what?

Her thoughts whirled.

What would have been important to the ruler of the known world? Wealth? Power? Territory? His title?

There were too many options, too many choices, and not enough time.

She heard Mason take a deep breath and knew the water had just risen over his face. She had less than a minute or two.

With one last desperate attempt, she tried again. If she was wrong this time, she wouldn't have another chance.

Once Mason collapsed she wouldn't be tall enough to reach the disk.

She spun the last letter into place and felt the water creep up over her knees.

Mason had been submerged for a minute and a half.

A grinding noise filled the chamber and the door in front of them burst open, carrying them forward in the rush of the current.

35

Annja went under in the sudden flood and was swept away from Mason. She felt herself slam into a few objects and got tangled up in them, but couldn't tell what they were as she was carried several yards into the room by the receding waters.

In moments it was over.

Wet, tired and very thankful that she remembered the name of Temujin's first, and favored, wife, Borte, she came to rest on the stone floor.

Something large and heavy lay atop her.

With her torch gone, she opened her eyes into darkness. Her left hand was pinned beneath the weight but she could move her right and she used it to pull her flashlight from the cargo pocket of her pants and turn it on.

A mummified Mongol face stared down at her from just a few inches away, its blackened flesh shrunken against the bones of its skull, its eyes deep in their sockets and dried out like oversized grapes.

Annja screamed.

"Annja!"

The mummy was suddenly pulled away and Annja found herself looking into Mason's concerned face. "Are you okay?" he asked.

She nodded, still too surprised to speak.

Having an eight-hundred-year-old corpse leering at her was not something she'd expected after escaping from the flood.

Mason helped her climb to her feet and together they shone their lights across the space around them.

Mummified Mongol warriors were scattered everywhere around the room, thanks to the force of the now-drained floodwaters. They were all dressed in Mongol battle armor, and many still held the swords and shields they had been posed with so many centuries before.

Annja shone her light into the face of one of the mummies and bent over to take a closer look. The wide gash across his throat had been stitched shut, the haphazard way it had been done removing even the smallest doubt that the repair had been anything but postmortem.

By letting her light play over the other figures nearby, Annja could see the same wounds on each. She suspected they had gone to their deaths knowingly, ready to follow their Khan into whatever world came next, and that only made it all the more unnerving.

Annja had excavated quite a few ancient burial sites in her career. She'd even had the pleasure of seeing the Terra Cotta Army while visiting China and marveling at how the figures had appeared so lifelike. Every single soldier had differing facial features, as if they had been modeled after living individuals. Here, deep in this mountain passage in the heart of the Great Taboo, there had been no need for models at all. These soldiers were real. Here, the honor guard that had probably stood in orderly rank and file had once lived and breathed. It brought a strange and eerie presence to the place, as if the dead had come to life and now walked about the place on silent feet.

Shining their lights down the length of the passage showed another set of wooden doors at the very end, opened by the force of the water that had passed through them.

Without a word Annja and Mason stepped over the tangled ranks of the dead piled up near the doors and crossed the threshold.

The final set of doors opened into a massive, natural cavern. If Annja hadn't been so mesmerized by its contents, she might have amused herself for hours looking at the way nature had carved its own little hideaway from the bare rock.

As it was, she could barely take her eyes from the rows upon rows of warriors organized in regular columns of ten, three to a side.

Like the warriors in the entry hall, these were mummified, as well. So, too, were the steeds on which they rode.

She had found the fabled "sixty," the warriors who had accompanied Genghis Khan's body on its long journey back to the homeland and who had given their lives in order to keep the location of his tomb a secret.

The silent ranks stared back at her and for a moment she could almost feel the challenge in their dead eyes, could almost hear the snort of the horses and the clank of the armor as the warriors moved slightly in their saddles, could feel the anticipation they held as they prepared to ride forth for their Khan.

"Hey!" Mason's hand on her arm brought her back to herself.

"You okay?" he asked. "You looked a little woozy there for a moment."

She smiled what she hoped was a reassuring smile. "I'm fine. Just still catching my breath, I guess."

And as she turned away from him to glance at the soldiers once more, she saw it.

An enormous tent stood all on its own just beyond the squads of mountain warriors. It was easily ten times the size of the *gers* Annja had seen being used outside the city limits and must have required half a dozen carts or more to transport its materials.

Those who'd lived in such a place must have lived like kings.

Or queens.

She knew she was right the minute the thought occurred to her. After all, they had found the sixty members of the missing honor guard, those who supposedly stood watch over the sixty brides, if the message was still to be believed. That meant the massive *ger* had probably been erected to fulfill another element of the prophecy.

It was to be the living quarters for the harem that had followed Genghis into eternity.

Of course, there was only one way to find out.

Taking a deep breath, Annja crossed through the ranks of the dead, mounted the steps leading to the entrance of the *ger* and, pulling back the heavy felt doors, she stepped inside.

36

Raised sleeping pallets lined the interior of the *ger,* each one covered by its own draped canopy of silks. A dark shape occupied the center of each platform.

Annja stepped up to the nearest one and drew back the silk curtains, shining her light inside.

The mummy of a young woman stared back at her from the center of the bed, its wrinkled face and hardened eyeballs framed by a long, luscious swath of black hair. The mouth was partially open, which, when combined with the protruding eyeballs, gave the corpse the appearance that she was about to speak.

Annja wondered what the girl would say if she could.

A quick count of the sleeping platforms told Annja her suspicions were correct.

They had found the sixty virgins.

This one was dressed in the remains of a traditional faded blue *del,* blue being the Mongol color of eternity, and on her feet were a pair of brocade slippers that Annja suspected were part of the plunder Genghis Khan had taken from somewhere in China. She looked peaceful, as peaceful as an eight-hundred-year-old mummy could look, she thought.

Mason and Annja went around the room, drawing back the silk curtains one by one, looking for anything that might possibly contain the final directions they needed to locate the Khan's grave site. In each bed they found the same thing, a lovingly dressed mummy of a young Mongolian woman, that was all.

No clues.

No map.

No hidden verses.

They were running out of options.

The final section of the *ger* was sectioned off by intricately designed *tangkas* that looked as if they had been made by the same craftsman who had crafted the one in which the black *sulde* had been stored. They had the same recurring patterns, the same symbols scattered throughout, the same colored fabric.

With nowhere else left to look, Annja pulled back one side of the thick fabric and looked into the inner sanctum just beyond, as Mason peeked over her shoulder.

A platform about the size and height of a pool table rose out of the floor, as if it had been hewn from the living rock. Even that couldn't hold their attention, though, for their eyes were drawn immediately to the object it supported.

A figure lay atop the platform and even from where they stood they could see that it was dressed in armor that hadn't seen the light of day in hundreds of years. A thick coating of dust coated it, but Annja could still make out the vibrant colors that had been painted on the leather plates, the sheen of the silver rings that made up the mail coat beneath, the snarling wolf's face that had been painted on the shield that was hung on the wall behind the body, along with a sword and a bow. Both arms were crossed over something resting on the corpse's chest, but from where she was she couldn't make out what it might be.

Rising up behind the platform like a ceremonial flag was a *sulde,* identical to the spirit banner they had found at Shankh except for one respect—this one was white.

It was the *sulde* the Khan had used in times of peace.

Annja heard Mason's shocked gasp from behind her.

"Is that…?"

She didn't know.

But she had to find out.

Slowly, almost reverentially, she stepped closer to the funeral bier.

A helmet rested atop the head and she recognized it immediately as the kind worn by Mongol warriors after the unification of the empire. It had a headpiece made of iron and flaps of leather that came down over the ears and the back of the neck to protect them from attack.

A square piece of silk covered the front of the helmet and, as a result, the face it rested on, as well.

Annja's professionalism warred with her curiosity. She wanted to know what was under that cloth but at the same time didn't want to disturb the scene until it had been properly documented. In the end, given all the time and hardships she'd endured to get there, her curiosity won out.

Her heart was beating so hard her hands were shaking as she gently picked up the edge of the silk covering and drew it to one side.

A blank, featureless face stared back at her.

She recoiled in surprise. He has no face, she thought, and then realized that she wasn't looking at a body at all, but just a primitive mannequin made from bundled cloth.

They had not discovered the body of Genghis Khan.

Disappointed, she stepped back to let Mason have a look. As she did so, her gaze fell on the thick book the corpse held in its hands.

It had clearly been in that position for some time. dust and cobwebs ran across the gauntlets of the mannequin and over the book they contained. The book's leather cover was stained a deep blue and a series of words had been branded into its surface. She could recognize the writing as Mongolian, but that was all.

With a start, she realized she might be looking at the Great Yasa of Genghis Khan.

Because of the vast diversities among the tribal units that made up the core of his empire, Genghis chose to allow local leaders to govern the way they traditionally had, provided that their rulings did not violate the universal laws that the Khan put into place. The laws did not cover day-to-day life on the steppes, but rather dealt with only the most troubling aspects, those that could cause the most discord. The laws were written on white paper and bound in blue to match the color of the eternal sky above. In time, the book itself became known as the Great Yasa, the Great Law.

Being careful not to damage anything, she lifted one of the corpse's gauntlets and slid the book out from underneath it before returning the hand to its proper place. Turning away from the platform, she took a deep breath and blew as much of the dust off the cover of the book as she could.

Satisfied that she wouldn't get any dirt on the pages,

she sat down and very gingerly opened it, leafing through the pages. She noted the careful writing, the orderly hand-written script. There wasn't a single correction. Not a single mistake. Whoever had written it had taken extreme care to be certain it was perfect.

That supported her belief that it was the Great Yasa, the written text of Genghis Khan's universal laws. She'd know for certain once she had Nambai look at it, for the written language of the Mongols had changed little in all the inter-vening years. Archaeologically speaking, it was likely the find of the century.

But to Annja, it was somewhat of a disappointment.

It wasn't what she had been looking for.

She let her gaze sweep the room, trying to figure out what they had missed, where she had gone wrong. She just didn't understand. As far as she knew she'd interpreted each line of the coded message correctly, going from one clue to the next. She'd found the *sulde* at Shankh and used that to lead them to the hidden chamber inside the cliff face containing the map. The map had led them to what was clearly the Tomb of the Virgins. If the coded message was correct, the tomb was then supposed to lead them to…

Wait a minute. Where was it supposed to lead them?

She pulled out the card she'd been carrying around in her pocket for days and reread the last few lines of the message.

The sixty brides rode sixty steeds
And now rest beneath the watchful eyes of those
who came before

In their arms is the truth you seek
The way to all that was and more

Then climb to the place where Tengri and Gazan meet
It is there that the Batur makes his home

She read it again, this time aloud.

The last two lines made sense. Tengri was another name for eternal blue heaven and Gazan was the name for earth mother. So, where Tengri and Gazan meet was where the sky met the earth. That could only be Burkhan Khaldun— God Mountain—the highest point in the region, especially if you took into account the reference to climbing. And Batur was simply a Mongol word for clan leader or chief. So the clan leader, in this case the Khan, made his home on God Mountain. The tomb was somewhere on God Mountain.

But where?

That's what the tomb, or rather the clue hidden in the tomb, was supposed to tell them.

Except it didn't.

Annja read the lines over again.

"*'In their arms is the truth you seek, the way to all that was and more.'*"

She wasn't certain who the lines were referring to—the sixty brides or the soldiers, listed as "those who came before"—but what was clear was that the next clue was supposed to be in their arms.

They'd examined each of the bodies carefully and hadn't found anything.

That's when it hit her.

She hadn't noticed it before but looking at it repeatedly she saw that there was a distinct break between the last two stanzas. Unlike the earlier portions, which seemed to flow from one to another, there was something disjointed about how the fourth stanza flowed into the fifth. *"The way to all that was and more"* was followed by *"then climb to the place where Tengri and Gazan meet."*

They didn't go together. It was almost as if there was a line or two missing.

A sinking feeling filled the pit of her stomach. She had made a mistake, had missed something. That was the only possible answer.

37

Despite all they had found, disappointment filled Annja and Mason with their failed search so they made the decision to return to the others. They retraced their steps, heading back through the hall of warriors, as Annja was now calling it, and into the connecting tunnel where they had nearly drowned, only to meet the others coming through in the opposite direction.

The stone slab that had previously blocked their escape route was gone. Davenport told Annja and Mason about how he and the other three had been sitting on the far side, trying to think of some way through the barrier, when it just quietly slid back upward into its previous location. Fearful that it might close on them again, they had gone back and brought their makeshift bridge down the tunnel with them, using it to brace the stone in its upright position just to be safe. They had just finished doing so.

Word of what they found fanned the curiosity of the rest

of the team, so Annja agreed to take them back inside the cavern to give them a chance to see for themselves. Mason chose to remain behind; he'd seen enough mummies for one day apparently.

While he waited, he tried to come up with a plan as to what to do next.

They had accomplished so much. They had found the Khan's *sulde,* long thought lost to antiquity and the ravages of war. They had used it to locate the voice in the earth and the map chamber with it. They had used the clues in the map chamber to bring them to the legendary Tomb of the Virgins. They were so close he could taste it.

But now what? Mason thought.

Without that missing clue, they could flounder around for weeks without finding anything.

And yet...

Short of heading back down the mountain, the only option he could see was to check out the region on the other side of the rope bridge. It had been built for a reason and so it seemed the natural course of action to take.

What did they have to lose at this point, anyway?

When he laid out the plan for the others upon their return, they agreed that it made sense.

The bridge it would be.

There was probably just enough daylight left to get the group across the bridge and to find a decent place to camp for the night, so they wasted no time in dragging the bridge back down the tunnel, setting it into place and then using it to get them all over to the other side of the chasm. After that, it was simply a matter of rappelling down to the base of the cliff and heading back down the trail.

WHEN THEY REACHED the cemetery clearing they decided to take a five-minute rest break.

Mason was turning to say something to Annja, clearly intending to try and pull her out of her funk if the smile on his face meant anything, when the sharp report of a rifle echoed through the trees.

Annja watched an expression of confusion cross his face and then they were both looking down at his chest where an angry red flower was rapidly blossoming. Two more shots rang out, both of them striking Mason in the back, and then the light was fading from his eyes as swiftly as his body was tumbling to the ground.

Time seemed to stop for Annja as her combat reflexes took over, her unconscious mind recognizing the ambush for what it was before her conscious mind had gotten over the shock of seeing Mason gunned down in front of her.

She threw herself sideways into Davenport, knocking him to the ground, as the rifle fire was replaced with the chatter of automatic weapons and Williams and Vale were practically torn apart by the fusillade.

The gunfire stopped and silence fell.

Annja heard a voice shout, "Throw down your weapons and come out with your hands over your heads!"

Fat chance of that, Annja thought, as she raised her head off the ground to try to get a look at what they were up against.

More gunfire came their way as a result and Annja crawled behind a nearby boulder. Davenport had already taken cover in the same location. If they crouched very close together, the stone was just big enough to cover both of them.

Bullets whipped through the trees and smacked off nearby rocks.

If they stayed there they were dead. Annja knew it was as simple as that. Some of Ransom's men would pin them down with gunfire while sending others around to flank them on the sides. Eventually, the enemy troops would simply walk up and shoot them both in the heads.

She had to get them moving!

She waited for another lull, then jumped to her feet, dragging Davenport with her.

It was now or never.

"Run!" Annja yelled.

She shoved Davenport ahead of her, forcing him to move, and headed down the left trail, away from Ransom and his thugs.

Gunfire split the air and bullets whined around them like giant prehistoric insects, but thankfully none of them found their marks. The thick trees and the suddenness of their rush for safety protected them in those first few seconds, before the winding nature of the trail took them out of the ambush team's sight.

Annja knew that it wouldn't take them long to come after them, however.

Ahead of her, Davenport stumbled and fell forward, but Annja reached him before he could hit the ground and hauled him back to his feet, practically dragging him after her as she sprinted down the trail.

If they could reach the bridge, she thought, they might have a chance to cross to the other side and then drop it into the gorge behind them, temporarily separating them from Ransom and his men. Hopefully that would give her enough time to figure out a plan to get them out of this alive.

Visions of Mason being cut down by the enemy's gunfire rose in her mind, but she chased them away angrily.

You don't have time for that right now, she told herself. Mourn for what might have been later. For now, concentrate on getting the two of you out of this alive.

It was a feat that was going to take all of her concentration.

Both of them were exhausted. They'd been climbing all day, only to face the disappointment that they had overlooked a crucial element. In the midst of that blow to their morale had come the attack. The emotional impact of the sudden ambush was almost as bad as the physical one. Losing Mason was even worse. She didn't realize how much she'd come to rely on his calm leadership and good sense until it was abruptly stripped away from her.

Davenport was her responsibility now and she'd do her best to see to it that he survived. As the bearer of Joan's sword, she could do no less. And the first thing they had to do was increase the distance between them and Ransom.

She realized that she had no idea what had happened to Nambai. She hoped he'd managed to get away from Ransom and his thugs as going back for him was out of the question at this point. None of them would survive if she did.

Their headlong rush down the meager trail continued, brushing aside low-hanging branches, stumbling over rocks partially hidden in the thick undergrowth, their breath pluming out around them in the high mountain air.

Before they knew it, the trees abruptly gave way, leaving them exposed on an open stretch of ground that ended at the lip of the ravine. Annja's innate sense of direction hadn't failed her. The bridge she'd glimpsed on the way up was directly ahead of them.

The two of them plunged ahead.

There was a good twenty yards of open ground between the tree line and the bridge, Annja calculated. The bridge itself was probably a hundred feet in length, so make it two hundred feet total that they had to cross before Ransom's men caught up with them. She knew that if they were caught in the open they were done for. Ransom's goal was to prevent them from getting word about the Khan's tomb out of the country. Once they had, he wouldn't be able to muscle in with a claim. That meant they were better off dead than alive to him. If they were caught here, his men could gun them down with impunity and no one would be the wiser.

They had to get across that bridge!

The few moments it took to cross that open stretch of ground felt like hours to Annja, but then her feet hit the wooden slats holding the bridge together and she had more important things to worry about.

The bridge seemed ancient. Two thick ropes served as railings on either side above the narrow walkway constructed across the ravine. The rope and wood slats that made up the walking surface of the bridge were worn smooth from years of use in some places and missing entirely in others.

The sound of the raging river far below could be heard clearly, a testament to its power and strength.

Annja went first, gripping the rope rail on either side tightly, knowing that if her feet slipped off the slats the railing lines would be the only thing keeping her from a long plunge into the raging river below. Behind her, Davenport struggled along as best he could. He stayed about ten feet back, not wanting to unbalance her with his own shifting weight, as the bridge rocked to and fro with their movement.

The narrow gorge acted as a natural wind tunnel, so that they were buffeted by gusts that shook and moved the bridge beneath their feet. Annja kept her eyes on the far side, trusting her balance, not wanting to be constantly reminded of the sheer drop beneath her.

She was about three-quarters of the way across the bridge when a horse burst out of the trees on the other side. Its rider stood high in the stirrups in the manner Mongolians had ridden for centuries, guiding the horse with his thighs, leaving his hands free for other things.

In this case, one of those other things included pointing an arrow directly at Annja's head.

She froze, astonished by what she was seeing. The man on the horse looked as if he'd just stumbled out of the history books. He wore armor made from cured leather and overlapping metal plates over a thick coat and had a sword hanging from the belt at his waist. Dense boots of leather and felt protected his feet and a helmet complete with a plume of horsehair covered his head.

A small round shield was strapped to his lead arm, ready to be put to use in defense if need be, once he'd loosed the arrow currently in his bow.

His face was relatively broad and flat, with a high forehead. His hair was dark, if the edges peeking out from under his helmet were any indication. She was also close enough to see that his eyes were a deep gray in color, a striking change from the dark brown eyes she'd seen in so many Mongol faces since arriving here.

The rider's gaze met hers.

Very clearly, so that there could be no misunderstanding, he shook his head.

His message was obvious. *You are not welcome here.*

He tucked his head back down and sighted carefully

along his bow, lining it up with her so that she could not mistake the warning.

Annja knew just how deadly accurate those bows could be in the right hands. Historically, Mongol children were taught to use them as early as age four, which was also about the time they began to learn how to ride. By the time a warrior reached middle age, he was extraordinarily proficient in both skills.

While she debated what to do about this new arrival, several other riders emerged from the trees behind him. They quickly spread out into a semicircle at his back, marking him as their leader. All of them were armed in a similar fashion, many with bows pointing in her direction, though some suddenly shifted position and aimed at something back in the direction she and Davenport had come.

Annja turned and looked behind her, only to see Ransom and his men emerging from the woods. They spotted the fugitives, and the Mongol cavalry, almost immediately and, in response, fanned out in unconscious imitation of their foes, shouting in defiance and taking a few potshots at Annja and Davenport.

The Mongols took that as an act of aggression and, their leader's signal, let their arrows fly.

Suddenly, Annja and Davenport were caught in the midst of a savage firefight. Bullets and arrows flew back and forth around them and the air was filled with the painful cries of the wounded and the dying. Davenport's hat was knocked off his head by a low-flying arrow and a bullet snatched at Annja's coat, punching a hole right through it when the wind lifted it away from her body.

As if that wasn't enough, a thunderous roar suddenly filled the canyon.

Annja turned to her left just in time to see Ransom's

helicopter rise up out of the depths and hover in line with the bridge itself, looming there like some great dragon out of legend. The downdraft of the chopper's massive rotors sent the bridge bounding left to right like a drunken partygoer. Annja was so close that she could see herself reflected in the dark Plexiglas that covered the cockpit. She could just imagine the expression of glee on the copilot's face as the chain gun mounted under the helicopter's nose turned in their direction.

38

The chain gun went off with a thunderous roar, but amazingly neither Annja nor Davenport was hit. A sudden gust of wind had tossed the helicopter to one side as if it were nothing more than a piece of flotsam caught in the tide, causing the gunner to miss his target.

Instead of knocking Annja and Davenport to their deaths, as had been intended, the bullets ripped through the cluster of Mongol warriors gathered on the far side of the bridge.

At the same time, the helicopter came dangerously close to smashing into the edge of the canyon. Only the quick action of the pilot as he yanked back on the stick kept the aircraft from becoming an early casualty of the fight.

Annja watched it lift up and out of the narrow confines of the canyon, knowing beyond a doubt that it would be back.

She knew that she didn't want to be there when it returned.

Annja glanced at the far side and realized this was their chance. The helicopter attack had thrown the Mongol formation into chaos. They were far too concerned with helping their wounded to watch the fugitives on the bridge.

If they were quick enough, they might just make it across, Annja thought.

Her gaze met Davenport's and she knew he was thinking the same thing.

Annja threw herself into motion, doing all she could to get across the remaining third of the bridge without being hit by gunfire from Ransom's men or being seen by the Mongols.

Fate chose that moment to step into the fray.

The next plank looked sturdy enough, but it gave way the moment Annja stepped solidly onto it. She plunged downward, her leg sinking deeper into the hole while she scrambled frantically for a purchase to stop her fall.

When she had, she found herself trapped, her leg pushed through the shattered plank all the way up to midthigh, the other one bent at the knee, while she clutched frantically to another plank several feet ahead.

"Annja!" Davenport cried, the fear looming large in his voice.

"I'm okay," she answered, fighting to stop her heart from popping out of her throat.

That had been too close.

But Davenport hadn't seen her fall; he hadn't even been looking in her direction, Annja discovered, as she twisted around to look at him.

Instead, his attention was captured by the sight of the helicopter thundering toward them in an attack run from above.

Time slowed.

Annja could hear the pounding of her heart mixing in counterpoint with the thunder of the helicopter's rotors, the two booming in syncopation. She could feel the gentle breeze from the evergreens caressing her face, teasing her nose with the smell of pine laced with the stink of aviation fuel. She could see Davenport's mouth open, could hear his furious scream, as he threw himself toward her.

As the helicopter dove toward them, Annja closed her eyes.

The 12 mm slugs went off with a roar, cutting through the bridge like a knife.

For just an instant Annja and Davenport hung in space, the bridge around them seemingly intact.

Then the badly damaged structure broke in two and plunged downward, taking the two of them with it.

Davenport's hand brushed against her own and instinctively she grabbed for it, catching him about the wrist just as they started their fateful plunge.

The bridge fell in two sections. The far edge carried the two of them away with it. Their weight sent it hurtling toward the cliff face below where the Mongols were now firing what seemed like everything they had at the passing chopper.

Annja had time to think *this is going to hurt,* and then she was slamming against the side of the chasm with what felt like bone-crushing force.

Miraculously, Annja did not let go of Davenport despite the impact.

She gritted her teeth in pain; her arms screamed in agony with the weight they were suddenly supporting, but she refused to let go.

Do. Not. Let. Go, she told herself.

When they stopped moving, Annja was hanging by one leg upside down in the remains of the bridge with Davenport slung beneath her, the only thing connecting them their mutual holds on each other's wrists.

He looked up at her, the fear bright in his eyes.

"Don't drop me," he said in a whisper.

Annja couldn't even find the energy to speak against the pain roaring through her arms.

She knew they couldn't stay like this for long…

IN THE HELICOPTER, Ransom leaned forward with eager anticipation.

"Did you get them?" he asked.

Santiago peered anxiously through the windscreen and then shook his head.

"They're hanging on the remains of the bridge, about fifteen feet below the rim."

"Make another run. This time don't miss."

Ransom's voice was filled with savage satisfaction.

Before the pilot could carry out his employer's orders, however, the helicopter came under fire again from the Mongols on the cliff's edge. Arrows, spears and bullets smacked into the frame and the windscreen. The pilot reacted accordingly, doing what all pilots did when their aircraft was in pressing danger.

He got the heck out of there.

"Where are you going?" Ransom screamed, spittle flying from his mouth in his fury.

"Sir! We're under attack. I'm—"

"I don't give a rat's ass what you think, you idiot! Get us back down there. Now!"

Wordlessly, the pilot spun the helicopter around and made another run at the spot where Annja and Davenport were hanging on for dear life.

ANNJA SAW DEATH COMING for them down the length of the chasm.

Just another few seconds and the chain gun would let

loose again. At that range, it would be hard for them to miss.

She knew their options had just been severely limited. If they stayed here they were going to be killed.

She had to do something and she had to do it quickly!

All this flashed through her mind in the space of a split second as she weighed options and tried to determine the best course of action.

Annja looked down toward the water far below.

It was an extreme long shot, with probably less than a one in a hundred chance of survival, but that was still better than their odds of staying where they were. Even if her arms managed to remain firmly in their sockets, something that was looking less and less likely by each passing second, that helicopter would rip them apart the moment it started shooting again. She didn't know why it hadn't done so already.

There really was only one choice open to them.

Mind made up, Annja looked down at Davenport and found him looking up at her, the fear etched across his face.

"Brace yourself!" she cried.

Annja reached into the otherwhere with her free hand and drew her sword. Davenport's eyes widened at the sight of it, then they got even bigger as she swung the weapon toward the guide rope on her right.

The rope parted with an audible snap.

Davenport opened his mouth to say something, but whatever it was was lost in the roar of the oncoming chopper and the howl of the wind in her ears. Twisting the other way, Annja lashed out with the sword a second time.

The blade cut through the other guide rope, sending them and the short section of bridge they were attached to plunging toward the roaring river far below.

RANSOM WATCHED IN satisfaction as Davenport and Creed dropped into the chasm, their forms quickly disappearing in from view in the mist and spray from the river far below. He would have preferred to blow them all to hell himself, but he'd settle for this if he had to. Besides, the idea that they were likely conscious for the entire fall only added to his glee at their demise.

He looked up, intending to share his congratulations with Santiago, and froze.

Behind his second in command was a window, and through it he could see one of the Mongol warriors rushing out of the woods with something long and slender in his hands. As Ransom watched, the warrior knelt and pointed the tube directly at the helicopter.

For just a moment their eyes locked.

Then the warrior pulled the trigger and the Soviet-produced rocket-propelled grenade, an RPG-7, sent a high-explosive antitank warhead, commonly known as a HEAT round, spiraling up toward them.

Ransom didn't even have time to shout a warning.

The warhead struck just as the cockpit proximity alarms began blaring, tearing through the tail boom, severing the tail rotor and sending it spinning off into the chasm below.

Without the tail rotor to keep the aircraft flying straight, it began to rotate around itself, the main rotors spinning it about like a child's toy top gone suddenly, drastically, out of control.

Inside the chopper both Ransom and Santiago braced themselves with hands and feet against the nearest solid surfaces as the pilot sought frantically to get control of his aircraft, something that just wasn't going to happen with a gaping hole where the tail rotor used to be.

The sky whipped past once, twice, three times, and then Ransom had an excellent view of the forest coming up quickly outside the same window he'd looked through before.

With a thunderous crash, the helicopter slammed into the treetops, skittered along for several hundred yards as its main rotor slashed everything before it and then plowed into the ground with all the force of a missile.

RANSOM REGAINED consciousness slowly. One eye was crusted shut with what he thought might be dried blood, but the other one worked just fine, and in the dim light he could see that he was hanging upside down from his harness in what was left of the helicopter. His chest hurt where the straps had yanked themselves tight on impact, and his left arm felt like the Jolly Green Giant had been playing tug-of-war with it, but other than some minor cuts and bruises, he was intact, as near as he could tell. He had blood in his hair and on his shirt, but he didn't know if it was his own or someone else's.

There seemed to be only one way to find out.

With a shaking hand, he reached across his chest and tripped the harness release mechanism.

Ransom fell onto what had once been the interior ceiling of the aircraft with a thud and a flash of pain. He lay still for a moment, catching his breath, but then pulled himself to his knees. From that position he was able to look around the cockpit.

The windscreen was gone, torn away by the shards of one of the rotors. So, too, was the pilot's head, though his body was still strapped in place, his hands on the controls.

Santiago seemed to have fared better. Ransom couldn't see all of him but what he could see didn't appear to have any major bodily damage, nor was he leaking a pool of blood onto the floor.

The wreck was filled with acrid-smelling smoke and the stink of aviation fuel, so Ransom decided it was best to get out of it as soon as possible.

On hands and knees he crawled over to the edge of the wreck where he could see a wide band of sunlight shining in. The hole was just big enough to crawl through if he got down on his stomach and wriggled in. He did just that.

Feetfirst, he pushed himself through the opening and into the clean air outside.

When his head at last passed through the gap and he sat, up he found himself surrounded by the Mongol warriors he'd seen back at the pass.

He caught movement out of the corner of his eye, felt something slam into the side of his head and then darkness snatched him in its icy grip.

39

For what seemed like the longest time, they fell.

Annja managed to hold on to Davenport for the first few seconds of their drop, but then his weight started to pull her off center and she had no choice but to let him go. It was for his safety, as well as hers. If they hit the water horizontally, rather than vertically, neither of them would survive. They were already taking a huge chance as it was.

She had a moment to wonder what would happen to Roux and Garin if she didn't survive the fall, and then her feet hit the water, the impact freeing her from the troublesome plank and plunging her deep into the river's icy depths, the shock of the water's temperature nearly driving the breath from her lungs. She clamped her jaws tightly shut in response. The current took her immediately, tossing her about like a leaf in the wind, twisting and turning her until she didn't know which direction was up.

Her jaws ached from the effort of keeping her mouth shut as her lungs kept trying to tell her brain that she needed air and that she needed it now, but she knew it was all over if she gave into that urge. Still, she couldn't hold out much longer.

Just when she thought she couldn't take it anymore, her head broke the surface of the water and she sucked in great gasps of air. Almost immediately the rapids sucked her under again.

She caromed into something unyielding, a rock, or a tree maybe, she didn't know, nor did it really matter; what mattered was fighting her way to the surface again. The water was close to freezing and it was rapidly leeching the warmth from her body. She had already lost a lot of the feeling in her feet and lower legs and she knew her arms would go next. Once that happened, she wouldn't have any means of keeping herself above the flow and it would only take the river a few minutes to finish the job the cold had begun.

She didn't have much time left.

The current twisted her body around and sucked her under again. She was shoved violently to one side and her head struck something solid. This time she wasn't so lucky. The impact left her dazed, robbing her of her sense of direction, and she felt herself spun around, unable to right herself.

Her thoughts were fuzzy, her vision distorted, and she couldn't remember what she was doing here. She was in the water, that much she knew, but why? How had she gotten here? What was she looking for? Why was she struggling so hard? Maybe she should just relax a little, relax and rest, let the water carry her in its embrace wherever it wanted to go, rest and relax…

She crashed into something for the third time, the pain jarring the deadly fuzziness from her thoughts for just a second, but a second was long enough. As she rebounded from whatever it was she had hit she lashed out with her hands and managed to grab hold of it. She was hanging there, fighting to hold on, her fingers all but frozen, when a hand reached down out of nowhere and seized her wrist.

It was a good thing, too, because less than half a second later she lost her grip and would have plunged right back into the deadly current.

She was only barely conscious as she was dragged out of the water and dumped onto a rocky beach. She remembered a figure looming over her, a flash of eyes dark as slate, and then the darkness claimed her and she knew no more.

ANNJA REGAINED CONSCIOUSNESS abruptly, uncertain of where she was or what she was doing there. She remembered the chase through the forest and how Ransom's men had shot at her and Davenport. She remembered the rush across the bridge and the fear she'd felt as they had been caught between Ransom's men on one side and the Mongol warriors on the other. She remembered the helicopter attacks and the bridge and the long fall into the water and…the water!

She had to get out of the water!

Annja surged up off the bed she was lying on, fear setting her heart to pound like a jackhammer, and would have scrambled away from wherever she was if a strong pair of hands hadn't reached out and grabbed her just below the shoulders.

The position brought back other memories and she gasped out, "Mason?" in surprise and wonder.

The man who had been patiently sitting next to her for the past few hours, waiting for her to wake up, shook his head. "No, it's not Mason," Davenport said gently. "Mason's gone."

Memories of all they had been through crashed over her like the tide and it took her a few moments before she could find her voice.

"Where are we?" she asked. "How did we get here?"

Davenport shrugged. "Your guess is as good as mine. When I came to, I found you lying there unconscious. There's a guard at the door who won't let us leave, but I haven't seen anyone else."

Annja swung her feet off the bed and sat up, realizing only as she did so that she was naked beneath the blanket. She made a quick grab for the covering and managed to keep from exposing herself, but only just.

"What the heck happened to my clothes?" she demanded.

Davenport blushed. "Sorry. Meant to warn you about that."

He got up and crossed to the center of the room where a metal stove sat framed by two orange posts. Annja let her gaze follow them upward to where they met a roof made from a lattice of wooden strips covered with what looked to be layers of canvas and felt. The walls around them were constructed the same way, but instead of the plain, undecorated fabric used in the construction of the roof, these were covered with designs in bright, rich colors.

Clearly they were in a *ger,* the traditional tentlike home used by the nomadic Mongols for centuries.

Her clothes were neatly folded in a pile on the low table that stood near the stove. Davenport carried them over to her and then turned his back while she carefully dressed.

As she did so, she took a thorough look at her injuries

and tried to make an accurate assessment of her condition. She was bruised and battered, but otherwise hadn't suffered any broken bones in their unorthodox escape attempt. Her head hurt and when she reached up she discovered a thick bandage wrapped around her skull. Must have hit it on something while I was in the water, she thought.

Well, at least they had tended to her injuries. That was a good sign. Better than killing her outright, anyway. Now to see about getting out of here.

She got up and walked over to the doorway. When she pulled aside the thick felt covering that served as the door, she found herself looking into the face of a large Mongol warrior standing just outside. He was dressed like the other warriors she'd seen from the bridge, in a long *del* and armored coat. A sword hung in a scabbard at his hip.

"Excuse me," Annja said and moved to go past him.

The guard, for that was what he was, stepped in her way.

"Ugui," he said sharply, putting a hand on the hilt of his weapon.

Annja had been in Mongolia long enough to recognize the word *no.*

She tried again, this time moving around him in the other direction, but he stopped her again, repeating his command more loudly and shaking his head to clarify his point.

Annja knew she could take him down if she wanted to; he was seeing only an unarmed and apparently injured woman, no match for a trained Mongol warrior. But there was nothing to be gained by giving away her secret at this point, so Annja decided to play nice and see what happened. She could always bust them out later if need be.

"All right. Okay," she told the guard. "No need to get uptight."

Without taking her eyes off him, she backed up and returned to the tent.

"The guard's still out there, I take it," Davenport said, when she came back inside.

"Yep. And as ugly as ever."

Her comment got a quick smile out of Davenport, which was what she was hoping for. If they could keep their spirits up, they'd be more prepared when the time came to get out of here.

There was tea on the stove and a covered platter that turned out to be some kind of noodle dish with chunks of meat, maybe lamb or mutton, Annja wasn't sure. But she was hungry and that was all the excuse she needed to dig in. She convinced Davenport to have some, as well, not knowing when they might get another chance to eat. It was always best to keep their strength up in situations like this.

"Who are these guys, Annja? What do they want with us?"

She'd been thinking about that herself. Legends stated that the tomb of the Khan had not only been hidden from human eyes but that a special guard, the Darkhats, had been posted to watch over it for all eternity. She had put that story right up on the shelf next to the one that said that Genghis would return to the Mongol people as their leader when they needed him most; both of them had seemed ludicrous to her. Maybe at one time there had been such a group, and perhaps they were the reason everyone but the Khan's descendants had stayed out of the Ikh Khorig, or Great Taboo, but to expect that group to continue their duties for eight hundred years or more was crazy.

Of course, so was a mystical sword that could vanish into thin air.

Maybe she had to reevaluate her thinking on the matter.

She explained about the Darkhats to Davenport and suggested that maybe these people were the descendants of that original group.

As she was finishing her explanation, the door was pushed aside and four men entered the *ger*. The leader, a short thin-faced man with a wide scar on his left cheek, rattled off a long sentence in Mongolian.

Unable to understand anything he was saying, Annja and Davenport simply stared back at him.

He repeated it, and then said something sharply to the men standing behind him when his captives still didn't understand what he wanted. The three men moved around and behind Annja and Davenport and, using their arms, began herding them toward the door.

"I think they want us to go with them," Davenport said.

Annja refrained from thanking him for stating the obvious, though it was a close call.

Outside, the sun was high in the sky, letting Annja know it was at least a day, maybe more, after she'd taken the plunge into the river. Around them, camp was being dismantled. Groups of Mongols were breaking down and storing nearby *gers* that were practically identical to the one they'd just left. Horses were being loaded and a few dogs roamed freely about, looking for scraps.

As they passed by, the workers stopped and watched them with impassive faces. There was neither welcome nor anger in their eyes, just a casual indifference, as if they had already ceased to exist, and that worried Annja a bit more than she let on. She had a feeling things were going to get worse before they got better.

The *gers* had been set up in an orderly fashion, two long rows of them on either side of the encampment, leaving a makeshift road down the center aisle that led to a larger, more ornate tent that probably belonged to the leader of the group. Apparently they were going to find out if she was right, for it was toward this that they were being led.

They were almost to their destination when another group emerged from the right and joined their own. There were ten men in the group, eight Mongols and two foreigners. The first was a muscular Hispanic man with a carefully trimmed goatee, the second a nondescript sandy-haired man in his midforties. Annja didn't recognize either of them, but Davenport did. He leaned in close to her so the others couldn't overhear.

"The one on the right is Ransom. The other man is his bodyguard, Santiago."

Seeing the architect of all their trouble so close at hand enraged her. Her mind was already calculating the angles, deciding who she had to take out first to get close enough to strike at Ransom, and then decided it wasn't worth getting split in two by a Mongol sword for the trouble. Ransom would get his; she'd make sure of it, one way or the other. She just had to be patient.

The trouble was that patience wasn't one of her virtues.

40

As they drew closer to the final *ger,* a man came out to greet them. Annja recognized him immediately as the one who had confronted her at the bridge. He still wore his armor, but he had removed the feathered helmet, which gave her a better view of his features. Even from here she could see his deep gray eyes as he looked them over, the anger clear on his face.

The captives were marched to the end of the pathway to stand in front of the wooden platform on which his *ger* had been constructed. The added height required them to look upward to meet his gaze and Annja almost laughed at the obvious psychological ploy it represented, but then decided being in his good graces was probably best for the near future.

Much to her surprise, the leader spoke to them in English.

"I am Holuin, the Voice of the Wolf. It is my duty to inform you of the charges against you and to ask how you plead."

"Wait just a minute, you stupid, arrog—"

Holuin gestured slightly and one of the escorts next to Ransom drove his elbow viciously into the other man's gut. Ransom stopped in midsentence, his lungs paralyzed by the sudden strike, and he toppled over as he fought to regain his breath.

"I will read the charges."

The leader read out a long list of charges, or, at least, what Annja thought were charges, for the recitation took place in Mongolian and she couldn't understand more than a word or two. She did notice that the escorts around her grew angrier as the list continued.

This was not good.

To her surprise, when he was finished, Holuin repeated the charges, this time in English. Now she understood what had gotten the others riled up; the list included trespassing, grave robbing, disturbing the dead and murder.

Annja listened just long enough to understand that she wasn't going to be able to talk her way out of this one easily. She was eyeing the edge of the platform in front of her, deciding whether she could draw her sword and make it up there before she was dragged down by the crowd around her, when the leader finished speaking.

His gaze drifted over her, lingering for just a second, as if he could tell exactly what she was thinking, then honed in on Ransom and Santiago. "How do you plead?" he asked.

One of the escorts dragged Ransom back to his feet, where he spent another minute or two trying to catch his breath. When he finally managed to do so, he straightened and told the man exactly what he thought of his charges and where he could put them.

A crowd had formed around them by this time, as word spread through the camp about what was happening. The

Mongols cheered, though for what Ransom had said or for what the Voice of the Wolf was going to do about it, Annja didn't know.

Somehow, she suspected the latter.

She shot a glance at Davenport, but he was watching Holuin and didn't notice. She looked at the platform again, gauging the distance, planting her feet so that she would be ready when the moment was right.

"Bind them," the leader ordered and her opportunity vanished in an eyeblink.

Still, she tried, anyway, kicking out with her legs as those around grabbed her arms and attempted to wrap them with rope. For just a moment she thought she might stand a chance, might be able to fight her way clear enough to draw her sword and cause some real damage, but then several of those closest to her simply threw themselves onto her and she went down beneath their combined weight. An elbow, or maybe it was a knee, smacked her in the head and darkness closed in for the second time in as many days.

WHEN ANNJA CAME TO, she was on her knees next to Davenport at the edge of a wide circle in the forest behind the camp. Her legs were numb, so she must have been kneeling in the cold for at least ten minutes or more. When he sensed she was awake, Davenport used his hands to ease her up off of him and it was then that she realized that each of them had their hands bound together in front.

A shout rang out, grabbing her attention, and she looked around groggily to find Holuin standing off to one side. Next to him was a line of eight archers. All of them, the leader included, were looking at something on the other side of the circle.

What she saw when she turned in that direction wiped any sense of confusion from her mind, letting her see and hear everything with stunning clarity.

Ransom and Santiago had been tied to two trees directly opposite the archers, their arms and legs stretched out so that both men resembled human *X*s. As Annja watched, the two men stopped struggling against their bonds and instead began to try to reason with their captors.

"Look," Ransom said. "I'm sorry for what I said earlier. I'm sorry for anything I've done to offend. Can't we talk about this, work something out?"

Annja could see the thick sheen of sweat on his skin even from this distance, and she knew he had to be terrified, though he was obviously trying hard not to show it.

Santiago, on the other hand, didn't care who knew he was scared out of his mind. He was already pleading, begging them to let him go; he was sorry; so sorry, he'd go away and never come back and would do whatever they wanted him to do to make up for what he had done; he'd never meant to hurt anyone and—

The leader barked out a command and the archers raised their bows.

Santiago's pleading turned to a mewling cry as he twitched and twisted, trying to get himself free, his eyes on the arrows now pointed in his direction. Ransom had more backbone, standing still and watching to see what would happen next.

Make it quick, Annja thought, surprised at her own sense of mercy toward her enemies.

But it was far from quick.

As far as they could make it, in fact.

When Holuin's arm flashed down, all eight archers released their arrows as one. They had chosen their targets well and every single projectile found a home. How could they miss, at this distance? Annja thought. Rather than striking some vulnerable area and ending things instantly, however, each and every arrow struck at some point on the captives' outstretched limbs, digging their sharpened points into hands and wrists, feet and ankles.

As the pain ripped through their bodies, both men screamed.

They were still screaming when Holuin gave the command again.

This time the arrows moved a bit farther down each limb, striking elbows and biceps, shins and knees.

He must have been in agony, but somehow Ransom summoned his strength. "Wait," he said. "Just wait. I can make you all incredibly wealthy. I can make you princes, kings…"

It was no use. The leader shouted again, and once more the arrows flew, once more the captives screamed.

Annja couldn't watch any more. She turned away, burying her face in her hands.

IT TOOK BOTH MEN a long time to die.

At last there was silence and Annja looked up to find her former enemies impaled by scores of arrows, so many that it was hard to recognize which man was which.

Next to her, Davenport was praying under his breath.

No way was she going out like that. No freakin' way! Think, Annja, think! she told herself.

Her hands were bound in front of her, allowing her to draw her sword, but what good would it do against so many? She'd be cut down by those archers before she took two steps.

Better to die with your sword in hand than as a human pincushion, though.

But she wasn't ready to die, not if she could find a way out of this.

Nothing came to her.

She was still trying to come up with something, anything, when Holuin spoke again.

"Bring the other captives forward."

As the guards closed in toward her, Annja surged to her feet, and stumbled forward, drawing her sword as she did so.

Hope surged. She would get out of this or die trying!

The exertion was too much, though. She was suffering from a concussion, possibly even a skull fracture, and she'd been kneeling in the cold for who knew how long? The strength had slowly leeched from her body, her legs cramping into immobility, and the combination finally took its toll. The sword flashed into being in front of her at the same time her legs decided they no longer wanted to cooperate and down she went.

The impact with the frozen earth knocked the sword from her grasp and it disappeared as quickly as it had come.

Hands grabbed her, dragged her unceremoniously to her feet and hustled her toward the other end of the clearing where the bodies of Santiago and Ransom still hung against the trees.

"Help! Somebody help us!" Davenport was yelling, as if there was someone to hear him in the middle of the Mongolian wilderness.

Think, Annja, think!

In an attempt to gain more time, Annja let her whole body go limp. Her guards weren't expecting the sudden increase in weight as she toppled forward into the snow.

They were relaxed as they bent to pick her up, probably

believing she had fainted with fear, and that was all the edge she needed.

She waited, knowing timing was the key, and when the one on her left was close enough she reared backward as hard as she could, striking the bridge of his nose with the back of her head. There was an audible crunch as his nose broke and the guard toppled to the side, howling in pain.

Annja barely noticed. She was already moving again, swinging both hands like a club toward the guard on her right. He was staring at his partner in surprise and never saw it coming; he caught the blow right across his temple.

His eyes rolled up in his head and he dropped to the ground like a felled tree.

Dazed and nauseous from the blow to her head, Annja stumbled to her feet, using both hands to draw her sword as she did so.

She had a split second to see the surprised look on Davenport's face as she drew her sword out of thin air and then she was turning around to face her enemies, stumbling a few steps to the side as dizziness threatened to overwhelm her.

There was a loud rustle as the archers fitted their arrows and drew back on their bows.

In that split second, the solution came to her like a bolt of lightning from the eternal blue heaven.

"I claim the Right of Challenge!" she called out, in as loud a voice as she could manage. She staggered again and only the fear that she would be dead before she hit the ground kept her on her feet.

Her shout hadn't sounded very loud to her, and she was getting ready to call out a second time, when she realized the clearing around her had gone eerily silent.

Wearily, she raised her head.

The crowd was staring, but not at her. Following their gaze she saw that the archers were still standing in their staggered line, still facing her with drawn bows, but their leader stood with one clenched fist in the air above his head.

Everyone was watching him expectantly.

He made sure the archers knew they were to hold their fire and then he walked toward her, his boots crunching through the snow.

To Annja, it seemed to take forever for him to reach her.

"What did you say?" he asked patiently in his excellent English.

Annja took a deep breath and then said it again, "I claim the Right of Challenge."

She said it confidently, almost regally, as if knowing he couldn't deny her. She just hoped history had it right, that such a thing had indeed existed under the Khan.

Holuin was silent for a moment, thinking, and then replied in a cold, angry voice, "Only the People of the Felt Walls may claim the Right."

He turned around, preparing to return to his place in the line, but Annja had heard the slight hesitation as he had answered her and wasn't about to let him off that easily.

"You lie," she said, and then repeated it louder so that everyone else could hear.

Apparently a few of the warriors spoke English, for her words sent a ripple through the crowd.

"The Great Law was for all men, not just members of the clan. It applied to Mongols and foreigners alike. Otherwise, it would not have prevailed. No man was above the law and no man was beneath it!" Annja shouted.

"What do you know of Chinggis's laws?" he replied haughtily.

Belatedly, Annja realized that she had trapped herself. If she admitted to leafing through the Great Yasa, then she would effectively be admitting her guilt with regard to several of the charges against her, such as grave robbing and disturbing the dead. But she quickly came to the conclusion that the charges no longer mattered; they were about to execute her, anyway. What did she have to lose?

"I've read the Great Yasa. I know the truth. I demand the Right of Challenge!"

Holuin stared at her silently for a long time. Was that respect she saw in his eyes? A grudging recognition of her bravery? She didn't know, didn't care. Just as long as he granted her request.

The leader turned and spoke to the crowd for a long time in Mongolian. They listened to him respectfully and then began cheering when he finished. Annja had no idea what was said, but the tightness in her chest eased somewhat when she saw the archers lower their bows.

He turned back to face her. "Very well. You shall have your challenge. It will take us an afternoon of hard riding to reach the Wolf's den. There you shall face your opponent. If you win, you and your companion will be set free."

With that, he turned and walked away, leaving her guards to help her to her feet.

"Are they going to kill us?" Davenport asked, from where he stood several feet away, flanked by his own set of guards.

Annja stared at Holuin's departing back.

"Not just yet," she replied.

But considering what was ahead for her, she wasn't certain if that was a good thing or not.

41

The next several hours seemed to pass slowly, something for which Annja was grateful. She knew that the longer she had to recover, the better off she would be. Her head had started to hurt less, but she knew she was a long way from being healed. At least the dizziness and nausea had subsided. She just hoped she could keep them at bay long enough to defeat whoever it was she was going to have to face in combat when they arrived at the Mongol's permanent camp. If she couldn't, well, she wasn't going to have to worry about a headache anytime after that, that was for sure.

After being returned to their *ger* and having their hands and feet untied, Davenport demanded an explanation for what had just happened. Annja did her best to help him understand.

"Genghis built his empire not on the basis of blood-lines, as the old clans had done, but on the basis of ability. Those who performed well rose to the top. Those who didn't, regardless of their heritage, fell to the bottom.

"Over time, as his empire grew and he couldn't personally handle every single issue that arose, he began to codify a set of laws that would govern as much of societal conduct as possible. He let regional and clan rulers still govern by local custom only if that custom did not violate his overarching laws, which would become known as the Great Yasa, the Great Law."

"Sort of like the difference between state and federal laws," Davenport remarked.

"Right. But remember, war was a fact of life for the people of the steppes and there were certain customs that reinforced their martial heritage, customs Genghis rightfully knew he couldn't do without. One of the older customs that he kept intact was the right of the accused to challenge his accuser in front of the court."

Davenport nodded. "Just about every civilized culture has discovered that this makes sense. It's why we have both a prosecution and a defense in our courts today."

Annja smiled gently. "Yeah, well, despite all their advances, this particular custom isn't going to win any awards for being at the front of the civil rights movement. When you challenge someone in the Mongol culture, it is a fight to the death. If you win, you get to go free. If you don't…"

Her companion stared at her with horror on his face. "My God, Annja," he said. "What have you done?"

"What I had to do to get us out of this mess," she said.

In hindsight, though, she was starting to have doubts. It had bought them some time, that was for sure, but would it be enough to save them?

Fully healed and with a decent meal in her gut, she was confident she could handle the best the Mongol leader could produce to face her. But she was far from any of those things and that sent more than a few shudders rippling down her spine.

She'd just have to take it a few hours at a time and hope for the best.

After being allowed to rest for a short time, Annja and Davenport were given a hot meal and a change of clothes to keep them warm on the journey deeper into the mountains. The leggings, shirt and jacket Annja was given stank of sweat and unwashed male flesh, but she didn't care. It kept out the cold and would provide some cushioning for her bruised body on the long ride.

The guards came for them shortly after that.

Holuin was waiting just outside the *ger*. He was mounted on one of the short, stocky horses so common to the Mongolian steppes, and there were two other horses next to him for Annja and Davenport.

"The trail is rough and dangerous at this time of year. You are going to need your hands to navigate the trip. Do I have your word you won't try to run?" he asked.

At first it seemed a strange request, but then Annja remembered that honesty and forthrightness were praised as virtues among the Mongol people. If a Mongol warrior gave his word, he would rather die than break it. Annja had exhibited knowledge of the Great Yasa and as a consequence Holuin was treating her as he would any other member of the clan. If she gave her word and broke it, her life would be immediately forfeit. If she gave her word and Davenport broke it, the same would hold true. It was not a simple request.

Nonetheless, Annja answered for both of them. "You have our word," she said.

THEIR JOURNEY TOOK THEM about an hour and ended at the far end of a long series of switchback canyons. A sea of *gers* greeted them as they rounded the final turn and entered a deep alpine valley complete with its own renewable water source in the form of a magnificent waterfall that spilled into a narrow lake along the valley's southern edge.

The men in their company were greeted warmly by wives and children who came out to meet them and they, in turn, were clearly glad to be home. Annja and Davenport were treated to what seemed to be a never-ending series of curious stares.

"Don't get out much, do they?" Davenport asked, and Annja had to laugh at his attempt at bravado. They'd have enough to be serious about shortly.

Holuin rode back down the line and spoke to their guards for several minutes before turning to them.

"It will be dark soon. I've instructed my men to see to it that you are given shelter for the night and a hot meal," he said, indicating the two warriors who stood nearby. "You will be given the opportunity to train in the morning, if you like. Unless the Wolf says otherwise, the challenge will take place after midday tomorrow."

They were taken to an empty *ger* and ushered inside. A local woman, probably the wife of one of their guards, brought them food and showed them how to use the stove and where to get water. With hand gestures she showed them where the latrine area could be found and then left them alone.

Davenport waited until the woman left and then said, "Okay, what's the plan?"

Annja frowned. "Plan for what?"

"To get out of here, of course."

"The only plan I have is to eat some food and get a good night's sleep."

"What?" Davenport stared at her in disbelief. "You can't be serious. We've got to put our heads together and figure out a way to escape."

Annja dropped down on one of the beds and began to take off her boots. "And go where? Last time I checked, we were surrounded by a couple of hundred Mongols in the middle of heaven knows where. Even if we managed to get out of camp unseen, we'd still be lost on the mountain in the dark with no idea of where we were going. We'd be lucky not to stumble into a crevasse and die."

"But we can't just sit here, Annja!"

She nodded. "You're absolutely right. We won't." She lay back on the bed, her eyes closing. "We'll lie here instead."

And with that, she fell asleep.

SHE WOKE THE NEXT MORNING to find the same Mongolian woman bustling around their stove preparing breakfast. Annja excused herself to use the latrine, making sure to give Davenport a nudge as she went out.

Thankfully her head had stopped pounding and she was able to move without it feeling as if someone was using a sledgehammer inside her brain. Good thing, too, for unless a miracle occurred she'd be in for the fight of her life later that day.

When she returned, she found Davenport sitting at the small table in the center of the *ger* being given a language lesson by their host. She pointed at a food product, said the name, then waited until Davenport repeated it back to her. If he didn't get it right, she went through it all again. *Kruurshuur* were fried little pancakes stuffed with mutton. A dish that was basically chunks of barbecued mutton was called *shorlog*. There were bowls of noodles and chunks of a soft white cheese known as *byaslag*. Finally there was the ever-present *suutei tsai,* milk tea with a pinch of salt. Annja enjoyed listening to Davenport trying to wrap his tongue around the foreign words almost as much as she enjoyed the breakfast dishes themselves.

When they were finished they were taken to a wide area on the north edge of the camp where a group of warriors had gathered to practice their martial skills. By way of hand signals and pantomime, the guards indicated to Annja that she was free to use any of the weapons set out on the nearby tables to practice if she chose to do so. Not wanting to be surprised by any limitations the blow to her head might unexpectedly have left her with, Annja decided to do just that.

She picked up a thick-bladed sword from the nearest table and, heading out to a clear area, began to move through her kata, testing her limits, looking for areas of weakness, things that she couldn't do or should avoid doing if she wanted the fight to go on as long as necessary.

After thirty minutes of hard work, she paused to rest and noticed a commotion going on to one side of the training ground. From where she stood she could see one man being attacked by five, maybe six, others. All of them held wooden practice staffs and, as she watched, the man fended off attack after attack without apparent effort. The only sound was the clack of the staves and the occasional grunt of pain as the man in the center took down his opponents one by one. It was like watching a master at work; first he played with them, to give them a chance to test their own skills, then he showed them what a true warrior could do. It was an astounding example of martial prowess and Annja felt the urge to share her appreciation with the fighter.

As she drew closer, she realized that the man who had defended himself so successfully was none other than Holuin. She shouldn't have been so surprised; who else but the best fighter in the group would be the Wolf's right hand man?

She waited while he spoke to the younger men surrounding him, no doubt offering encouragement and pointers for improving their own skills. As the others drifted off, she moved closer.

"You fought well," she said to him.

He grunted an acknowledgment of her statement but didn't say anything more.

Irritated by his seeming dismissal, Annja opened her mouth to say something about his attitude when a horn sounded over the encampment and echoed eerily off the surrounding cliffs. To Annja, it sounded like the voice of the whippoorwill, mourning its lost love.

But to Holuin, it had an entirely different meaning.

He waited for the sound to die away and then turned to face her.

"Come," he said. "It is time for your challenge."

Davenport, who until now had been standing to one side, avoiding Holuin, shot her an anxious look. She did her best to return a reassuring one. She couldn't blame him for being nervous, but he wasn't the one having to face a fight to the death.

Then again, she didn't have to face the archers if she lost, the way he would.

In her mind, she was getting the better part of the bargain, despite the fact that she'd already be dead.

42

Holuin led them across the camp to where a large circular ring had been laid out on the ground in front of an oversize wooden platform. The sides of the circle were made of piled stone that came up to about midthigh. The center was packed dirt that was frozen rock solid this time of year. Atop the platform stood a large *ger* fashioned of blue felt; it wasn't quite as big as the one they'd discovered inside the Tomb of the Virgins, but it was close.

Annja guessed that it belonged to the Wolf, the mysterious clan leader they'd been hearing about but had yet to see or meet.

Holuin crossed the circle, climbed the steps to the platform and then disappeared inside the *ger,* leaving her to wait with Davenport and her two guards at the edge of the circle.

After several long, anxious moments, the horn sounded again. This time it blew three long notes, which was a signal for the clan to gather together. They began to arrive shortly thereafter in twos and threes, finding places along the edges of the circle.

The door on the blue *ger* opened and Holuin stepped back out. Behind him, Annja caught a glimpse of an older Mongolian man seated in a chair by the doorway, looking out through the thin silk inner door.

The guards indicated that Annja should enter the circle, so she climbed over the wall and walked into the center.

Holuin pinned back the heavy door of the *ger,* leaving only a thin semitransparent covering over the entrance. When he was finished he came down off the platform and explained the rules to her, of which there were few.

"This is a fight to the death. The winner proves their worth to the clan and walks away. The loser joins his ancestors. Each fighter may use one weapon. As challenger you have first choice, though your opponent may choose the same blade if he desires."

He paused, as if to wait for questions.

"Who am I fighting?" she asked, looking around for her opponent.

Holuin waited until she turned her attention back to him and then grinned. "Me."

It was not the answer Annja had been expecting, nor was it a welcome one. She had seen him take on six opponents earlier as easily as if he'd been facing only one, and she knew she was going to need every ounce of her talent and skill to come out of this alive.

For the first time, she doubted her strategy was a smart one.

Too late now.

A table had been set up to one side of the ring and it held a series of weapons. Annja walked over to inspect them. Holuin kept back a respectful distance, not wanting her to use any of the weapons on him in some misguided attempt to escape probably, but that was fine with her as it gave her the opportunity she needed.

If I'm going to fight, I'm going to do it with my own sword, thank you very much.

Pretending to be examining the various blades, she picked them up and put them down again, piling them up to one side. When the pile was large enough to hide what she intended to do, she reached into it while at the same time summoning her own blade from the otherwhere, hoping the tangled mess would hide the sudden appearance of her sword from their eyes.

When she turned to face the group, no one said anything about it.

She carried Joan's sword, her sword, with her into the center of the circle and waited while Holuin chose his own blade.

He selected a bejeweled weapon with a long narrow blade. It was slightly shorter than her own, but probably lighter, as well, which, when combined with his speed, eliminated any advantage she might have from her longer blade. It was a good choice and Annja's respect for his ability went up a notch.

Holuin took up position in one half of the circle and Annja did the same in the other. From where she stood she could see over Holuin's shoulder and noted the figure standing just inside the entrance of the *ger,* watching them through the gossamer curtain.

Hello, Wolf.

On impulse, she raised her sword and saluted him.

She was just turning her attention back to her opponent when the horn sounded for a third time that afternoon, signaling the start of the fight.

Holuin didn't waste any time; the moment the horn sounded he moved in swiftly, perhaps hoping his larger size and years of experience would allow him to end things sooner rather than later.

Annja, however, wouldn't be so cooperative.

As he swung at her midsection, she dropped the point of her sword and met Holuin's blade with the edge of her own, channeling the energy of her attacker's strike away from her and toward the ground instead. She twisted and brought her own weapon up in a semicircular motion that sent it swinging back toward Holuin's neck, hoping for a lucky strike to end it all before it had barely begun.

But her opponent was too good to be taken out that quickly and he easily blocked her strike, in turn.

He went low suddenly, his blade flashing out in a strike intended to cut her off at the knees, but Annja easily leaped over the blade, slashing with a strike of her own even before her feet were back on the ground.

Houlin was forced to step back, out of the reach of her blade, in order to avoid it but came back at her quickly in a flurry of blows, trying to overwhelm her with his strength and brutality.

Annja, however, had been in more than her fair share of sword fights lately and she recognized what he was trying to do. She gave ground before him, letting him think he was driving her backward, and then, when he was committed to his next blow, she sidestepped suddenly, letting his momentum carry him past her. She struck out with her right foot in a near-perfectly executed side kick, catching him in the small of the back and sending him stumbling forward.

As she moved to take advantage of her opportunity, he turned his stumble into a shoulder roll, twisting around as he went so that he came back up on his feet to meet her attack without looking the worse for wear.

This was not going to be an easy fight, Annja thought.

The strikingly similar look he gave her let her know that he was thinking the very same thing.

So be it.

Back and forth they went, blow after blow, twisting and turning, moving about inside the confines of the circle, each one striving to gain the upper hand and deliver the winning blow.

Holuin drew first blood, catching Annja with the tip of his sword as she spun away from him and carving a thin line across her left hip.

The crowd around them cheered to see their champion wound his opponent.

It wasn't long before she returned the favor, however, catching him with a slashing blow that cut through the meat of his shoulder, and they cheered just as loudly for her.

Apparently, all the spectators wanted was a good fight.

Houlin and she were well matched. Every time she thought she'd found a chink in his armor, he managed to get away. Every time he thought he was about to deliver a killing strike, she was no longer where he expected her to be. It went around and around like that for some time.

Annja knew a longer conquest would favor her opponent. She could feel herself getting tired already, her muscles not responding as quickly to the commands her brain was giving them as they had at the start of the battle. Despite the difference in their ages, he fought and trained in this weather and altitude every single day, which gave him a distinct advantage. If it came down to a battle of sheer stamina, he would win. Annja had no doubt about that.

She, of course, had to do something to prevent that from happening.

Her life, and Davenport's, depended on it.

She began to favor her left side, keeping it back slightly and being just a hair slower when turning in that direction. She knew he would see: what she wanted him to see; a tired opponent with an injury she was trying to favor.

Most fighters would shield that region, trying to protect it. The savvy fighter knew that was exactly the wrong strategy to use, however, as it telegraphed your problem to your opponent and left you vulnerable in other areas as you devoted all your energy to defending your injury.

Annja hoped Holuin's ego would get the better of him, that he would think of her as inexperienced and take the bait.

Thankfully, he did.

He came in with determination, trying to make her fall back on her injured limb, probably hoping she would stumble and drop to the ground if he pressured her hard enough.

Their blades flashed in the sun and rang against each other with every blow.

Annja's world narrowed down to just her and her opponent. No one else mattered.

She bided her time, waiting for just the right moment, all the while allowing Holuin to force her backward, letting him think she was growing even more tired and weak.

Then, when the moment was right, she stumbled, making it look as if her leg had just failed her.

As expected, Holuin came in with a horizontal strike designed to slice her throat wide open, or force her to put weight on her injured leg in the hope that she would fall over backward when it failed to support her.

Annja leaned back at the waist, letting Holuin's blade pass by her face before meeting it one-handed with her own, forcing it farther forward and down, preventing him from doing a quick reversal. At the same time she pushed off her "bad" leg, using it to propel her forward with much more force than Holuin expected.

She had a moment to catch the surprise on his face as he realized she'd suckered him and then her left elbow was coming around with all of her body weight behind it. She struck him in the head, felt the shock of the blow reverberate back up her arm, knew even before he began to stumble backward that it had been a good, clean strike.

But Annja wasn't done yet.

She kept moving, left foot planted hard against the dirt, using the momentum of her strike to whip her body around in a full circle that brought her right leg up and over in a vicious strike that connected with her opponent's exposed throat.

Holuin's sword went flying as he was flung to the ground by the force of the blow.

Annja was on him in a second, the point of her sword held against the tender flesh of his throat.

Point. Set. Match.

He looked up at her without fear.

"Go ahead," he said calmly, through his bruised and battered throat. "You have no choice. You must end it. The law of the Challenge will not let them release you while we both still live."

For just a moment, she was tempted. The anger and frustration she felt over all that had happened since she'd left the dig in Mexico needed an outlet and, just seconds before, this man had been doing his best to try and kill her. Now he lay beneath her blade, unarmed and helpless. It would be so easy, too; just a few extra ounces of pressure against the hilt and that would be that.

She raised her gaze and looked out over the crowd.

They were completely silent, watching her, waiting to see what she would do. Even Davenport was spellbound. It was as if the whole world was holding its breath, waiting, wondering, watching.

In the end, though, she had no choice but to disappoint them. Killing a man who is trying to kill you is one thing. Killing a man who was at your mercy was another. It wasn't right and her conscience wouldn't let her do it.

She pulled her sword away from his throat and stepped away.

"No," she said. "There's been enough killing."

The crowd erupted, shouting and yelling, though she had no idea what they were saying. Holuin hadn't moved. He stayed flat on the ground, watching her with wide eyes, as if he couldn't believe he was still alive.

Annja turned to face the crowd. "I will not kill him," she yelled in English, then followed it with one of the few Mongolian words she knew. *"Ugui,"* she said. "No."

She turned around and started walking toward Davenport. If they wanted to kill her they would. There wasn't anything she could do about it. But she wouldn't be a party to any more killing.

She was halfway across the circle, suddenly exhausted now that all the adrenaline had left her system, and she was doing all she could to stay on her feet, when Davenport's eyes popped open wide and he shouted at her.

"Look out!"

Annja whirled around, her sword coming back up, knowing she was already too late.

She found her opponent just a few feet away, his

weapon already raised over his head in preparation for the downward strike, his muscles tensing as he brought his arms forward.

His blade fell toward her face as her own swung upward.

From the look in his eyes and the smile of triumph on his face she knew she wasn't going to be in time.

"Ugui!"

The shout was loud, jarring, and with the unmistakable force of command.

Holuin froze in midmotion, his muscles straining at the force needed to stop his killing blow.

Annja gazed at him in stunned disbelief, amazed that she wasn't already dead as her own sword swept harmlessly through the space between them.

A long stream of angry Mongolian filled the air. It was coming from the old but fit-looking man who now stood in front of the entrance to the blue *ger,* the same one she had seen looking out earlier during the challenge.

Holuin's response was immediate. He put his weapon down and bowed to her. He held that position, his neck exposed to her blade.

Confused, she looked over at the Wolf, wondering just what on earth was going on.

The leader of the Mongols drew a finger across his throat.

That was one symbol that didn't need interpretation; he was offering her Holuin's life for his attempt at striking her when she had already won the duel.

Annja kept her sword where it was and shook her head.

The Wolf gestured at her again, this time with more emphasis, as if he thought she hadn't understood.

Again, she shook her head. To show she knew what he

was telling her, she jabbed her sword into the ground and then stepped forward. With a hand on Holuin's shoulder, she drew him upright.

For just a moment she could see the cold sense of relief in Holuin's eyes and then the mask he typically wore fell back over his emotions, hiding his true feelings once more.

Again, the Wolf stared at her. Annja decided the Mongol leader was well named—she felt like a rabbit caught in the stare of a predator determined to make her its dinner.

Much to her surprise, the Wolf blinked first, turning away and shouting something over his shoulder as he re-entered his *ger*.

"He wants you to join him."

Annja stared at Holuin, incredulous. "You can't be serious?"

For some reason, the defeated Mongol found that amusing. Through his laughter, he assured her that he had never been more serious.

The Wolf wanted her company. Now.

Holuin had just been ordered to see to it that she joined the Wolf in his tent.

"What about my companion?" she asked, casting a fearful look at Davenport who stood still flanked by several guards.

"You have my word he will not be injured."

Oddly enough, Annja trusted him, despite his having just tried to kill her.

Annja reclaimed her sword and handed it to Holuin. She knew he would never allow her to take it into the tent with her. Besides, it wouldn't help her in any way once she was inside. If any harm befell their leader, the Mongols would never let her leave. Nor could she just make the weapon vanish in front of everyone without being branded a witch or worse. So she handed it over without concern, knowing she could make it vanish back into the other-where at any time.

So with what could only be described as a sense of utter surrealism, Annja crossed to the base of the platform with Holuin at her side and then climbed the steps.

At the top of the platform she cast one last glance at Davenport, gave him a shrug and then stepped forward into the Wolf's den.

43

Annja cautiously entered the *ger,* remembering to step across the threshold with her right foot first as was the custom, not wanting to insult the Wolf before she knew what he wanted.

What she saw took her breath away.

The interior was richly decorated with all types of artifacts—from Chinese teak cabinets to Ming vases, from a complete suit of Japanese armor to what looked to be the hood ornament of a Mercedes hanging on the wall in a glass case. There was a Greek statue of Aphrodite standing in front of a Monet painting hanging on the wall. A ship's astrolabe sat next to an ancient text that she could see was written in Latin and included hand-drawn images in the margins. The variety in the objects themselves and the places they came from was astounding and she had a hard time taking it all in on first glance. She was reminded of how both Garin and Roux collected objects in a similar fashion. What was it about such things that made men hoard them so?

A light, crisp scent filled the air, though she couldn't find the incense burner amid all the other items that occupied every square inch of display space in the *ger*.

The man who had invited her to join him stood in the middle of the *ger,* on the far side of the little table that formed the traditional eating area.

"Sain Bainu uu," he said to her. *"Minii nerig Temujin."*

She shook her head. She'd only understood one word. Temujin.

Genghis Khan's birth name.

Not all that surprising, she reasoned. Who better to name a male child after than the man who had put their culture on the map?

Aloud she said, "I'm sorry. I don't speak Mongolian." She said it in English, without much hope that he would understand her.

Much to her surprise, he replied in kind.

"Well, then, we will talk in the language of your fathers instead of mine. Please, sit." He indicated the pile of cushions arranged on the opposite side of the table from where he stood.

Seeing no reason why she shouldn't, Annja did.

Once she was seated, he followed suit.

They studied each other for a few minutes, neither of them saying anything.

He was one of those people whose age she had a hard time determining; he could have been forty just as easily as seventy. He looked fit and healthy, though his skin had that leathery look common to those who spend so much time in the wind and sun. His face was creased with age lines but there was a light in his eyes that suggested a personality that had yet to be weighted down by the demands of the world. His hair had probably once been dark, but now it was gray-white and worn long, as was the thin mustache that drooped down either side of his lips.

Yet he felt far older than he looked. That was the only way Annja could describe it to herself. He had an air of age about him, a sense that he had seen it all and heard it all, that he had been around since the world was young. She felt the way she had on her first dig, when ruins that hadn't seen the light of day for thousands of years had been unearthed. Just being in the same room with him made her feel that same air of wonder and awe.

It was a strange reaction to have to an individual and it made her uncomfortable.

She kept looking at him, trying to put her finger on what caused her to feel that way but with no luck.

He watched her watching him and smiled in response. She was reminded of a hawk, the keen eyes missing nothing.

"Would you like some tea?" he asked.

"No, thank you."

"Perhaps some *airag* instead?"

She'd heard of the drink made from fermented camel's milk and decided that having anything alcoholic at this point was not a good idea. Politely, she declined, but did accept a glass of water.

"You fought well. Like a true Mongol. Your clan must value you highly."

For a moment the comment stung. Having been raised in a Catholic orphanage in New Orleans, Annja didn't have a clan to be proud of her. The Wolf had no way of knowing that, however, and so she knew it was not meant as an insult.

"Thank you," she said.

He paused for a moment, gathering his thoughts, and

then smiled at her. "Tell me. Do you know how the camel lost his tail and his antlers?"

The question caught her off guard. She'd been expecting questions about why she was here or what her expedition had hoped to find, and instead she's asked about a camel's antlers?

"Camels don't have antlers," she said, before her brain caught up with her mouth.

"Not after losing them, they don't. But do you know how they lost them?"

Annja shook her head.

"It's quite an interesting tale. You see, long ago the camel had a magnificent pair of antlers, as well as a lush, gorgeous tail. The camel was known as a generous animal and sometimes others took advantage of him."

Temujin paused to refill his cup of *airag* from the cloth bag hanging nearby.

"You wouldn't know it to look at them today, but the deer was born with a bald head and the horse had only a thin, raggedy tail. One day at the watering hole, the deer asked to borrow the camel's antlers for the day, claiming he was going to a big celebration that night and didn't want to be ashamed of his bald head."

Annja was sure there was a lesson in this story, just as there is in most folktales, but at the moment she didn't have a clue where he was going with it.

"Being the kind soul that he was, the camel said yes, on the condition that the deer return them the next day. As the deer went on his way, holding his head up high to show off the new set of antlers he had gained, he ran into the horse and explained what had happened.

"The horse decided this would be an excellent time to get something for himself, so he, too, went to see the camel and asked to borrow his tail, using the same story as the deer.

"The next morning the camel returned to the watering hole, expecting to get back his antlers and his tail, but neither the deer nor the horse ever showed up. To this day, whenever the camel takes a drink, he will look out over the steppes, hoping to catch sight of the deer and the horse, but he never does."

Temujin watched her face for a moment and then asked, "A sad story, is it not?"

"Only for the camel," Annja replied.

"What lesson do you think the camel learned?"

He asked the question casually, but Annja's instincts were suddenly on high alert. There was a message here, one she would do well to understand.

"The camel learned that being too generous is not always a good thing." She watched his eyes for a reaction, but he gave nothing away.

"So which animal are you? The camel, the deer or the horse?"

There it was. The trap she'd been expecting. If she claimed to be either the deer or the horse, she would have a problem, because stealing was against the Mongol code. While neither she nor Davenport had been in possession of the Great Yasa or the Khan's *suldes* when they were captured, the Wolf's men had probably informed him that the artifacts had been removed from their prior locations. In effect, they had been stolen, just like the camel's antlers and tail.

Claiming to be the camel wouldn't help her, either, because he had been too generous and had been taken advantage of; she did not want to make herself look like a fool for saving Holuin's life, despite the fact that she knew it was the right thing to do.

She pondered the problem for several long moments, searching desperately for an answer that wouldn't get her in worse trouble than she was already in.

It wasn't until she sensed that he was getting impatient that she figured it out.

Taking a deep breath, knowing her life could quite possibly hinge on her saying the right thing in the next few moments, she replied, "I'm neither the camel, the deer, nor the horse. I am the Wolf, who rules the steppes and who, in his wisdom, spares the lives of the other animals at the watering hole."

Silence filled the *ger*.

Temujin stared at her, expressionless.

Then he giggled.

The giggle turned into a laugh, which, in turn, became a full-fledged cackle. He laughed so hard that he fell over backward, spilling his *airag* all over the floor.

Annja didn't know what to do. She hadn't meant her answer to be funny, never mind hysterically so.

She decided the best course of action was to wait for him to get himself together again, which he eventually did, wiping the tears from his eyes as he sat up again.

"The Wolf indeed!" he cried, which almost resulted in another laughing fit, but he managed to control himself in time. "A most excellent answer, Annja Creed."

The realization that he knew exactly who she was did not sit well with her. How had he found out? What else did he know?

Somehow, she knew the answers to those questions would not be forthcoming.

Once he had calmed down, the Wolf turned serious again.

"You won the match with Holuin and, like the camel,

you gave away something of value—your freedom. After all, the rules were simple. In order to gain your freedom, only one of you could leave the circle alive. Yet when given the chance, you chose not to kill him. Why is that?"

She didn't even have to think about that one. "Because it wouldn't have been right," she answered hotly. "He'd been defeated. What use would taking his life have served?"

"A wise answer, for one so young. You have the wisdom of the ages about you."

Not knowing what to say to that, Annja chose to remain silent.

"But wisdom is not alone. Destiny has her claws in you, as well, I think."

Annja was too surprised to answer. She wondered if all conversations with Temujin were like this—jumping from subject to subject, knowing there was a pattern beneath it all but being unable to see it until he'd surprised you with something else.

He didn't appear to notice her consternation. "Yes, destiny has claimed you as her own. A harsh mistress she is, but one that cannot be easily ignored." He smiled. "Trust me, I know. So what are we to do with you, Annja Creed?"

She didn't hesitate. "Let us go. The men you punished were criminals in your world as well as mine. They will not be missed, nor will we mention what happened to them if we are asked. When we leave here I give you my word that we will not return."

"Even if the answers you seek can be found here and nowhere else?"

Davenport would be disappointed, but she was convinced even he would recognize the necessity of agreeing with the Wolf's request. Besides, there was more than one way to skin a cat.

"Even then," she replied.

He gazed into her eyes and Annja was overcome with the feeling that he was not just looking at the surface of her flesh, but looking deeper, somehow seeing into the depths of her very soul, searching it for a sign that she was being less than sincere.

She was suddenly thankful that she hadn't lied.

He would have known; she didn't doubt it for a moment.

This time his smile didn't hold any frivolity but was more the smile of one resigned to something that could not be avoided and trying to show a brave face. "Fate has much in store for you, Annja Creed. And those who choose to argue with fate never win. I shall not set myself on that road."

He clapped his hands suddenly, startling her.

"So be it. I shall have my men escort you to the edge of the Ikh Khorig, with the understanding that you will be killed on sight should you cross into our territory again in the future."

Annja felt the weight on her chest lift and she breathed easily for the first time in days.

She stood and gave a quick bow. "Thank you. For my life and the life of my companion."

Assuming the audience was over, she turned and made her way back to the door. As she reached out to move the thin curtain aside, the Wolf spoke once more.

"What you are looking for cannot be found, Annja Creed. It does not exist in the way that you think. Chinggis is at rest. The Eternal Blue Heaven wishes that it remain that way and so it does. Do you understand what I am saying to you?"

She glanced back at him, looking for hidden meaning in his words but seeing nothing but that wily smile and the stark intelligence in his eyes.

"I understand," she said, though, in truth, she did not.

She knew he was aware of that, as well.

He nodded and then turned away, which she took as her cue to leave.

She wasted no more time before doing so.

44

Holuin and a squad of six Mongol warriors escorted them down the mountainside shortly thereafter. Annja and Davenport had each been given a horse to ride, with instructions to set them free once they reached the edge of the steppes; the horses would find their own way home or return to the wild, as the eternal blue heaven saw fit.

They left the mountain by a different route than the one they had used on the ascent. This time it was easier for Annja to note landmarks along the way. By the time they reached the foot of Burkhan Khaldun she was all but certain she could have retraced her way right back to the door of the Wolf's den.

It didn't matter, though. Somehow she knew that if they ever managed to find their way back to that particular canyon again they would find it empty, all trace of the clan having vanished into thin air as if they had never been.

The Wolf was too wily to remain where his enemies could find him so easily.

As they rode, she found herself thinking about the legend of the Darkhats and comparing it to what she knew of the Wolf and his people. Clearly they had some contact with the outside world; both the Wolf and Holuin spoke near-perfect English. In fact, it was good enough that she knew they must have either been trained by a native speaker or spent significant time in an English-speaking country. And the range and variety of the artifacts in the Wolf's *ger* suggested someone who had traveled rather extensively.

But if your job was to protect the tomb of your nation's greatest leader from any and all who came looking for it, wouldn't it behoove you to understand just what the outside world was like? What the people who lived in it were capable of? To pay attention to the growing tide of interest in Genghis Khan and the tomb itself as Mongolia came out from under the Communist thumb?

Of course it would.

But then there was the comment the Wolf had made just before she took her leave of him. "What you are looking for cannot be found," he'd said. Did that mean that the exact location of the tomb had been lost through the ages? Or that the tomb didn't exist at all, which had been her original belief?

She didn't know and probably never would.

Just one more puzzle in a life full of mystery.

It was close to sunset when they reached the place where the river split into three separate waterways and where the voice in the earth had led them to the map. It was there that Holuin and his men intended to leave them. The trucks the expedition had driven in from Ulaanbaatar weren't far from this point and Annja was certain she could find her way without difficulty.

The distant cry of a gold eagle, rare in these days even in Mongolia, reached them and, looking up, they saw a lone rider sitting atop a horse high on a nearby bluff. In his hand was a white *sulde* and Annja could see the horse-hair blowing in the wind, gathering power for the standard bearer and determining his destiny.

The rider's face was in shadow, but she didn't need to see it in order to know it was the Wolf.

For whatever reason, he'd come to see her off.

His voice echoed in her mind.

Destiny has claimed you as her own. A harsh mistress she is, but one that cannot be easily ignored. Trust me, I know.

And just like that the pieces fell together in her mind like dominoes, the pattern revealed as the fog of confusion rolled away.

The missing page from the journal containing the final clue.

The lack of a body in the Tomb of the Virgins.

The use of the Wolf moniker, which was clearly a reference to the Mongolian folktale that their people were descended from the gray wolf of the steppes. As well as the name of the clan from which their greatest hero had descended.

And finally, the name.

Temujin.

It was outrageous to even think it, but so was the idea that a broken sword could repair itself or that both Garin and Roux had been alive since the time of Joan of Arc, yet she knew both of those things were true.

One thing she had learned since becoming the bearer of the sword was that, sometimes, life is stranger than fiction.

She stared up at the rider and felt his eyes upon her, as well.

Someday I will return, she told him silently, and we'll have that talk about destiny.

Yours and mine.

But for now, farewell.

Genghis Khan.

The Don Pendleton's
Executioner®
SALVADOR STRIKE

A WARRIOR'S PLAYGROUND

The star witness and the prosecuting attorney for the case against the lethal MS-13 gang have been murdered, leaving the trial in shambles. With the situation critical, Mack Bolan is called in to fight fire with fire. MS-13's leaders have a plan to terrorize suburban America and it's up to the Executioner to stop them—showing no mercy.

Available February 2010 wherever books are sold.

GOLD EAGLE®

www.readgoldeagle.blogspot.com

GEX375

TAKE 'EM FREE

2 action-packed novels plus a mystery bonus

NO RISK

NO OBLIGATION TO BUY

SPECIAL LIMITED-TIME OFFER

Mail to: Gold Eagle Reader Service

IN U.S.A.: P.O. Box 1867, Buffalo, NY 14240-1867
IN CANADA: P.O. Box 609, Fort Erie, Ontario L2A 5X3

YEAH! Rush me 2 FREE Gold Eagle® novels and my FREE mystery bonus (bonus is worth about $5). If I don't cancel, I will receive 6 hot-off-the-press novels every other month. Bill me at the low price of just $33.44 for each shipment.* That's a savings of over 15% off the combined cover prices and there is NO extra charge for shipping and handling! There is no minimum number of books I must buy. I can always cancel at any time simply by returning a shipment at your cost or by returning any shipping statement marked "cancel." Even if I never buy another book from Gold Eagle, the 2 free books and mystery bonus are mine to keep forever.

166 ADN EYPE   366 ADN EYPQ

Name	(PLEASE PRINT)
Address	Apt. #
City State/Prov.	Zip/Postal Code

Signature (if under 18, parent or guardian must sign)

Not valid to current subscribers of Gold Eagle books.
Want to try two free books from another series? Call 1-800-873-8635.

* Terms and prices subject to change without notice. Prices do not include applicable taxes. Sales tax applicable in N.Y. Canadian residents will be charged applicable provincial taxes and GST. Offer not valid in Quebec. This offer is limited to one order per household. All orders subject to approval. Credit or debit balances in a customer's account(s) may be offset by any other outstanding balance owed by or to the customer. Please allow 4 to 6 weeks for delivery. Offer available while quantities last.

Your Privacy: Worldwide Library is committed to protecting your privacy. Our Privacy Policy is available online at www.eHarlequin.com or upon request from the Reader Service. From time to time we make our lists of customers available to reputable third parties who may have a product or service of interest to you. If you would prefer we not share your name and address, please check here. ☐

GE09

Don Pendleton's Mack Bolan

Betrayed

**Powerful enemies plot to derail
a rescue mission in the Middle East…**

Working toward a peace breakthrough in
the Middle East, Dr. Sharif Mahoud is being
hunted by purveyors of terror who are
threatened by his efforts. The Oval Office
sends Mack Bolan to get him to safety—
but hostile forces dog Bolan's every move
as the enemy will do whatever it takes
to turn a profit on blood and suffering.

*Available March 2010
wherever books are sold.*

Or order your copy now by sending your name, address, zip or postal code, along with a check or money order (please do not send cash) for $6.99 for each book ordered ($7.99 in Canada), plus 75¢ postage and handling ($1.00 in Canada), payable to Gold Eagle Books, to:

In the U.S.	**In Canada**
Gold Eagle Books	Gold Eagle Books
3010 Walden Avenue	P.O. Box 636
P.O. Box 9077	Fort Erie, Ontario
Buffalo, NY 14269-9077	L2A 5X3

Please specify book title with your order.
Canadian residents add applicable federal and provincial taxes.

GOLD EAGLE®

www.readgoldeagle.blogspot.com

GSB132

JAMES AXLER

DEATH LANDS

Blood Harvest

Welcome to the dark side of tomorrow. Welcome to the Deathlands.

Washed ashore in the North Atlantic, Ryan Cawdor and Doc Tanner discover two islands intact after Skydark, but whose inhabitants suffer a darker, more horrifying punishment. When the sun goes down, mutants called Nightwalkers manifest to unleash a feast of horror…which Ryan and Doc must struggle to survive.

Available March 2010 wherever books are sold.

Or order your copy now by sending your name, address, zip or postal code, along with a check or money order (please do not send cash) for $6.99 for each book ordered ($7.99 in Canada), plus 75¢ postage and handling ($1.00 in Canada), payable to Gold Eagle Books, to:

In the U.S.	In Canada
Gold Eagle Books	Gold Eagle Books
3010 Walden Avenue	P.O. Box 636
P.O. Box 9077	Fort Erie, Ontario
Buffalo, NY 14269-9077	L2A 5X3

Please specify book title with your order.
Canadian residents add applicable federal and provincial taxes.

GOLD EAGLE ®

www.readgoldeagle.blogspot.com

GDL91

Don Pendleton

SEASON OF HARM

**Stony Man severs a narco-link leading
straight to Russia's highest office....**

When a routine FBI raid on a New Jersey warehouse
turns into a bloodbath, an explosive link between
Asian heroin smugglers and Russia's newly elected
strongman president emerges. With new satellite
technology, Stony Man unleashes relentless
fury against an army of narco-lords and a highly
protected political kingpin poised to take the
motherland—and the world.

STONY MAN®

*Available February
wherever books are sold.*

Or order your copy now by sending your name, address, zip or postal code, along with a check or
money order (please do not send cash) for $6.99 for each book ordered ($7.99 in Canada), plus
75¢ postage and handling ($1.00 in Canada), payable to Gold Eagle Books, to:

In the U.S.	**In Canada**
Gold Eagle Books	Gold Eagle Books
3010 Walden Avenue	P.O. Box 636
P.O. Box 9077	Fort Erie, Ontario
Buffalo, NY 14269-9077	L2A 5X3

Please specify book title with your order.
Canadian residents add applicable federal and provincial taxes.

GOLD EAGLE®

www.readgoldeagle.blogspot.com

GSM105

James Axler
Outlanders®

REALITY ECHO

A shape-shifting assassin and a cannibal army threaten the future's last hope….

The Bluegrass range hides the operating base of a race of monstrous genetic mutations, faithful servants of an ancient overlord. As Kane and the rebels stage their reconnaissance, the shocking new face of an old nemesis enters the fray and—replicating himself as Kane—aims to wipe out the mountains, and their inhabitants, from Earth permanently.

Available February wherever books are sold.

Or order your copy now by sending your name, address, zip or postal code, along with a check or money order (please do not send cash) for $6.99 for each book ordered ($7.99 in Canada), plus 75¢ postage and handling ($1.00 in Canada), payable to Gold Eagle Books, to:

In the U.S.	In Canada
Gold Eagle Books	Gold Eagle Books
3010 Walden Avenue	P.O. Box 636
P.O. Box 9077	Fort Erie, Ontario
Buffalo, NY 14269-9077	L2A 5X3

GOLD EAGLE®

Please specify book title with your order.
Canadian residents add applicable federal and provincial taxes.

www.readgoldeagle.blogspot.com

GOUT52